Anna Kent has worked as a journalist, magazine editor and book editor as well as enjoying a stint as a radio producer. She's written for numerous publications at home and abroad, including the *Daily Telegraph*, where she was a contributor for six years. Brought up in the South East, she loves to travel while maintaining a base in Gloucestershire. She's married with two children.

THE HOUSE OF WHISPERS

ANNA KENT

ONE PLACE. MANY STORIES

HQ
An imprint of HarperCollins*Publishers* Ltd
1 London Bridge Street
London SE1 9GF

www.harpercollins.co.uk

HarperCollins*Publishers*
1st Floor, Watermarque Building, Ringsend Road
Dublin 4, Ireland

This edition 2021

21 22 23 24 LSC 10 9 8 7 6 5 4 3 2 1
First published in Great Britain by
HQ, an imprint of HarperCollins*Publishers* Ltd 2021

Copyright © Annabel Kantaria 2021

Annabel Kantaria asserts the moral right to be
identified as the author of this work.
A catalogue record for this book is
available from the British Library.

ISBN: 978-0-00-843015-3

This book is set in Fournier

Printed and bound in the United States of America by
LSC Communications

THE
HOUSE
OF
WHISPERS

Transcript of interview with Mr Rohan Allerton, husband of Abigail Allerton: 20 December 2019

'So, let's rewind right to the beginning. When was it that you first suspected that something might be wrong?'

'It's really hard to say. Abi's always been a bit of an oddball. It's what I love about her. She has what I call... "quirks", but I put that down to her being so talented. You know she's an artist? Her work is sublime, and I always think that, with such talent, comes a degree of... [cough] "individuality"? "Uniqueness"? [pause] I guess what I'm saying is that it's hard to tell where that ended and... Look: I thought things were pretty normal, given that one of us was an artist. I wasn't looking for signs. I wasn't on high alert.'

'But if you had to pin it down? How long ago are we talking?'

'I guess last summer. Do you remember how hot it was? God. Our house is old. It traps the heat. It rises, right up to the attic where she works. Maybe that had something to do with it. Stuck up there all day, stewing in the heat. I don't know. Even my mum said she wasn't herself.'

'And did she have any ideas on what might be the root of the problem?'

[Laughs] 'Let's not go there! But, yeah, I suppose it was the summer when I knew something was up with Abi. I felt she might be hiding something from me… To be honest, I thought she might be pregnant.'

'And would that be a problem? Something you would describe as "wrong"?'

'Oh God, no. Not at all. It would be right. All right. We've been trying for over a year.'

'I see. But she wasn't pregnant?'

'No. She wasn't pregnant.'

One

I didn't tell Rohan straight away that Grace was coming back. The morning that I got her email, I started to tell him, but then I held the thought inside me, like a breath. Inviting her to stay with us was a huge decision. I knew it would change everything.

It was 7.30 a.m. and already the air in the kitchen was stifling; residual heat from the long days of the heatwave was an unwelcome guest trapped in the ceilings and walls of the house, like a ghost. London was suffocating.

'Darling,' I'd begun, thinking at that point that I would tell him – not just about Grace, but everything – the whole story. Ridiculous, really, but it was honestly what I was thinking that sweltering morning. We were sitting at the small table in the kitchen, and the back door was propped open to suck in what reluctant breeze there might be. I was nursing a coffee and my husband, ready in his work shirt, his silk tie slung over his shoulder, was eating scrambled eggs on toast. Already I could see the fabric of his shirt darkening under his arms.

But he hadn't heard me. Maybe I hadn't said it loud enough; maybe I hadn't said it out loud at all – I don't like to think he ignored me. The unresolved issue of what we were going to do about New York hung in the air between us, crackling like an electrical charge. I was still upset with him and he knew it. The fine hairs on my forearms tickled under a sheen of sweat. A fly, gleaming metallic blue, circled lazily over the fruit bowl. The coffee made me sweat more; I pushed it away.

'So, what are you up to today?' Rohan said. 'More pets?' He shook his head and tutted, but he was smiling. 'I don't know why you do it. You should be focusing on your real work: going to galleries, looking at books – I don't know. Nobody ever got inspired painting dogs. And no gallery ever bought *Rufus – the Series*.' He laughed.

I closed my eyes as I let out an imperceptible sigh. We'd been here before. 'As Picasso said,' I told him, '"inspiration exists – but it has to find us working."'

Rohan moved his head in time with the words; he'd heard that before, too.

'I'm doing a home visit today,' I said.

His eyebrows shot up. 'A home visit?'

'Yep.'

Rohan looked at me then, his head tilted; the ghost of a frown lining his forehead. 'I thought they were supposed to upload photos. Wasn't that the whole point of the website?' He shook his head and smiled indulgently. 'You're too soft.'

I went over to him and put my hands on his shoulders, feeling the heat of his skin under his shirt as I gave him a little massage.

'It's a one-off.'

Rohan leaned back into my hands. 'Yeah, that's good. Right there.' He groaned as my fingers released the tension in his muscles and I realized that, with one thing or another, we hadn't touched properly for a day or two. That was unusual for us; New York really was taking a toll.

'Look,' Rohan said, 'you're the best judge, of course, but I really think you need to focus on your next collection and stop messing about. You've exhibited in London, hon. It was a sell-out! You can do it again!' His voice softened. 'You're good.' He reached up and squeezed my hands. 'I hate it when you sell yourself short.'

He stood up and touched his lips to mine. The tension went out of me as I relaxed into the kiss and, for a few moments, there was no New York, no Grace, no house, no masterpiece waiting to be painted – just the feel of my husband's mouth on mine and the familiar smell of his skin. But then he pulled away reluctantly, stroking a finger across my cheek as he did so.

'Hold that feeling, gorgeous. Save it for tonight.' His hand slid down my body, round my waist and across my bum. 'I've got to run.'

He winked as he looked around for his keys and his briefcase, and that was it: the moment to bring up the topic of Grace was lost. But what I didn't realize then was that the longer I held the information inside me, secret and burning, the harder it would be to tell him. Rohan didn't know Grace, or the effect she had on me, but I did.

I'd lived with her before.

Two

Rohan closed the front door with a bang, leaving a shocked silence that reverberated through the house. I sat for a moment, with my head in my hands and my eyes half closed, and let my mind wander. Under my eyelids, I could see the kitchen as it used to be – before we coated its walls with glossy units and smothered the old lino floor with laminate; before we fitted the built-in appliances and the gleaming new oven.

It was all there: the foundations of the old Victorian house, as well as the transient energy of those who'd occupied it throughout the past century. If I concentrated hard enough, I could sometimes catch echoes of them; a snatch of the adults who'd lived and loved within these four walls; of the children who'd grown up here. Their breaths had brushed this very ceiling; had become a part of the fabric of the house. Their thoughts and emotions had impregnated the walls. To my mind, these people still existed, trapped in layers, like coats of paint, behind the cabinets and the shiny glass tiles.

In the hall, the grandfather clock we'd inherited with the house ticked off the seconds, each tick a textured drop of sound that swelled and burst, adding its own shape to the canvas of the house. My breathing slowed and, between my half-closed lids, I pictured the girl who'd lived here before slip into the kitchen, her hair in a ponytail, clean uniform on, ready for school. I watched as she poured cereal into a bowl, added milk, taking care not to spill it, closed the old pine-fronted fridge, and sat at the table to eat her breakfast. She was sweet, and I could tell by the pride she'd taken in her uniform that she was conscientious, too. She read while she ate: one of the thicker Harry Potter tomes. It was advanced for her age, which I took to be seven or eight today, and I smiled my admiration, proud like a mother – not that she'd see me, of course.

But this was no time for daydreaming. I pushed my chair out from under me with a scrape and stood, bringing our new kitchen back into focus. The heat was still stifling; the clock still ticked its metronomic beat; that lazy fly still circled. I picked up the fly swat that had taken up residence on the kitchen table since the heatwave began and gently swooshed until I could edge the fly back out to the garden and off away over the hedge. As my second coffee ran through the machine, I leaned on the counter and reopened the email on my phone. Not that I needed to read it again; already I knew it by heart.

Hi Abi, how are you? I know – long time! How have you been? How's the art coming along? Have you exhibited again?

I've had a blast in Australia. I've moved around a bit and seen some different places but my last job came to a natural end and, after lots of soul-searching, I think it's time to come home. You can only wander for so long, right? I've decided to look for a job in London, maybe do some volunteering or something where I can make a real difference. Are you still in London? It'd be great to hook up and, if you have any leads on places to stay, that'd be great. I'm back next month. Cheers, Grace

Grace. Grace, Grace, Grace.

She'd been the first person I'd met at university. It had been my very first afternoon and I'd sensed her before I'd seen her, as if her presence had charged the air itself. Dad had dropped me and my suitcases at the Halls and left, muttering about parking meters and rush-hour traffic, and I'd found my room, unlocked it and heaved my stuff inside. It wasn't anything much: the scuffed grey paintwork was the colour of rain clouds and, without any personal stuff, it was as bare as a prison cell. I could still give you an inventory of what was there when I arrived: bed, desk, desk chair, easy chair, wardrobe. I added the contents of two suitcases and, later, an easel, canvases, paintbrushes, turpentine. Two dinner plates, two side plates, two bowls, two mugs, two glasses, two sets of cutlery.

'What if you have friends over to eat?' Dad had asked.

'I won't have friends over,' I'd said. *I don't have friends.*

I'd lain on the bed that first afternoon, staring at the pages of a book, my eyes scratchy with unshed tears; my ears unable to drum out the unaccustomed roar of the London traffic and the sounds of London life: engines revving, sporadic shouts, sudden bursts of police sirens that left my heart thudding. I felt naked — more than naked; I felt as if my skin had been torn off, leaving me red raw and vulnerable; my sense of self as warped as a Picasso. I'd lain on the bed and tried to picture a force field around my body — a buzzing line of light that would keep the world, with its horrors, away from me. I hadn't learned, then, about PTSD. I hadn't learned how to deal with it.

From inside the building I could hear voices: my fellow students. They were in the corridor, talking and bonding, flirting, getting to know each other; chatting about where to go for dinner.

Vacuous. No cares in the world. I pictured them leaning casually against the walls, dirty shoes marking the paintwork; someone's door open, music coming from inside, and I longed to be with them; one of them. There was the occasional voice raised in mock offence, and too much laughing. Something deep inside my head had thrummed and then, when I heard the rap of knuckles on my door and the excited voices stopped outside my room, I'd held myself statue-still, not breathing. Even the earring I liked to twist between my fingers fell still.

'Is she in?'

'I thought she was.'

'I didn't hear her go out.'

'Maybe she popped out for something to eat?'

'Knock again.'

I visualized the force field, crackling and electric outside my door; a barrier of energy to repel them and, after a few interminable moments, I heard the shuffling of feet retreating.

'We tried.'

'Never mind. Another time.'

I'd slumped back on the pillow, the corridor once more silent. My window was open to the warm September evening but then, right outside my room, the air was rent with the sudden and hostile blare of a car horn that sent my heart scudding. When it had calmed, I'd turned my attention back to the book I was trying to read, my eyes going over the same paragraph I'd read ten minutes previously, and then the hairs on the back of my neck prickled. I froze.

Someone was outside my room; I felt it. I waited, motionless, for the knock but, as the pause extended, I slid silently off the bed and crept towards the door. I'd held my breath, waiting for the person outside to make a move, and I'd stood there for almost a minute, then, when nothing happened, I'd ripped opened the door and there – looking as surprised to see me as I was to see her – was a student about five feet six tall, with shiny, dark hair, tortoiseshell glasses, pale skin and freckles. I still remember what she was wearing: grey skinny jeans, a white T-shirt with a scarf knotted artfully around her neck and the same scuffed white Adidas we were all wearing in those days. Over her shoulder she'd slung a stylish leather bucket bag, which had made me instantly rethink the backpack I carried everywhere.

We'd stared at each other for a moment, then she'd said, simply, 'Hi, I'm Grace. Can I come in?' and the force field had really failed me there because I'd stepped back and let her walk right into my life.

And, to be fair, they'd been happy days, just the two of us hanging out. Sure, to begin with, I'd had to back away when her boyfriend, Alex, came up to visit, but I was her North Star – 'the fridge to her magnet', as she used to say – the one thing she'd always come back to with a knock on the door and a smile. She'd slink into my room in her lounge pants and her glasses with neither apology nor explanation, and there we'd be again, just the two of us.

Grace and Abs. Abs and Grace.

It soon became apparent that Grace was popular. And why wouldn't she be? A keen and brilliant medical student, she had everything going for her – brains, beauty, emotional intelligence by the bucketload. Her dimpled smile won everyone over, from professors and students to grannies on the bus. She was the type of girl who'd dance or sing with buskers in the stuffy tunnels of the Underground before blowing a kiss and giving them her last fiver; she was on first-name terms with all the *Big Issue* sellers we ever passed; and she shouted 'thank you' to bus drivers. She gave off an aura of loveliness in which everyone wanted to bask – yet she chose to attach herself to me.

'Go out with your friends,' I'd tell her. 'I'm fine on my own' – and that was the stupid thing in all this: I really was. I was happy to be alone, to lie in my filth and revel in my misery, but she'd roll her eyes and punch my arm, and joke that I was stuck with her now. If Alex wasn't coming up to stay, she'd bound into my room on weekend mornings, tearing open my curtains and say, 'Come on! Get up! Let's go on an adventure!' She'd suggest ice-skating, tap-dancing, going out to dance Zumba, or taking the train down to the Kentish coast to eat ice cream with Flakes down by the sea.

She told me everything – all the details of her life, even her love life, assuming, incorrectly, that I, too, was no virgin, and I'd look at the floor and flush as she told me about this position and that position and how she liked it best. The intimacy was unnerving. Overwhelming. All-consuming. Flattering. We were chalk and cheese but, somehow, it worked.

For a while.

The coffee machine beeped, startling me from my thoughts and I stared at the email, still not believing that Grace had written to me; not believing that she was coming back. It had been four years since she'd left, just before my gallery show – just before I'd met Rohan. By then I'd lived with her for five years, through university and beyond, until she'd disappeared – *pouf!* – like a pantomime genie, off to Australia with her latest boyfriend.

I should invite her to stay with us, of course. That's what she wanted – that's what was expected, but then… I stared into space as I weighed up the dilemma. I was older now. Stronger. Married.

Living in a lovely home. Although she was as familiar to me as a favourite old shoe, there was no space for Grace in my life. I picked up my phone and clicked 'reply'.

Dear Grace, I wrote, thumbing the words before I lost my resolve.

Lovely to hear from you! Sounds like you had a wonderful time in Australia, and how exciting to be moving back to London. Yes, I live in North London now, with my husband. I'm very busy with work but I'd be very happy to help you find somewhere to stay – if you give me an idea of budget and the sort of area you want to be in, maybe I could see what's available. When are you planning to arrive? Cheers, Abi

Upstairs, a door slammed, and the noise ripped through the house like a gunshot. I jumped in my seat and Alfie, our cat, shot into the room, his claws skittering on the hard floor.

'You got a shock, too?' I said and he prowled, his tail fluffed up like a squirrel's. Outside, the trees rustled, the first wind we'd had in days – weeks, it seemed. 'It was just the wind,' I said. 'Nothing to be scared of, you wuss.'

I turned back to my phone and read the email again to myself, as pleased with myself as an alcoholic pushing away a drink, then I put the message into the 'drafts' folder – it was time to visit Mrs Keyson. Her husband was one of my patients at the hospice: a sparky, ex-fighter pilot, he was one of my favourites, but he didn't have long left, and he missed his dog, Bruce. It was way beyond my remit as a volunteer, but I was going to paint a portrait for him to keep by his bedside.

Three

It was midday by the time I'd finished photographing the dog at Mrs Keyson's and got off the bus at the High Street. I was sweating, my T-shirt damp against my back; the music in my AirPods drowning out the sound of whatever birds might have been singing. Summer was never easy for me; things that other people loved – the scent of a flower, or the slant of light at sunset – had the potential to tip me into a full-blown panic attack. I knew that now. I dealt with it.

At the bus stop, a woman fiddled with a tube of sunscreen and a dotty pink parasol that protruded from the handlebars of her pushchair. The buggy was close to the kerb, its wheels facing the road, and I looked away, uncomfortable. You saw these random accidents all the time on the news. 'It happened in the blink of an eye' or 'I only turned away for a second'. Children run over in their own driveways; toddlers slipping under the water of holiday swimming pools; kids running out into the street to catch a ball. But the woman spoke, forcing me to turn around and pull out an AirPod as I pressed 'pause' on my iPod. She was slim with long dark hair, not much more than twenty, her face bare of make-up.

'D'you think it'll rain?' She nodded up to the sky as if scanning for invisible clouds and, for a moment, I froze. Talking to strangers wasn't something I generally did. I looked up at the sky, too, my mind working to frame a reply.

'Feels like it might,' the woman said, and I knew what she meant – the morning's wind had dropped to nothing, and there was a ripeness in the air; a feeling that something might pop and that that pop would bring the relief the very fabric of the city was waiting for.

'How long can this go on for?' she continued, unbothered by the fact I hadn't replied, and then her bus hove into view, announcing its arrival with a long, drawn-out squeal of brakes, and I turned away.

The pavement was unusually deserted, the thrumming heat that bounced off the shop fronts and up from the tarmac of the road presumably having driven people to stay home during the hottest part of the day. Even the birds had fallen quiet. The heatwave had gone on so long people were adopting the *siestas* and late *al fresco* dinners of their European cousins, sleeping during the day and eating light suppers in gardens and on terraces as the sun's warmth teased out the evening scent of the vegetation.

Only the occasional car passed me now, one or two throwing out the startling thwump of a Euro-beat from open windows; the others hermetically sealed, locking in the air-conditioning as they swished silently past on tyres pliant with heat. I skirted the edges of the buildings, seeking what little shade there was until I found myself outside the window of one of London's best-known estate agent's. I stopped abruptly, as if that had always been my plan, and searched the 'for rent' ads, just wondering what sort of thing Grace might be able to afford, should she decide to live in my neck of the woods. It was all so expensive. There was a movement inside the shop; I looked past the ads and caught the eye of a woman at a desk. She smiled and tilted her head and, before I knew it, I was pushing through the door into the cool interior.

'Is there something I can help you with?' the woman asked, rising and holding out her hand. 'I'm Katie.'

She was wearing a sleeveless cream-coloured dress that had creased across her hips. Her tan spoke of summer weekends spent lounging in the garden. Her hair was blonde, her lipstick a bright pink. I shook her hand and her tricep wobbled.

'I was just trying to get an idea of ballpark prices for a friend.'

'To rent or to buy?'

'To rent. Just something small. For her. One bedroom. But she's not here yet. I was just looking.'

'Do you know what her budget is?'

'No. I just wanted to get a sense,' I said, but Katie was already rummaging in her filing cabinet. She pulled out some papers. 'These are all the one-beds we have for rent at the moment. Hmm. Whereabouts are you looking?'

'As close to here – and the station – as possible, I suppose. She'd like to be reasonably close to me. I'm in Albert Road.'

'Oh?' A barely noticeable nod told me she was impressed. 'Nice... Which house is it, if you don't mind me asking?'

'Semi on the corner. Fifty-nine.'

Katie's chin lifted and fell in another nod. 'Oh yes. I remember that one.'

'One person's misfortune is another's good luck, right?' I said brightly and Katie exhaled through her nose.

'Sad story, though, wasn't it?' She tapped her nails on the desk.

I nodded. 'And they just upped and left the house as it was. As you would, I guess.' I shrugged. 'It was untouched for nine years and then… well.' I shrugged again. 'Anyway, it was a blank canvas for us. We've done lots.'

'Good,' Katie said. 'Well, if you're ever ready to sell…' she gave a little laugh and a wink, 'I expect you'd get a very good return on that one.' She sorted her brochures and pushed one across the table. 'Right. For your friend, we currently have this. It's very nice. Spacious. Recently redecorated. Walkable.'

I looked at the price and recoiled. 'Is that what a one-bed costs these days?'

Katie pursed her lips and nodded. 'Yep. It's commuter-belt. Good schools, too. We also have a few studios that would come in a bit cheaper. Do you think your friend would consider that?'

I waggled my head this way and that, already regretting coming in, and Katie slid over another brochure. The photographer had tried their best but even I could tell they must have had their back pinned to the wall to make the room look anything other than tiny. Despite containing a bathroom and a 'kitchenette', it wasn't much bigger than our rooms in Halls had been – all very well when you were eighteen and starting out, perhaps not so now.

Still, Grace did have a knack with interiors. She'd taken one look at the way I'd done my room in Halls and waved her magic wand over it. Shifting the bed up against the window and moving the desk to the side, she'd created a much more inviting area with more floor space. A potted plant here, a throw and a couple of cushions there, and she actually made the room look homely and welcoming. But I couldn't see what she could do to improve this place.

'Thank you so much,' I said, pushing the details back to Katie. 'Honestly, I don't really know what she's looking for so maybe it's best I leave it to her. But thanks anyway.'

'No problem,' Katie said, handing me her card. 'Get her to drop by or give me a call when she's here and I'll see what we can find for her.'

I practically ran out of the shop, shielding my eyes against the sudden blast of light. I owed Grace — we both knew that. It was why she'd written to me in the first place. I'd still do anything for her — as I always had. It's what was expected.

In my gut, I had that feeling I was cresting the top of a roller-coaster, my stomach clenched and my muscles tensed; my mouth open ready to scream as I plunged headfirst into the abyss. Walking quickly, I turned into Albert Road, glad to leave the High Street, Katie and the estate agent's behind.

Four

Albert Road marked the beginning of the older, more established, part of town, and the trees that towered above my head threw shade across the entire street, bringing the temperature down a notch. The roads on this side of the railway meandered in curves that were laid over a hundred years ago, Albert Road the backbone from which the other, narrower streets sprung like the broken ribs of an ancient skeleton. It was the most desirable part of this expensive satellite of London – a part that Rohan and I would never usually have been able to afford. But fifty-nine had been underpriced, largely – though not entirely – because it was what the estate agent had called 'a project'.

Rohan had been surprised I'd even looked outside our usual search area.

'Great location – but, bloody hell!' he'd said as we'd stood outside on the pavement, taking in the dilapidated three-storey house that sat eternally linked with its smarter twin where the street made a sharp turn left. The matching attic windows of the two houses gave the appearance of eyes that watched the comings and goings of the street ahead of them.

The front of the house was choked with ivy that stretched its tendrils towards and around the third-floor window and the front garden was overgrown, giving us only a hint of red brick and a glance of peeling paintwork around the edge of the front windows. Cast-iron railings ran around the edge of the plot, looking more as if their aim was to restrain the house and its residents than to keep out any undesirables; and a path of cracked terracotta tiles led to the porch. *Decrepit* was the word that came to mind. *Decayed*.

'It's a vacant property,' the estate agent said vaguely as he ushered us down the path, keys rattling in his hand. 'It's still furnished, and comes "as is", but you might not want...' he'd cleared his throat behind his hand. 'Well, see for yourselves.'

Inside, the theme of decay continued, the semi a far cry from the neo-Georgian new-builds that my husband coveted, with their gleaming new kitchens, plantation shutters and easy-breezy, open-plan layouts. Untouched since the owners' sudden departure, the interior spoke almost of a different age, its air loaded with the stale exhalations of people long gone. We'd explored its musty depths as the agent had spoken of 'original features', 'exciting potential' and a 'rare opportunity'.

'I know you're up for doing some work, but it's too much,' Rohan said as we contemplated the master bedroom. Busy floral wallpaper coated the walls from floor to ceiling and even suffocated the back of the door, closing up the room and constricting my lungs with the feeling that I might never find my way out. The agent had tugged at the heavy damask curtains, releasing a scattering of dead flies and a cloud of dust that made us all cough, and pointed out the original marble fireplace, the high ceilings, the sash windows and the stained-glass inlays that cast colours across the thinning green carpet. The double mattress, stripped of its linen, sagged.

Outside, the back garden was more overgrown than shady. It was dominated by a huge oak tree, the branches of which reached toward the house like greedy arms. At the back fence, I could just about make out the faded pink paintwork of a children's Wendy House, its roof now camouflaged with mildew. Its edges were indistinct, as if it were dissolving back into ancient oak and becoming a part of the garden's wilderness. With my forehead pressed to the window, I cut back the plants in my mind's eye. I trimmed the grass and sat on the wooden bench by the roses – in my head, I pictured a little girl in red shoes and a flowery dress make her way across the lawn to whisper secrets to her dollies at a Wendy House tea party.

'It smells like someone died in here,' Rohan said, looking dubiously at the bed's stained mattress.

I turned to face the room with a sigh then wandered back onto a landing fringed with ornate wooden railings and across into the big family bathroom. It was rife with peeling, yellowed wallpaper and featured a stand-alone bath so filthy I had to trail a finger through the dirt to see it was made of porcelain.

The second bedroom was smaller and darker, much of the light stolen by the oak tree. It was cool and I shivered as I entered. The room still contained the single bed and dresser of a girl – presumably the one for whom the Wendy House was built. It had a grey carpet, and lilac-and-white wallpaper that swirled and twirled, its pattern marked with the greasy smudges of old Blu Tack. The room had its own fireplace, functional rather than fancy, the ashes of a solid object still lodged in the grate. I bent down to look closer: a book of some sort; a diary maybe, perhaps 90 per cent destroyed by fire, but the swirl of handwriting was still visible on the fragment of a lined page that faced me. I reached out to touch the paper and it disintegrated. I jumped back up, goosebumps prickling my flesh.

Rohan was right: there was a smell about the place, but I could see through the detritus of the years to the families who'd lived there before; to the child who'd worked, played, lived and breathed in this very room. I stood back on the threshold and surveyed the room, imagining her again: I pictured her waking up in the morning, opening the curtains, looking out at the street; picking out clothes for the day; getting dressed and ready for school. I'd told the estate agent to keep the story to himself – there was no way that Rohan would buy the house if he knew about it. He and his mother were as bad as each other with their ridiculous superstitions. I inhaled deeply. Was it my imagination or could I pick up a shadow of the girl's scent; something sweet and flowery?

'Aww,' said Rohan when he joined me there. He slid his arms around me and nuzzled my neck. 'Are you getting all teary-eyed on me? I agree it's the perfect size for a baby.' He stepped past me, opened the wardrobe door and closed it again with a frown. 'But I really don't like older houses. I swear, they give me the creeps.'

'But just look at the proportions,' I said. 'A project would be good. It'll keep me busy. Maybe it'll unlock my creativity! And look at the area. We can renovate it bit by bit, starting with the kitchen and bathrooms.' I paused. 'If we bought this place, we'd have the budget to do that.'

Rohan sighed. 'I really don't know. It's a lot of work.'

'It'll be worth a *lot* more when it's modernized,' the estate agent said helpfully from the landing. 'If you can do the work, it's a great investment.'

It was only then that I saw the small wooden door, about three-quarters the height of a normal door, on the landing.

'Where does this go?' I asked but already my hand was on the heavy latch, the tickle of a cobweb trailing on my skin as I lifted it and pulled open the door, releasing air stagnant with heat. I craned my neck up to see a narrow, spiral staircase. Using my hands to steady myself as I climbed, I stopped in my tracks at the entrance to a third-floor attic bedroom, and I knew at once that there was something special about this space. High in the eaves with its sleepy eye looking down on the street, it was quiet and still, with an energy that was different to the rest of the house. It had clearly been used by the girl who'd lived there, perhaps as a playroom and maybe later as a study, because stencilled flowers danced around the walls and a desk and bookshelves were pushed up against the wall. In the corner were a few dusty cardboard boxes and a couple of old suitcases. Energy thrummed through me.

I closed my eyes and pressed my fingertips to my temples, feeling the vibrations echoing inside my head. It reminded me of the basement flat Grace and I had shared after I graduated. I'd done my best work there, and this attic had the same feel. It was perfect.

Rohan caught up with me, puffing slightly from the exertion of climbing steps almost as steep as a ladder.

'Wow,' he said. 'Studio?'

I nodded and he blew dust off one of the boxes. 'Looks like the last people left some stuff.' He opened the top box and pulled out a toddler's dress. 'Meh. Baby clothes. Shame it's not the family treasure.'

'We have to buy this house,' I said, heart thumping. 'Rohan, please. I really need to live here.'

Five

Funnily enough, I hadn't studied Art at university. Much as I'd wanted to.

'Nope,' my dad had said when I'd pushed him, again and again, to let me do something more interesting than Management Science. 'No way.'

We'd argued it this way and that over dinner, relentlessly, for months.

'You don't need a degree in Fine Art in order to paint,' he said. 'Did you see the graduate prospects on a Fine Art course? Seventy-one per cent. Compared to what? Ninety per cent on Man-Sci? It's a no-brainer.'

'Did you see the student satisfaction scores?' I'd retorted, because I'd looked at the website too. '4.03 on Management Science, and 4.52 on Fine Art.'

'*Pff,*' Dad had said. 'University courses aren't designed to make people happy. They're designed to get people qualifications and jobs – good jobs, careers – and set them up for life.'

'Sounds boring,' I'd muttered under my breath.

'You can paint in your spare time,' Dad said, over and over, like a broken record, like the words were a part of him, a part of his soul, his identity. In the end, I'd resolved to switch courses once I got to university, but then everything had happened and the fight had gone out of me and I'd ended up, empty as a soggy paper bag, on the Management Science course, and it had been Grace who'd helped me find my way back to painting.

She liked to watch television in my room. Every evening after lectures she'd slip into my room and flick it on. One evening, while she devoured whatever it was she was watching, I'd got my pencils and doodled a little sketch of her, enjoying the comforting rub of pencil on paper.

'What's that?' she asked as the credits finally rolled, and I shrugged and turned the picture away. 'Nothing.'

But she grabbed it from me and examined it, a wry smile lifting the corners of her mouth. 'You know, it's really rather good,' she said. 'You can actually draw. Weren't you tempted to study Art? I mean, seriously, why are you studying Management Science when you so clearly hate it?'

I picked at the skin around my thumbs and tried to come up with a better answer than 'because my dad told me to'.

'Because it'll be useful?' I said.

'No doubt about it.' Grace picked up a bottle of my nail polish and started languidly to paint her nails. She balanced the blue polish she loved so much precariously on a textbook on my duvet cover. 'But what about passion? I've known since I was twelve that I wanted to be a doctor, and my whole life since then has been spent working towards that goal. The subjects I chose, how hard I studied... the summer jobs I took. All to get me closer to where I want to be.'

'Wow,' I said faintly.

'But what makes *you* happy – what makes your soul sing – is art,' Grace declared. One hand done, she replaced the cap on the polish and looked up. 'So why aren't you painting? Just because you're studying Management Science doesn't mean you can't paint. It's not as if the two are mutually exclusive.'

She tilted her head and looked at me, waiting, and my mouth fell open. Dad may have said the same thing a hundred times, but this was the first time the words had actually reached me. Grace spoke again.

'And if I were you – if I had your talent, I mean – I would be bloody well nurturing it in my spare time, not sitting about feeling sorry for myself. I mean, let's be honest: we both know you could do with some *joy* in your lonely little life.' The words stung despite her laugh, but she shook up the nail polish, unscrewed the cap and continued stroking blue onto her nails. The next day I went to the art supply shop and bought what materials I could afford.

There was just about space for the easel in my room. I'd bought a pre-stretched canvas, primed and ready to go, and a set of acrylic paints: a box of tubes every colour of the rainbow, but it was the darker colours that called to me. On my virgin palette, I squeezed out black and grey, greens and browns and reds and oranges, and then I picked a brush and I dipped it into the paints and swirled and stroked the colours onto the canvas, knowing but not wanting to know what was coming. Knowing that it wasn't going to be pretty.

And, underneath my hand, a landscape started to appear – fields and hedges and trees and birds – but I couldn't stem the feelings that exploded through my brush and I lashed the colours onto the canvas, twisting the picture into something dark and angry; a visible ejaculation of fear, of horror and of shame.

It was only when I'd finished, as the students in the rooms around me started to wake, banging doors and shuffling off to breakfast, that I saw how far I'd demolished the landscape; how I'd warped the birds into dribbling beasts of horror; how the flowers, the golden fields and the hedges had morphed into something dark, twisted and angry; how I'd given trees whispers of faces that observed with beady eyes and spiteful, pointy mouths; how I'd sucked up the beauty of nature and spat out something sick, which oozed malevolence, darkness and evil.

But, as I'd sat there, spent, and taken in the finished painting in its entirety, I'd realized that not only was there a beauty to that destruction, but that the act of painting it had taken away a sliver of the self-hatred that sat on my shoulder, ugly and dark, like a beast that needed constant feeding. From then on, when the feelings became too much to bear, I'd buy more supplies and start another picture, sitting up all night as my soul drained onto the canvas. These landscapes were the ones that formed the basis of the collection that was shown at my first exhibition.

It had been, in every sense, a triumph.

Six

After I'd had some lunch and made a bit of a fuss of Alfie, who was unused to me going out for so long, I climbed the stairs up to the second bedroom. The door was closed: Rohan and I had gone bit by bit with the house renovation – the kitchen and bathrooms our priorities, then the living area and the master bedroom. This room was still largely untouched; a space neither of us had cause to use. I stood outside the door for a moment and took a breath, then pushed it gently open.

Inside, the air was cold and musty – neglected – yet I had the feeling that I'd disturbed something. Was there a rustling? Or the echo of a rustling? I peered at the room. The bed and dresser we'd inherited from the previous occupants looked dejected, as if waiting for their owner to return. I kicked the leg of the bed, thinking to send any potential mice skittering, but of course we had a cat so there were no mice, and the room answered with a silence that caused the hairs on my arms to stand on end.

I skirted around the bed and opened the wardrobe, catching as I did so an echo of the scent that had steeped into the wood – something floral, and soft, like talcum powder. A few wooden hangers still remained on the rail and, on the floor, there was a pair of flip-flops, the ancient print of a foot embossed on the thin, cracked rubber. I slid a foot gently into one. Cinderella.

Replacing the shoe carefully, I pulled out the fabric of the flowery curtains and sneezed. The pattern was faded from bearing witness to thousands of sunrises, but the fabric was sound – with a good vacuum and a clean, they'd do. I pushed open the window, letting fresh air rush into the room, and looked around. A spring-clean, a lick of polish on the wardrobe... It wouldn't be such a big deal to invite Grace to stay, and if Rohan was going to be working in New York... I bit my lip and my heart thumped. Would he acually go without me?

The bed creaked a little as I sat down on the edge, then I swung my legs up and let myself sink back, my body suddenly heavy – pulled down by something more than gravity. It was as if the bed itself wanted to feel my weight on it; as if it were drawing me in, the mattress wrapping itself around the contours of my body as I settled into the dips and rises made by the past owner. My nose prickled with dust.

Lying on my back, I took in the room from this new perspective. Had the wallpaper danced in front of the other girl's eyes, too, the pattern appearing to move as it joined and separated from itself in an eternal, swaying dance? Had she lain awake at night, staring at it as she pictured her future and planned what she'd do with her life?

I blinked and rubbed my forehead to rid myself of the pattern imprinted on my retinas, then opened them again with a smile: the crazy pattern was just the kind of thing Grace-the-extrovert would like.

Despite the saggy mattress, the bed was comfortable and, the longer I lay there, the more I felt it pulling me in, sucking me deeper. I closed my eyes once more, and, slowly, something started to form in my mind's eye – an image of some sort. It was hazy, a will-o'-the-wisp that faded if I tried to focus on it. So I let it come, batting down the buzz of excitement lest it interfere: this was a feeling I knew; a feeling I hadn't had for a long time. I concentrated only on breathing in and out while I let my subconscious take form in my mind's eye, like a bubble from deep down making its way to the surface. And then, was it my imagination, or was there the lightest of touches on my arm – a hand, cold? I jumped and my eyes snapped open as a gust of wind tugged at the curtains and blew the room door open, slamming it against its hinges so it bounced.

I scrambled up and ran, without thinking, to the attic, where I picked out a canvas and placed it carefully on my easel. Without letting my thoughts interrupt what I was doing, I picked up my palette and squeezed out a few colours. I mixed a few – skin tones, I noticed – which I dabbled onto some rough paper and played with, using different brushes as well as my fingers, and experimenting with the way the colour might vary in different lights. Then, still not knowing what it was that was forming in my subconscious, I mixed a palette of complementary colours – a blue, some browns, a pale purple – and I dabbled them together on the paper, smudging them into one another. When Rohan's head appeared at the top of the stairs I barely processed his presence.

'Phew, hot day,' he said, loosening his tie, then he crossed the floor, kissed the back of my neck and took in what I was doing with his face level with mine.

'Ahh,' he said, standing back up, and I could hear both hope and admiration glittering in his voice as he recognized this almost dissociative state I was in. 'Does the artist work again?' He put

Transcript of interview with Mr Rohan Allerton, husband of Abigail Allerton: 20 December 2019

'I understand that it was that summer when Abigail first began working on a new portrait painting?'

'Yes.'

'How did you feel at that point?'

'I was hopeful. It was a good thing. She'd stagnated creatively for some time so I was glad to see her mixing paints for something other than a dog portrait. I really hoped she'd got her mojo back, not least because she had an exhibition lined up and she was running out of time. Francesca – from the gallery– kept putting the dates back and I got the impression that her patience was running out. I worried that if Abs didn't pull something out of the bag, she wouldn't be given another chance.

'So I was relieved when I saw her starting on something that looked like it might be more serious. I mean, she's a talented artist. If only she'd just focus and not spend her time pissing about – excuse me – with pet portraits.

'Her first collection was a massive success, you know. The critics loved it. It sold. Every piece sold. Have you seen it online?'

'Not yet.'

'It was dark; threatening. You can google it. It's scary. Looking back, I suppose that was a clue... but you don't know at the time, do you? You don't know where these things come from.'

'And you don't want to ask?'

[Pause] 'No. You don't want to ask.'

Seven

It was Rohan's idea that we had dinner with his parents a minimum of once a month. Though, when I say 'his parents', I really mean his mother. And, when I say it was his idea, I'm absolutely sure it was hers. I wouldn't be giving anything away to say that it's she who wears the trousers in my in-laws' marriage – an arrangement that suits my father-in-law, Clive, down to the ground.

Meena Allerton is a strong woman who usually gets what she wants in life, and Rohan is her only son – her pride and joy – a point which she'd made clear from the moment she first cast her eyes over me. While she never judged me, not openly anyway, I always had the impression she thought I was lucky to be with Rohan – never the other way around. Sometimes I wondered if she would have preferred Rohan to marry a 'nice Indian girl' for, although he is to all intents and purposes British, we both know that if you scratch a little deeper, he's laced through to his soul with the spirituality of Meena's Hindu background. Physically, he's a good mix of both his parents: his colouring and his aristocratic bone structure from Meena's side, and the blue-green eyes courtesy of the Anglo-Saxon input of the Allertons. A paler, bearded version of Hrithik Roshan, as Meena's always saying. I roll my eyes, but secretly I agree.

Meena herself is the only member of the family not originally from England. She was born in India and sent to the UK to study. It was here in London, while she studied for her degree, that she surprised everyone by falling in love with Clive, a quiet, unassuming Accountancy student. The stand-off about where they would live after marriage was the stuff of family legend: while Clive was happy enough to give India a try, my mother-in-law refused point-blank to go back, and so the Allerton family tree remained firmly rooted in North London, where it always had been. I often wondered if Meena missed the colours and life of India but, when I asked her, she said she missed only three things: her parents – both now dead; the warmth of the sun; and the 'perfect' *masala dosas* from a certain street-food shack.

In fact, her quest to find a *dosa* that rivalled these magical ones from India underscored the Allerton family's entire lives. Whenever we found ourselves in a restaurant that served southern Indian food, there would be a certain quickening as she wondered: could this be the one? She'd lick her lips and finger the menu nervously.

'For God's sake, don't do it,' Clive would sigh. 'Don't torture yourself, love.'

But still, a *dosa* would be ordered. Meena would taste it, delicately, as if it might contain something toxic, then her head would tip sideways and up as if asking the opinion of the gods, but then she'd shake her head and turn her lips downward. Seeing her shoulders sag with disappointment every time was strangely moving.

'Nope,' she'd say, pushing it away with a sigh, then she'd tell Rohan to order '*pav bhaji* or *chana puri* – and maybe some veg *samosas*?' instead. But, once the attention had moved away from her, she would slide her hand gently back out toward the *dosa*, pull it towards her and eat it greedily with the *sambar* running down her wrists. The first time I witnessed this decimation of the rejected *dosa*, I looked at Rohan with a laugh ready to burst, but he refused to meet my eye, and I learned right there and then that no one laughs at Meena Allerton.

Anyway, the dinner for which I'd had to pull myself away from my easel was the 'at-least-monthly' dinner we took with Meena and Clive.

Eight

Meena was already at the table when we arrived at the restaurant; there was no sign of Clive, but this was not unusual. Rather than reschedule if her husband couldn't make it, Meena would come without him, desperate, I'm sure, not to get out of the habit of the monthly meeting lest it set a precedent.

The restaurant had embraced the heatwave, its huge glass doors zig-zagged back to open up the place completely to the pavement. I was glad to see Meena was seated at a booth a little way back and to the side from this edge – blame the PTSD if you like, but I couldn't relax too close to the edge. Meena was dressed in pale-blue jeans and a *kurta*, which made her look almost ordinary and that created a dissonance inside me; 'ordinary' was not a word anyone would naturally associate with my mother-in-law, a formidable woman known in the community for her phenomenal ability to raise both funds and awareness for whichever causes she chose to champion: premature babies, abused women, cancer research.

When Meena saw us walk in, she stood up and clutched Rohan to her, hugging him tight and ruffling his hair as if he were a child home from his first day at school. I looked away until she was ready to let him go, then she and I had our usual slightly awkward hug and air-kiss — not that she didn't love me. Just not as much as she loved Rohan.

'Abigail, how are you?' she said, openly scanning me for signs of early pregnancy.

'Good, thanks. And you? Hot, isn't it!' I said, ignoring the sinking of the shoulders that showed she'd seen nothing of interest.

'Daddy has a meeting tonight,' she said in reply as we took our seats, and Rohan and I nodded as if we knew what she meant. Clive was long retired and, although he kept his fingers in some philanthropic pies, I suspected his Monday evening 'meeting' might involve the pub. Again, there were things that were never spoken about in this family; certain dignities that were upheld without questions being asked.

'Mili might come, though,' she added.

I nodded and Rohan said, 'Great.' Mili was his sister. Stunningly beautiful and achingly cool, she'd done everything 'right' in Meena's eyes; despite being a couple of years younger than Rohan, she was already married with a two-year-old daughter. I was glad she was coming; when Mili turned up with the baby, the focus of attention was generally on little Sofia and not on my own childless state.

I flicked through the menu while Rohan caught up with his mum. Outside, the sun was squeezing itself sideways through the gaps between the buildings of the High Street, its rays softer, kinder, than they'd been earlier in the day. A knot of drinkers mingled outside the pub, their voices rising to compete with one another so the overall sound that reached us here in the restaurant was loud, rowdy and punctuated with shouts. Music ebbed and flowed from the open windows of flats above the shops: the thump of a beat, the riff of a saxophone, the repetitive squawk of a child practising scales on the violin. Pedestrians strolled arm in arm in the uniform of summer: shorts, vests, slip-dresses and slopping flip-flops blackened by the city's pavements.

Suddenly I was aware of something moving faster than the prevailing speed of the street; something carving a way through the pedestrians and the mob outside the pub. I tensed involuntarily, but then I saw the signature scarf flying like a flag: Mili.

My sister-in-law surged along the pavement and into the restaurant through what would have been the window as if she'd been caught up in a hurricane, her hair flying loose, chiffon scarf swirling about her. She was wearing a classic 'Mili' cocktail of brightly coloured East-West clothes and eyes followed her as she swerved between the tables, hands raised in apology to those she bumped. Gold studs gleamed in her ears, a tiny diamond studded her nose, and all her fingers were ringed in gold. Mili worked as a buyer at John Lewis, in the homeware department, and was one of those people who 'had an eye' for fashion and style – I knew no one who could throw things together as randomly as her yet somehow make everything look so well put together.

'Hi-hi-hi,' she said, giving her mum a quick squeeze and a showy kiss on the cheek. 'And, hi, Love's Young Dream.' She gave Rohan and I each a proper hug before sliding into the seat next to Meena. 'How's it going?'

I watched Rohan's face drop with a thud that hit me in the gut. 'No Sofia tonight?' he asked.

'School night,' Mili grinned. 'She's at nursery now. Needs to get into a routine. So, no. Jay's on Daddy duty.'

'I don't know. These nurseries,' Meena shook her head, 'breeding ground for sickness. You mark my words, she'll be sick all the time now. You should have...'

'. . . left her with you,' Mili interrupted, rolling her eyes. 'Yeah, yeah, I know, but it's just not practical. I work four days a week. You wouldn't be able to do anything if you had her with you. Think about your charity work! Anyway – let's not go over that again. I'm *starving*. What are you all having?'

'We haven't looked,' said Rohan, although I knew exactly what both he and his mum would order.

'Hmm, maybe the pepperoni?' Rohan licked his lips. 'And what about you, my love? My gorgeous artiste?' He pronounced the word with a long 'ee' as he looked at me over steepled fingers.

'Ooh,' said Mili, who never missed a trick. 'Are you painting again?'

'I caught her mixing colours this evening,' Rohan said, nodding as if he were my manager. 'I think she might be onto something.'

'Another dog?' Meena said with a little laugh. Her fingers fiddled with the paper napkin.

'No,' said Rohan slowly. He looked at me with narrowed eyes, a tilted head and the hint of a smile. 'I could see something was bubbling inside her. The colours – they looked like skin tones. What do you think it's going to be? I'm thinking a portrait? Am I right?'

I shook my head vaguely. I hated talking about my work, especially when it was still in this opaque state.

'Oh, come on! You must have some idea,' said Meena. 'What was in your head? You can tell us.' She leaned further towards me, eyes wide and I pictured her on the phone to her coffee-morning friends telling them I was painting again. These are women who inhale Chinese whispers like oxygen: by mid-morning I'd have painted a whole collection; by the afternoon, I'd be 'exhibiting'; by this time tomorrow, my entire collection would be 'pre-sold'.

Patience. I closed my eyes, inhaled deeply, exhaled, then said, 'Rohan's right.' I smiled at him. 'I think it might be a portrait.'

Mili nodded. 'A departure. Good. It's good not to get typecast, so to speak.' I smiled; she knew nothing about art, but then she said, 'Do you have a muse?' and I stared at her with my mouth half open as things slid into place in my head and I thought: *you know what, Mils, that's actually a really good question.*

Grace, I realized right then and there, was my muse. Not only was it because of her that I'd started to paint back at university, but it was as a result of her encouragement that I'd managed to secure that first gallery exhibition, the one that had launched my career. She'd pushed me out there to meet people in the industry; she'd forced me to approach gallery managers. But there was also something far less tangible about her influence. Something to do with the way she challenged me. She fired me to places I would never otherwise have gone. She did something to my head; allowed me access to things I otherwise couldn't see.

There was also the fact that, once upon a time, she'd saved my life.

Rohan, Mili and Meena were all looking at me across the table. Meena's head was tilted sideways, her face hungry to receive the information that would be transmitted like a news bulletin to the aunties on her WhatsApp groups. Mili's face was open with curiosity and a genuine interest, and Rohan was smiling indulgently with his eyes half closed. It was the perfect chance to say, 'Actually, yes, she's called Grace and, hold onto your hats, because she's coming to stay!' but I couldn't do it – not here, not like this.

'Nah,' I said, scrunching up my forehead. 'I don't have a muse. Well, not that I know of.' I laughed, and they laughed with me.

'Yes, let her hit the big-time, then she'll get a muse,' Meena said. 'But, first, she needs to have a baby!' She rubbed her hands together and Mili looked at her watch.

'Ten minutes,' she whispered to me. 'Not bad.'

'Anyway, *beta*,' Meena said to Rohan, innocently, I think. 'Did you decide whether to take the job in New York?' and it was as if the world stopped turning. Every sound fell away: the scrape of knife on plate, the clatter of crockery, the shouts from the open kitchen, the sound of the cars passing, the buzz of conversation in the restaurant – even the din from the pub across the road – everything faded away as I held my breath and waited to hear what Rohan would say.

Nine

I'd been in the kitchen the night Rohan had come home and told me he might need to move to New York – 'might', I soon learned, being an understatement as it turned out because there was no 'might' about it. It was just before the heatwave began and the weather was still unremarkable – the usual British summer of four seasons in one day. It seems odd now to think of weather that wasn't a talking point; weather that hadn't taken on a character of its own, baking the house, the street, the city and its residents – but I remember it wasn't raining, neither was it sunny. The windows were closed. The sky was nondescript and the light was fading although it wasn't yet dark enough to switch on the lamps. In this dreary light, the house felt brooding and shadowy – fully expressing the legacy of its Victorian roots, despite what we'd done to bring it up to date.

Rohan had been for a post-work meeting and I was halfway down a bottle of wine by the time I heard his key in the door. I waited for the pause as he threw his jacket over the bannister, then tracked the steps of his work shoes along the tiles of the passageway towards the kitchen. When he was at the threshold, I jumped up and squeezed my arms around him, pinning his own inside my embrace as I kissed him.

'Hello!'

'Give us a chance to get through the door!' Rohan protested, and I tasted beer on his lips and smelled the pub in his beard as we kissed again, slower this time.

'I can't help it if I missed you. How was the meeting?' I let him go.

Rohan pulled a beer out of the fridge and popped the lid. 'Cheers!'

I raised my glass.

'Well,' he said slowly. 'Funny you ask. It seems I may have news.' He paused. 'Tell me... what do you think about moving to... New York, New York?' He put the beer down and did jazz hands.

'What?' I said, struggling to catch up as my insides fell through me. 'Are you serious?'

'Yes. They want to send me to New York – initially for a couple of months but it could easily be extended if we decide we want to stay. What do you think?' My mouth opened and closed, utterly speechless. 'I'm thinking six months,' Rohan continued. 'Upper East Side pad – trendy brownstone – a loft maybe? Just think, Abs: Fifth Avenue, Madison Avenue, Central Park, MOMA, the Guggenheim... the Metropolitan Museum of Fine Art... and your birthday in New York!'

And I was thinking, just not of the good things but of the horrors of a city – a city I didn't know, at that. Traffic, sirens, congestion, crowds, the subway and the sweaty, suffocating stench of a humid, New York summer. Terrorists. 9/11! Guns! Fear oozed through my guts; it slid around my organs and fired up my heart.

'We can't go. No way,' I said, and my voice came from far away, but it was too late. The panic had already gathered, a burning ball in my abdomen, scorching my insides and making sweat break out on my forehead. It swelled inside me and ballooned up towards my throat, squeezing my chest until I struggled to breathe. I grasped the counter as the kitchen swayed.

'No!' I gasped. 'Just say no.'

'But Abs…' Rohan said. He breathed slowly in and out with his eyes closed, then pinched the bridge of his nose and shook his head. 'I already said…'

'You said…?' I slumped onto the counter, my head in my hands, my mouth gasping for air.

'Abs,' Rohan said carefully. He put a hand on my back. 'Breathe for me. In and out. In and out. Nice and steady. Come on. Sit down.' He led me to a chair and I fell hard into it as my knees buckled.

'Let's just calm you down. You're having one of your "moments",' Rohan said and I didn't have the breath to defend myself. All I could hear was the racing of my blood as it coursed through my body.

'I have to go,' Rohan said quietly. 'With or without you.'

I pushed my hand against my chest, pressing, pressing, as my eyes beseeched him: *don't go. Don't leave me.*

We stared at each other and I saw the hesitation in his eyes; the question of whether he really could leave me. After a long moment, he changed the subject, but the issue had sizzled between us ever since, an unseen echo of the stifling heat of that interminable summer.

'Yes, darling, what did you decide?' I asked sweetly as Meena and Mili looked at Rohan. He rubbed his moustache and peered at me through a narrowed gaze I wasn't sure I liked. I knew he was trying to gauge whether I was about to have a 'moment', and weighing up how bad that would look in front of his mum.

'Well...' he said slowly.

Meena cocked her head at him. 'We're waiting!'

'Well,' said Rohan again, and I took a sip of water. 'We talked about it,' he said carefully. 'It's obviously something they really want me to do, but Abi can't get away from the hospice.'

He looked at me as if seeking my reassurance, and I nodded, relieved. He'd stay! I'd have to tell Grace she couldn't come after all, and everything would be fine. 'They're short on volunteers as it is,' Rohan said, and I nodded again: this was all true, though I only volunteered once a week.

'So you're not going?' Mili asked. 'Well, hello, career suicide.'

Rohan traced a pattern on the paper mat with his fingertip. 'However, they really, really need me there by the start of September and they've agreed it can be only for six weeks, so...' He pursed his lips. 'I'll come back for a couple of weekends whenever I can... kind of like commuting...'

His words hit me like a punch in the gut. Six weeks? Had I heard him right? I stared at my wine glass, not daring even to move.

'What?' snorted Mili, jolting the table as she banged her hands down on it in a way that made me jump, heart skittering. 'You're *commuting* to New York? Oh my God, you're my hero! You absolute legend!'

But Meena was shaking her head, her face serious. 'Oh no, *beta*, no. You can't leave Abigail. There must be some other way.'

'I have to go, Mum,' Rohan said quietly and Mili nodded, one eyebrow raised. Meena inhaled deeply then tilted her head and looked at me.

45

'What's wrong with New York, Abigail? You should go. It will be good for you.'

I opened my mouth but Rohan took the words before I could say them. 'She's needed at the hospice. And she's painting. It's too disruptive. I can fly back after four weeks for a long weekend.'

Meena looked from him to me and back again, her antennae for marital troubles quivering. She frowned at me.

'Go with him, Abigail. I know you do good work at the hospice, but he's your husband! And it'll be good for you to have a break, relax… How do you expect to start a family when you're always so… busy?'

'He chose to go, not me,' I muttered.

'What, Abigail? What did you say?'

'His choice.' I gave a tight smile and looked out toward the street, and then Meena leaned further towards Rohan and me, and said:

'Anyway, I've just remembered. Speaking of children, I've something to tell you.' She paused, making sure she had our attention, then continued. 'So, I was at a coffee morning the other day – just a small one, a charity thing where they sell goods made by those ladies in villages all over the world? You know, like that embroidered bookmark I got you? Anyway, this time it was quite good. There were hats – what do you call them? Panama, like the canal? Oh, and earrings. Very nice earrings. I got some for myself, actually.' She touched her ear but realized she was wearing her usual gold studs. 'Anyway, where was I? Oh yes, coffee morning. So the point is – Jyothi Aunty was there.'

She said this last bit with an exaggerated nod that made me think I was supposed to know the significance of Jyothi Aunty being there. My eyes slid to Rohan. He was only half listening since he was accepting the drinks from the waiter; directing the glasses of white wine to Mili and me, the juice to his mum and taking a long swig of his own pint of lager.

'Okay,' he said, rolling his lips to remove the froth.

'So,' said Meena, as if she was starting to tell a really interesting story. 'Do you remember Jyothi Aunty's son, Anouj?'

'Mmm-hmm,' said Rohan. 'How could I forget? All those times you rammed us together at dinners and weddings. Wonderful Anouj.'

'*Accountant* Anouj with the "good prospects" and the "Mercedes saloon",' said Mili with an eye-roll.

Meena glared at both of them. 'Anyway,' she said, 'Anouj is married now – to a very nice girl – and his wife's just announced she's expecting.' She sat back with a big smile as if Anouj's purpose in the world was now complete.

'How lovely,' I said.

'But – the interesting thing is,' Meena continued, 'and this is confidential, of course, because I'd never gossip about such things – but apparently they'd been trying for over a year. And then they saw a doctor, a very well-respected specialist – and look, the proof's in the pudding – or the bun in the oven!' She laughed at her own joke then carried on, 'Because she's now passed her twelve-week scan.'

'You make it sound like a degree,' said Mili darkly.

'Okay,' Rohan said. 'That's great news. Do wish them well from us.'

'Harley Street,' said Meena, nodding. 'I got his number. I hope you don't mind. He's not cheap, and he has a long waiting list, but it's worth a try, wouldn't you say?' She leaned back with a big smile and a nod, and folded her arms.

'You told Jyothi Aunty we needed this guy's number?' Rohan said, throwing his hands up. Meena bit her lip in a 'sorry-not-sorry' manner. 'For God's sake, Mum. You know we'll be the talk of the aunties now. Everyone will be gossiping.' He sat back in his seat. 'All the coffee mornings will be, like, "That wife of Rohan's can't have babies. She's too this, she's too that."'

Meena laughed. 'Oh, come on now, Ronu. No one thinks like that. Anyway, it's not as if they don't know… You've been married for three years now and,' she waved her hand at my belly, 'still no baby. Goodness, it's no secret. Maybe it's time to accept some help.'

She scrabbled in her handbag and took out a scrap of paper with a number on it and, despite his protestations, Rohan reached out and took it.

Ten

Grace was always going to have babies. She was one of those girls who just assumed that it was her destiny to have it all – career, husband, kids – and, when she got together with Alex in Year 12, it was as if the universe had come together to grant her wishes. According to Grace, Alex was the archetypal boy next door: handsome, clever, sporty and popular. Their parents even knew each other.

'Not just know each other but *love* each other!' she told me. 'When I told my mum I was going to lose my virginity to Alex, she actually took me shopping to Victoria's Secret.' Grace giggled, and I squirmed, unable to imagine such a moment with my dad. 'She helped me choose a special set of *lingerie* to celebrate.' She pronounced it properly, her French impeccable.

Alex was good at maths and science, apparently. He was at Manchester, studying Engineering. Serious, focused and utterly in tune with each other, the lovebirds studied together throughout A-levels, hung out together, finished one another's sentences and spent their spare time planning their future together. The two families even holidayed together. Grace made the pair of them sound like the best-matched couple the universe had ever seen, which made me all the more surprised when I first met him.

'Alex, this is my friend Abi,' Grace simpered, as she pushed her boyfriend ahead of her into my room. 'Come on, don't be shy!' and then Alex was there, too big for the space and not at all what I'd expected from the glowing description.

Yes, he was handsome if you liked that type, but also scruffier than I'd imagined, his dark hair dirty and a bit too long, and his jeans slung too low, gathering in pools above his grubby Converse. His skin was pale and one arm was heavily tattooed in a way I just wouldn't have associated with Grace. But what concerned me was the flightiness I sensed. There was something reckless in his eyes that spoke of infidelity and heartbreak, but Grace was blind to it.

'We've got our whole future mapped out,' she told me as we lolled about in my room, and I tried to imagine the man I'd met agreeing to her saccharine plans. She had a folder in which she kept her notes, thoughts and contacts relating to her wedding, reception, dress and honeymoon. When she wasn't studying or watching TV, she was on Pinterest, looking for ideas and adding them to the folder.

'Why don't you wait till you graduate, and then see how things go?' I suggested. 'You never know what curveballs life might throw at you, and your course is five years. It's a long time.'

But Grace yippered on as if I hadn't spoken.

'The wedding will be small.' She flashed me a picture of an elegant stone-clad house. 'This is actually the registry office where I live, can you believe it, and the photos happen on this lawn right outside.' She pointed to the lawn as she pictured herself smiling into the camera with her darling Alex. At least his suit would cover those tattoos. 'It'll be chic: just us and close family. Small but perfectly formed! No meringue nightmares! No frocky horror bridesmaids!'

Their friends would be invited to a wedding reception at the pub.

'You too!' she laughed, poking me. 'You'll have to get a dress! We're going to have fish and chips and apple crumble with custard – none of that fancy stuff. I'm no Bridezilla, so please tell me if you ever think I'm going over the top. I just want the people who mean the most to us to be able to have fun sharing our day. After all, isn't that what it's all about?'

She and Alex were already saving up for the honeymoon. They would travel to Goa with backpacks – yes, she even had a folder of those on Pinterest – and stay as long as they could afford; they were going to travel about, 'see a bit of India', then come back and get jobs. I didn't like to ask her how that worked when you were a doctor. If there licensing requirements and so on. Anyway, after a few years, when they'd saved up enough money – she didn't mention it, but I bet she had a spreadsheet – they were going to have two children, ideally girls. I envied her certainty on that bit. What if they couldn't have kids? What if they had a boy? Triplets? But the point was there: Grace and Alex had planned out their perfect future. It was decided. Everyone knew.

Eleven

Rohan held my hand as we walked home from the Tube station after the dinner with Meena and Mili, carefully avoiding the shortcut through the graveyard of St Michael's, as we always did. The sun had finally set but there was still an echo of light in the sky to the west and the warm air slid over my limbs, giving me the smothering sense that I was swimming underwater. The High Street lay on a high point of town and there was a spot opposite Mr Ho's Chinese from which, if you looked to the right, you could snatch a view down towards the spreadeagled tangle of Central London. It was second nature to face that way as we walked – to take in that view – and, tonight, as we looked, a shard of lightning speared the distant sky, illuminating for a moment the spikes of the skyscrapers that reared like jagged teeth from the urban sprawl below. We both jumped at the flash.

'Whoa. Finally!' said Rohan. 'We need this weather to break.'

I counted in my head, waiting for the crack of thunder, wondering if the drama of a thunderclap was the push I needed to confront Rohan about why he'd taken the number of the fertility specialist from his mum, but the silence dragged on, and we turned into Albert Road, where the trees now added not shade but an extra layer of darkness. The leaves rustled and my insides shrivelled at the thought of bats going about their business just above my head, their veiny wings and bulging eyes swooping over us, their stringy legs and long toes clinging to the branches. Sometimes I'd squint my eyes half closed as I walked in this part of town and try to picture how the road could have looked in Victorian times; sometimes I fancied I heard horses' hooves echoing across the centuries.

The average house price in Albert Road was higher than anywhere else in town. I knew this for no reason other than because Rohan was constantly monitoring it, like a surgeon monitoring his patient's vital signs. A few more steps along our street and his head swivelled right to take in the house he most coveted: the symmetrical, red-brick, new-build 'Georgian' that looked almost rude thrust in a modest plot among the Victorian semis. I could tell just by looking at the family paraphernalia that littered the garage that it wasn't coming up for sale any time soon – not that we'd ever be selling number fifty-nine.

The leaves rustled again as the edge of a breeze picked up and I looked down, concentrating on the uneven paving stones while I figured out how to bring up the topic of the fertility specialist. In taking the number, Rohan had admitted to his mother, to Mili, and to me that he thought there was a problem; funny how such a small thing as reaching out your hand could change so much. At the far end of the street, our house loomed in the semi-darkness, its eyes watching, unblinking, as we approached. In the attic window, something moved, caught by the breeze, maybe. I pulled my hand out of Rohan's and squeezed it into a fist.

'So, you took that number from your mum,' I said when I was sure I could get out the words without them strangling me.

'I don't have to call the guy.'

I focused on the pavement. 'Why didn't you just tell her to butt out?'

'Because… oh, for God's sake, Abi. It's just a number. I can tear it up if you like. Throw it away. I just took it to shut her up. All right?'

'You took it to make her happy. Because that's what you always do. You never stand up to her.'

Rohan spun to face me and stopped in my path. I stared up at him, surprised myself at my words because I usually liked Meena. I don't know what Rohan saw in my eyes because, when he spoke, his words sent chills through me.

'Hold on,' he said slowly. 'This isn't about my mother, is it? It's about you.' He nodded, realizing he was right, and I thought: *No. Not now. Not like this.*

'Don't you want a baby?' Rohan asked. 'Is that what this is about? Because if you don't, I think you need to tell me.' His face twisted as he fought to control his emotions. Lightning flared again, lighting us and the street for a fraction of a second as bright as the brightest day. Rohan and I stood frozen in a tableau. His hands were on his hips and he took up most of the pavement space. As the darkness after the flash released us, a dog barked a volley of howls and the trees above us rustled. I tried to sidestep Rohan, to dive towards the house, but my husband had an agility that surprised me.

'Well, Abi?' he said, blocking my way, and we stared at each other. His hopes, his dreams, his need to be a father shone out of his eyes; there was a desperation there, too. I swallowed.

'Of course I want a baby,' I whispered to the street but I felt as if the trees, the houses and the paving stones themselves could see through me. Again, out of the corner of my eye I caught a movement at the attic window and shame flooded through me. 'More than anything,' I said, and suddenly my eyes were full of tears and a lump sat hard in my throat. Rohan stared at me for a moment then pulled me to him.

'Oh, hon, it's okay,' he said, holding me tight, his hands in my hair. My tears soaked into his shirt, mascara blackening the fabric. 'I know it's difficult.'

I liked how his voice sounded with my ear pressed to his chest. I didn't want to move, to look up, to have to see that look in his eyes again.

'I just… I don't know,' he said. 'Sometimes I think it's only me on this train. Sometimes you just don't seem to be on board.'

'I am,' I said, muffled against him.

He hugged me tighter. 'I know, darling. I know. I'm sorry. I forget that you bottle things up inside; that you're not like me.' He inhaled deeply and exhaled the breath as a sigh. 'Can I tell you something else?'

I nodded.

'I'm quite worried about leaving you. When I go to New York. Will you be all right?'

A sob rose inside me and I swallowed it back down. In my mind's eye, I pictured the possibility of Grace being with me in the house; of Grace sleeping in the spare room; Grace sitting in the kitchen; Grace watching TV with me; and goosebumps pricked my skin. I didn't reply; just tightened my arms around Rohan's waist.

Transcript of interview with Mr Rohan Allerton, husband of Abigail Allerton: 20 December 2019

'So you agreed to work in New York for two months while Abigail stayed home. Were you worried about leaving her?'

'Yes and no. Look, you have to know I had no choice. My boss made that very clear. He basically tapped me on the shoulder and said he thought I had potential. But if I wanted to continue progressing within the firm, the only way to do it was to take an overseas secondment. [sighs] It's a tough business, competitive, and people have memories like elephants in that company. If you're offered a secondment and you don't take it, you'll be passed over not only for any other secondments, but for promotions. It's a fact of life that the people who get the promotions are the ones who have the overseas experience; the ones who've worked in the international offices, not the ones who stay put, whether that's in London, Beijing or bloody Timbuktu.'

'So, Abigail understood that you felt you had no choice?'

'Yes, I think so. And, look: you know she's an artist. You can't count on that as a regular income. Yes, she was due to exhibit, and the chances are the paintings would sell, but you can't depend on it. It doesn't pay the bills. She hasn't earned anything except pocket money painting bloody pets for the last four years so I'm basically supporting both of us, while trying to save money for the future. It's not easy. I need those promotions. I need to progress. I can't stagnate.

'But, to answer the question, yes, I guess I worried a bit. I know she's fragile. I know she doesn't like going out. I know she lives a lot in her head but, at the back of my mind, I knew I had my family – my sister, and my mum – who'd be more than happy to keep an eye on Abs. I was already planning to give a house key to my mum. [chuckles] If you need anyone to keep an eye on anything, you ask my mum.'

Twelve

Back at the house, Rohan went on up to the bedroom. I ran myself a glass of water and drank it standing at the sink. The floorboards creaked overhead as my husband moved around the bedroom taking off his shoes and socks and changing into his T-shirt ready for bed.

I stared out at the blackness of the garden, inhaling the scent of plants that had roasted all day in the sun. So Rohan was going to New York. There was nothing I could do to change his mind – that, I realized – which left me with three choices: go with him; stay home alone; or invite Grace to stay with me. I sighed. Why couldn't things be black and white? Grace was Grace, and it would be dancing with danger to invite her back into my life – but she also had an undeniably positive effect on my creativity. Would being with her be better or worse than being alone?

And then there was Rohan. My husband. I loved him and I didn't want him to worry. If he knew I was going to have a friend here, he wouldn't feel so bad about leaving me. Because he didn't know Grace, he'd picture me safe with my friend, the two of us cocooned together in the house reminiscing over old times, no doubt, and he'd stop worrying. He'd know there was someone here to look after me; to make sure I got up in the morning and went to bed at night; to make sure I bought the groceries and ate enough food; and – I shrank a little into myself as I thought this – to make sure I didn't drink myself unconscious.

But I didn't want to tell him about Grace until I'd decided for myself whether I was going to invite her to stay. If I mentioned the possibility, he'd insist that she came, and I needed that decision to be my own.

I swilled the water in the glass and sighed again. Having Grace around would certainly have its advantages. I shivered as the feeling of laying new colours on the paper earlier in the evening came back to me, thrilling me because I could feel that they were the start of something that could be immense. Was it a coincidence that I started to get my painting mojo back the very day that Grace's name reappeared in my life? Could having her back here be the catalyst I needed to paint a new series? My exhibition was looming and so far I had nothing to show.

Outside, the wind rustled the leaves of the oak tree and rattled the cat-flap door. With a huge sigh, I picked up my phone and over-typed the previous email.

Dear Grace. What a surprise! Sounds like you had a wonderful time in Australia, and how exciting to be moving back to London. Yes, I live in North London now, with my husband. We'd love to offer you somewhere to stay while you get back on your feet over here. When are you planning to arrive? All the best, Abi

I read the email one more time then sent it before I started my nightly checks. You never knew what tiny thing could trigger a full-scale disaster. *Cooker – off. Gas – off. Smoke detector – working.*

Front door — locked. Back door— locked. Blinds — closed. Key — in door. Escape routes — clear. Rohan had long ago stopped trying to do these things for me.

Checks done, I continued up the stairs to my studio while Alfie watched from the landing, inscrutable. I'd left the window open and everything not weighted down had been disordered by the breeze. Over at the easel, I looked again at the colours I'd mixed. There was a kernel of excitement knotted in my belly about this portrait. When it was done, it could be quite possibly the best thing I'd ever painted.

I reached out and touched the now-dry paint on the paper and the palette, my fingers tingling with the anticipation of continuing, of laying down the frame and the colours on the canvas itself. Something bubbled inside me, giving me a sense of potential I hadn't felt in years. I knew, quietly and calmly, that this would be one of a series, that there would be more. This was it. This was what I'd been waiting for and, for better or for worse, Grace would be the one I had to thank.

The temptation was there to sit at the easel, to close my eyes and let the portrait come, but I also knew I mustn't rush it. I did a quick scan of the upstairs windows, making sure they were locked and the keys accessible. In the bathroom, I reached up to the top cupboard, lifted down the old Nivea pot in which I hid my contraceptive pills, and popped one in my mouth.

Transcript of interview with Mr Rohan Allerton, husband of Abigail Allerton: 20 December 2019

'You mentioned earlier that you thought Abigail might be pregnant. Had you talked about starting a family?'

'Yes, we had. [pause] We both want a child. We're on the same page about that. [pause] It's what every couple wants, isn't it?'

'Yet it wasn't happening? Did you talk about it then?'

'No. We just kept going from month to month like a rollercoaster; you know, the hope and then the disappointment, and the hope again that next month would be the lucky month.'

'Had you considered any sort of intervention?'

'Well, not really, but one night at dinner, my mother gave me a phone number for a fertility specialist – you know, one of these Harley Street guys. Abs was *not* happy. I didn't realize it would be such a big deal. We'd been trying – I think everyone knew that; it's pretty unusual in our community to wait so long after marriage to have your first child. I don't know if Abs didn't notice it, or if she was just burying her head in the sand, but *everyone* was waiting for her to get pregnant. Literally hanging for it. So, when Mum handed me the number, I took it without really thinking about it. But, even if I had, I'd have assumed that Abi would welcome a bit of help. It's pretty dispiriting watching her get out her tampons each month, knowing that we failed again. I was worried that I might be the one firing blanks. Actually, I'd quite like to know... I didn't think I was doing anything wrong in accepting a bit of help.'

'You said Abigail wasn't pleased?'

'She freaked out. She was really pissed off. We had "words" about it that night. I didn't know if she was pissed off about me taking the number, or if it was more about it being my mother who'd given it to me. Sort of like it was her saying Abs wasn't up to the job; or couldn't do it on her own. She's always in this power struggle with my mum. I've tried to tell her life would be so much easier if she just accepted that Mum means well and went along with things with a smile. But I guess it's not in her nature. Anyway, the argument certainly wasn't about her not wanting kids – I have no doubts about that.

Thirteen

I never remember the dream itself, just impressions, feelings, a sense of throat-clutching horror, and then the scene remains in my head afterwards.

A pretty road snaking through a snatch of countryside. On the right, a low hedge and fields that roll as far as the eye can see, blanketing the ground in shades of brown, straw and green. There's the odd patch of bright yellow, too, vivid in the sunshine; rape fields. The grass verge below the hedge is scattered with wildflowers, some I know the names of, some not: purples, blues, yellows and whites, tangled among the overgrown greens of the various grasses. Daisy, foxglove, cow parsley, forget-me-not. I'm happy that they've been allowed to grow. Tree branches hang over the road forming a canopy, shade from the dazzle of the sinking sun. To the left a high hedge flanks the road, taking the twists and turns of this section as if marking the way from this part of town to the next. Above the fields, birds wheel and cruise on the thermals, wings spread wide. The air's thick with the happy chirruping of even more birds I can't see; those hidden in the hedges and trees, nestled with their food, their eggs and their babies. The scent of summer hangs in the air; with it, the sense of possibility, of longing, and the potency of adventures still to come.

But then the light goes flat and grey, as if the sun's slipped behind a cloud, only it's more than that and it's terrifying. Even in the dream, I know something monstrous is coming and I know what it is, and it paralyzes me with terror.

I wake up trapped in a silent scream, my heart pounding, my limbs pinned to the bed, a film of sweat icy on my skin. I know that, gathered in the hollow at my throat, will be a pool of sweat, deep enough to splash my fingertip. I wait, as I always do, for my heart to slow and my body to unfreeze itself; for reality to impinge once more on my consciousness. I breathe in through my nose, like I've learned; I hold the breath while I count to five, then exhale slowly. I repeat the calming breath, then I open my eyes and take in the familiar night-time shapes of the bedroom: the wardrobe; the dresser; Rohan's T-shirt slung over the easy chair; his work shoes, twin rats, just visible on the floor; the white rectangle of the door; the slug of the door handle. Outside, the moon is bright, backlighting the curtains.

'You're in bed, at home,' I say out loud, as I always do, though perhaps not that convincingly. 'Everything's fine.' It's a mantra, a routine, that means little to me anymore. When I can move again, I turn my head and see the dark bulk of Rohan, fast asleep. My terrors stopped waking him years ago.

Fourteen

I'd only just got back to sleep after the dream that night – or so it seemed – when Rohan woke me with a hand placed gently on my arm.

'Don't move,' he breathed into my ear. 'Someone's here.'

I froze, every fibre of my body straining to listen. Could I hear breathing? Feel the vibration of a soul? Mentally, I went through the doors and windows I'd locked last night. All of them. Not one left open downstairs – I knew it – not even a slit to let in the breeze. Could someone have climbed up the side of the house and let themselves in through an upstairs window?

'In here,' Rohan whispered. 'I saw them. I'm going to check.'

In one swift movement, he leaped up from the bed. 'Who's there?' he yelled, flicking on his torch and flashing it into the corners of the room. The furniture loomed under the spotlight, discarded clothes making shadows on the walls and floor.

'Mind your eyes,' Rohan said, and snapped on the bedside lamp. He got up, pulled on a pair of shorts and walked out onto the landing then downstairs, clicking on lights as he went. I tracked his movements down and then back up.

'Did you find anything?' My skin was clammy. 'A break-in?'

'Nope. Nothing.' He slid back into bed and ran his hands through his hair.

'Nothing at all? Maybe it was Alfie. He's heavy enough these days to make the floorboards creak.'

'No.' He flopped back onto the pillows. 'It was more than that. A person. I'm sure of it. I saw her – them – whoever – by the window.'

I curled my body around Rohan's to chase away my goosebumps. 'Are you sure? Are you sure it wasn't a dream? You know you sometimes get those dreams where you wake up and it seems so real but you're still dreaming?'

Rohan inhaled deeply and let the breath out again. 'I was dreaming… God, I can't remember. There was a… uh! You know I can feel it but I can't quite get it. There was a – I was – *shit*. It's not coming. But maybe. There's something. Maybe. Maybe it was a dream.'

'You did have a few beers tonight.'

Rohan sighed. 'Yeah, maybe.'

We fell asleep with our arms wrapped around each other, his breath hot on my hair.

Despite the broken night, I woke pre-dawn with the desperate urge to paint. Early morning had always been my most creative time and, now I had this purpose, that was all that mattered: the paint, the canvas, and the impressions that swirled in my mind. My fingers were buzzing, desperate to hold my brushes. In my head I was starting to see how the first portrait needed to look; it was as if a three-dimensional image hung in my mind's eye. I lay still, feeling the shapes and the ideas that were still as thin as gossamer; feeling inside myself the movements that my hand would make with the brush to get those images onto the canvas. It was impossible to nail down these feelings – to conceptualize them – at this point. I knew I simply had to let them absorb into my being. I had to trust the process.

So, while the feeling was fresh – before any thoughts and practicalities, any discussions about what had happened in the night, could creep in and ruin it – I got up, threw a sweater over my nightshirt and went straight to my easel. I gently traced my finger over the tight fabric, picturing where on the canvas the head would fall, and the proportions and dimensions I might use. Closing my eyes, I inhaled deeply and examined the image in my mind, then I started to mark, very lightly, the key points. Without looking closely at what I'd done, I mixed some acrylics and began the first ghostly layer of the underpainting.

It was going to be a child, I realized as I worked. A pretty little thing – bright and luminous. I'd play with light to give her the glow of youth. It was hard to make her stand still in my head: she was dancing, happy, carefree, with her whole life arching ahead of her in a glittering path of opportunity. It was the essence of this promise I wanted to capture in her face and in the light of her eyes. I narrowed my own eyes, trying to project the image in my head onto the canvas as I worked. I don't know how much time passed but it was fully light outside by the time Rohan appeared at the top of the stairs, fastening his cufflinks.

'Morning,' he said, planting a noisy kiss on my cheek. 'How are you?'

'Good.' I didn't move my eyes from the canvas.

'Good. By the way, I've been meaning to tell you: I think we need to get someone in to look at the oak. Did you hear it creaking in the wind last night? I don't think it's very healthy. I'm worried it might fall. Can you sort that out?'

'Sure.'

'Great. By the way, it's quarter past. Isn't it hospice day today? Tuesday, right?'

Now I turned to look at Rohan with the hazy image of the girl still in my eyes, my brain slow to understand the meaning of what he'd said. At the same time, Rohan focused on the canvas.

'Oh,' he said. Then 'oh' again. He started to back out of the room. 'I thought you were doing the dog. Stay here. Keep going. It's fine, I'll grab breakfast on the way. And I'll tell the hospice you're not coming, shall I?'

His words snapped me out of my trance. I looked at my watch: 7.15. I was due at the hospice by 8.00.

'Oh my God! No, I'm coming,' I said, quickly cleaning my brushes.

'They wouldn't mind if you missed it, just once…' Rohan said. 'You're so conscientious. Surely your…' he pointed to the canvas with his eyebrows raised, 'is more important?'

'It's a commitment,' I said. 'I can't let them down. I need to go.'

'But Abs…'

'It's okay,' I said. 'I know what I'm doing now,' and I knew I was right. It was as if my subconscious had unblocked in a torrent of image and emotion. Suddenly I could feel the series spanning ahead of me; I could feel where it might take me.

Rohan was out of the door when he turned back to me. 'Oh, who is it, by the way? You said a portrait, but you didn't say who.'

I paused, trying to find my voice – but my pause was too long for him because he said, 'Tell me later,' and disappeared down the stairs.

'No one,' I said to the empty doorway. 'No one you know.'

Fifteen

Given the strength of their love, and the belief they had in their future plans, Alex and Grace didn't take long to implode. They limped through the first half of the first term, lurching from visit to visit – but how long can a long-distance relationship survive when you're eighteen and living two hundred miles apart? I was surprised Alex went through the motions at all.

Grace, however, was one of those girls who really made an effort. Despite being, from what she said, the academically smarter of the two, she reverted to being a Fifties housewife around him, planning their weekends in meticulous detail: what she'd wear, where they'd go, what they'd eat, how she'd entertain him. To begin with, she'd come back from her time with him fresh-faced and bouncy, but soon the visits started to thin out.

'He's doing a lot of sport,' she said. 'The matches are at the weekends. It's fine. He's always thinking of me.' She tapped her phone and turned it to face me. 'See? *Miss you, Wish I was with you, How are you, gorge?* – short for gorgeous, obv. That was just this morning. He sends messages all the time.'

'Why don't you go up there?' I suggested. 'You could watch one of the matches? Take some pom-poms for the touch line?'

'Oh, I offered to go up, but he said there wasn't much point as

I won't know anyone and it's all very "teamie". You know, all that male bonding after. He doesn't want me to feel left out.'

Soon, even the messages started to dwindle. As the term continued, Grace's phone began to sit next to her as we lounged on my bed in the evenings, and the TV was silenced each time a message pinged.

'It's just you never seem to be around anymore.' Hats off to her, Grace tried not to whine on the phone. 'You tell me when's a good time to call… oh… right. Well, till then.'

She chucked her phone down. 'His course is really full-on,' she said. 'It's good he's throwing himself into it.'

'Medicine's not such a walk in the park, either,' I said, but she immersed us back in *Glee* and that was that until he failed to turn up for a weekend.

She'd gone to Euston to meet the train he said he'd be on. I could picture her waiting at the barrier as the passengers streamed through, bobbing her head this way and that to see through the throng; straining to glimpse her beloved, who absolutely must have been in the last carriage because almost everyone was off and… oh, I could picture the moment she realized there were no more people coming. The moment she turned, confused, searching the concourse in case she'd somehow missed him. I could see her pulling her phone out of her bag and dialling his number, pressing it to her ear, her head tilted and her index finger blocking the noise of the station out of the other ear as she listened to the tinny ring.

He didn't pick up. Just sent a message saying sorry, he missed the train and he'd see her next week. I found all this out only later because, in a very out-of-character act – and without the massage oils, mini scented candles and VS undies she usually had on hand when she was visiting Alex – Grace actually jumped on the next train to Manchester.

When she got back, she entered my room looking unusually fragile – hollow – as if the essence of her had been snuffed out. Her precious wedding folder was hugged to her chest.

'It's Alex.' She barely got the words out before her face collapsed and she threw herself onto my bed, clutching the folder as if it were a life jacket in the middle of the ocean. I sat next to her and rubbed her back and passed her tissues while she sobbed and then, when she could finally speak, she started to explain, between hiccups, a story even I hadn't seen coming.

'He says I don't have the head space for him anymore,' she said, and her tone was scathing, despite the tears. 'Apparently, I'm "too distracted" and he's making all the effort coming to London but apparently my head's not in it anymore.'

Tears leaked again from under her eyelashes, and she swiped at them with the sleeve of her sweater. She was one of those rare people who could cry prettily. I tried to smile with a modicum of sympathy. I felt for her, of course I did, but at the end of the day, I could have told her he wasn't going to go the course – even a blind man could see that – and some of us had greater burdens to carry than a failed relationship. But what she said next surprised me.

'*Apparently*, all I care about these days is my new friends.' She paused. 'New *friend*.' I stiffened, feeling the shape of blame looming over me; guilt already circling like a shark.

'We had a row,' Grace said. 'It was ugly.' She sniffled. 'We never fight. We always discuss things. I can't believe he was being so *mean*. I didn't know what triggered it but then he brought up your name and I realized that's what it was: he was jealous.'

'Jealous?'

'He said you're monopolizing me and that I should hang out with other people. That it was unhealthy to be so close to one person.' I opened my mouth to agree – I'd often thought the same – but she carried on. 'He said I'm always in your room and hanging out with you and he thinks it's unhealthy.' She paused. 'He said you're *weird*.'

'Weird?'

'I know! He said you're morose and a loner and it wouldn't surprise him if you were depressed. I said, what would he know? And, surely, if you were depressed you needed a friend more than ever, but he started going on about it rubbing off onto me and how I had to be careful, and I should be out living it up with lots of friends not moping about with you. He said you were like a drain; a "joy-sucker", Abs!' Another gulp and sniff. 'So I said I wasn't going to choose my friends for him and it was up to me to do what I wanted to do while I was at uni, and if it bothered him so much, he didn't have to be my boyfriend.' Her face crumpled. 'And he said, "Fine."'

I exhaled loudly. 'Whoa.'

'You should have seen the look on his face. I've never seen him look like that. All hard and flinty. I could see it was over. He made me choose – and I chose you. You need me more.' She convulsed with another sob. 'My God, two years together. All our plans ripped up. My future ruined!' She squeezed the folder tighter. 'He was my first love. The love of my life.'

She stopped sobbing and her eyes met mine. Without words, and despite the fact that Alex was always going to dump her, the message was clear: *it's all your fault.*

Transcript of interview with Mr Rohan Allerton, husband of Abigail Allerton: 20 December 2019

'You mentioned nightmares? Am I right in thinking Abigail has been having regular, or recurring, nightmares?'

[Sighs] 'Yes. She's had them as long as I've known her but, despite her waking up every night, she won't tell me what they're about, or what might be causing them. Trust me, I've tried.'

'So what happens?'

'Well, that's it in a nutshell. One minute we're both fast asleep, the next she's sitting up with her hands out in front like she's trying to stop something. Other times she's still lying down but soaked in sweat and with her eyes wide open, but there's usually a scream of some sort. I mean, yeah, it's not easy to live with.'

'Have you tried to tackle the subject with her in any way?'

[Sighs] 'I tried to get her to go for therapy, but she refused, so I tried asking her myself, you know, like a therapist might. I asked "open-ended" questions in a "non-confrontational" way, like when we were walking side by side. Things like, "Did you always have them? When did they start? What are they of? Did anything in particular trigger them?"'

'But she's an expert in shutting me down. Trying to talk to her when she doesn't want to talk is like playing that childhood trampoline game "crack the egg". Do you remember that game? She puts up this protective shell over herself, and there's nothing I can do to crack it open.'

'I see. So the nightmares continued?'

'Not for lack of trying on my part. I did everything I could think of to help her. I made her read before bed. I made milky drinks and herbal teas, massaged her back and ran warm baths for her. I bought a lavender pillow spray and I even got aromatherapy candles – which she moved to the bathroom. None of it seemed to have any effect. So I did what anyone who values their sanity would do: I learned to sleep with earplugs in; I like the foam ones that you roll up and squeeze into your ear. Boots often have them on three for the price of two. I get through a lot. They don't block out everything, nor do they stop me becoming aware of her thrashing but, eventually, my body learned to wake briefly – to recognize that she was as all right as she could be – and to fall back asleep. I've always been a deep sleeper.'

'Knowing what you now know, do you think the nightmares could have something to do with what happened with this... [ruffles paper]... Grace?'

'I'd say so, yes.' [softly] 'Definitely.'

Sixteen

I dreamed that night, not my usual nightmare, but that I was being chased.

I ran on the streets of a darkened city, dodging behind parked cars and into tiny alleyways but still I wasn't fast enough. I flicked off my shoes, shrugged off my coat and ran barefoot, thinking how much faster I'd be in trainers – why wasn't I in trainers? – as I jumped over a garden fence that ripped at my clothes and scratched my skin. I skirted around houses, darted down side paths and squeezed through gaps in back hedges to throw off my pursuer, and finally I pressed my back against the dirty wall of a dank underpass, the brackish water of a canal sliding right by me while my lungs heaved and the steps of my pursuer rang out on the road above my head.

I sagged with relief but it wasn't over. In the way of dreams, I was running again, across a field this time, my heart pounding and my neck tensed for a shot in my back as I strained to reach the cover of far-lying trees. I flung myself under a bush, face-down in the mud and clawed at barbed branches until I was hidden and blood from my shredded fingers seeped into the ground.

I flattened myself into the earth, something sharp digging into my ribs as my lungs pushed against the ground and I struggled to get my breath but then I was running again: in quicksand this time, my heart in my throat, air rasping in my lungs as I floundered ever slower and deeper, and then I was running through the university halls I lived in with Grace, the familiar smell of the disinfectant and institutional paint in my nostrils.

I reached my room and jabbed the key in the lock but it wouldn't turn and it wouldn't turn and the footsteps were catching me; they were louder and closer and louder and closer and, with a feeling of unsurmountable horror I turned to face my pursuer, and it was Alex. Grace's Alex with a knife raised to stab me.

I woke with a jolt, my limbs pinned to the bed and waited for my heart to slow. Yes, there were the shapes of our bedroom, everything in its usual place; Rohan's bulk exactly where it should be. Gingerly, I moved my head a little to the left and then the right, then flexed a leg and an arm. When my limbs were my own again, I slid myself up to sitting and took a sip of water. The sweat was rank on me; my nightshirt damp, and the terror of being pursued clung to me like fog.

Why was I letting Grace back into my life? After I'd got rid of her once. What was I? A mug? A complete idiot?

I went to the kitchen and opened my laptop, hoping to recall my email, but already there was a reply from Grace.

Thanks so much. Can't wait to see you. It'll be just like old times.

Now I'd have to tell Rohan.

Seventeen

I blurted out the news that Grace was coming back over dinner with Rohan. It was a week before he left for New York.

It had been a stiflingly hot day with no relief up in the attic, despite the fan. I'd taken off my clothes and worked in my bra and pants, laying down another layer of acrylic and, as that dried, turning to my palette to mix the first oil colours with the care of a surgeon preparing her instruments. I'd worked straight through lunch and well on into the afternoon, fuelled only by black coffee and, later, vodka from the drinks fridge Rohan had thoughtfully installed for me in the studio.

I liked a drink, that was no secret. I liked how it freed my mind; how it loosened the binds that tied me to the Earth. I liked how it made me forget things, and I liked it even more when I was painting: I loved how it stripped me of my day-to-day reality and bent the world into a better shape. Rohan found me in my underwear with the vodka bottle open beside me.

'Should I disturb you?' he asked, and I turned, surprised to see him there, flesh and blood, in his shirtsleeves.

'What's the time?' I'd taken off my watch since the sweat trapped under it irritated my skin. The air was humid and the birds in the tree – now I registered their racket – were agitated, restless – as if they could feel something that we couldn't yet sense ourselves. I looked out of the window: the orangey-purply sky was shot with white vapour trails. A canvas in itself. The air was ripe with the sense of…

'Seven,' Rohan said. 'It's date night. We're booked at Mr Ho's – if you still want to go?'

He stepped closer to me and ran his hands appreciatively over my bare skin, then pulled my hips against his so I could feel his hard-on, but my head was full of the weird sky, restlessness, Grace and the painting. Rohan's hands wandered up to and slipped casually inside my bra, sending a jolt of desire through me. He kissed me deeply then pulled away, his hands in the air like he was surrendering.

'That was just a teaser,' he said. 'The rest comes after dinner. If you still want to go…?'

I tore my thoughts back to reality: my husband, date night, Mr Ho's, and nodded.

'Yes, of course. Let's go.'

And so I cleaned my brushes and went down to the bedroom to find something to wear. The concept of 'date night' was something Rohan had brought to our marriage and – although I disliked the fact we'd become the cliché of the married couple who needed to carve out time for each other – I was the first to admit it was quite useful in as much as it gave us a chance to catch up properly; it gave structure to our week. Anyhow, I liked Mr Ho's despite its stiff pink tablecloths. It specialized in Indian-Chinese – a spiced-up version of the classics – and we were regulars. We'd sit at pretty much the same table by the window with the view of the High Street every time, and Rohan would open the menu, turn the pages while rubbing his chin, then close it with a bang and say, 'Think I'll have my usual, for a change.'

This night was no different.

'Have you decided?' Rohan asked as we sat at our table, and I shook my head, unable to say the names of dishes when all that was in my head was Grace. I put the menu carefully back down.

'Rohan,' I began, the thing so big in my head now I struggled to find words to contain it. 'My friend Grace...'

'As in, your university friend? The one you lived with?' Rohan interrupted.

I nodded, irritated. 'Yes, her. Well, I wanted to tell you that she's, uh, moving back to the UK.'

And that was it. The genie was out. The secret no longer mine.

'Oh, okay,' he said with a smile that showed me he had no idea how this would impact our lives. 'Well, that's great.'

I smiled weakly at him.

'So,' he said, peering at me, 'how do you feel about it? You've never really talked about any of your uni friends. Are you... pleased? Not pleased?' He moved his shoulders one way and then the other, hands open as if weighing something up.

I opened my mouth wide but nothing came out so I closed it slowly again.

'Pleased,' I said carefully.

Rohan looked at me sideways. 'You don't *look* so pleased?'

I exhaled. 'It's just...' I stared at him for what felt like the longest time: could I tell him I was looking forward to having Grace around but was also nervous? That I was wary of the effect she would have, not just on me, but on our marriage? That I was scared of how I might change once Grace came back?

'I've invited her to stay for a bit until she finds her feet,' I said carefully. 'The spare room's just sitting empty, and you'll be away most of the time.'

Rohan had been out when the new bedding had arrived. I'd bought a small chair, too, with a pine frame, that rocked – nothing fancy. It wasn't The Ritz, but I knew Grace would like it.

'Does she have family here?' Rohan asked.

I shook my head. 'Her parents died. It was quite sad, actually. One got sick – her dad, I think? And the other died within weeks.'

'Very sad,' Rohan agreed. 'But yeah – it would be good for you to have a friend around.'

'Mmm,' I said, and we lapsed into silence for a few moments.

'I've never met her, have I?' Rohan asked. 'What do I need to know about her? Or should I ask her for all the dirt on what you got up to?' He gave me a leery smile, though I knew he thought that the worst I could possibly have done would have been to miss a lecture.

We had to break off then because Mr Ho appeared at the side of the table, order pad poised.

'How are you today, Mr Ho?' Rohan asked. 'How's the family?' Although he was the owner of the restaurant, the patriarch, he wore, like all the other staff, white shirtsleeves, a black waistcoat and black trousers. He'd told us once that his father used to run the restaurant, and that he hoped to pass it on to his own children, though they hadn't shown much interest to date – one was doing Media Studies at university and the other was a jobbing musician. It was a source of great sadness to him to think he might have to sell the restaurant when he could no longer work.

'Nothing to report,' said Mr Ho, so Rohan ordered his food. 'And what about you, darling? The spicy chicken and cashew nuts?'

I nodded yes to the chicken. Mr Ho took the drinks order and left.

'So what does this Grace do now? Where's she been all this time?' Rohan asked. Underneath the table, his foot found mine and pressed against it. He'd done the same on our first date, and at every date night since.

'She's a doctor,' I said. 'She moved to Australia after we left uni, and she's been working there ever since. I'm not sure what she'll do here. Probably try to get a job as a GP. And she also said something about some sort of medical volunteering. She's the type who likes to "give back".'

'Oh okay,' said Rohan, nodding his approval. I could see him thinking: *respectable then, not some reprobate*. 'Is she married? Kids?'

I shook my head.

'Okay,' said Rohan, then he laughed: 'Should I be scared?' He laughed to show he was joking but my hesitation must have been more obvious than I thought.

'Mind you, I don't suppose she'll be around much,' Rohan said. 'If she's a doctor, she's not going to have a lot of spare time, is she? Don't they work seventy-hour weeks?'

I tried to smile but it came out more of a gurn. I took a sip of water. 'Yes, I guess.'

'Well,' said Rohan, squeezing my hand, 'it's good you'll have someone around—' and suddenly there was a flash and a crack that made me leap out of my seat, followed by a commotion outside as the people sitting at the three aluminium tables Mr Ho had put on the open veranda jumped up, clutching their drinks and moving their plates, and I saw that, finally, after this long run of hot, arid weeks, it had started to rain.

Transcript of interview with Mr Rohan Allerton, husband of Abigail Allerton: 20 December 2019

'How did you feel when you heard that Abigail's friend Grace was coming to stay with her?'

'I wasn't worried at all. Why would I be? I was pleased. Abi had refused point-blank to come to New York with me and I was a little concerned about leaving her alone while I was gone. But then she mentioned that this friend was coming to stay and, honestly, I thought, *thank God for that.*'

'You were relieved? Why were you so relieved?'

[Sighs] 'Look, Abs needs someone to look after her. It's like she lives her life in fear of some disaster that may never happen. For example, she can't go to bed without checking that everything in the house is secure: every window closed, the gas off, the door locked and so on. And I don't mean that in a normal way. It's like she's obsessed. No matter how late it is, or how tired she is, or where in the world we are, she'll do it, or she can't sleep. I wonder if it's OCD.'

'I see. She sounds quite difficult to live with.'

[Sighs] 'Yes, maybe. But I love her. She's beautiful – inside and out – and so talented. I have so much respect for her talent. And it's more than that.' [Pauses] 'When I first saw her, she was having a quick smoke outside the gallery on the opening night of her exhibition. She was wearing this sculpted black dress and high heels. I could tell she wasn't used to the dress or the shoes. And her hair – her crazy hair – she'd tried to tame it with this clip thing but it hadn't really worked. She was so clearly a fish out of water – so nervous and unsure of herself, but trying so hard. My heart just went out to her. She was – I don't know how to put it? Swan-like, elegant, fragile. Vulnerable. I just wanted to scoop her into my arms and protect her. And I have done ever since.' [Laughs] 'But she's not the most stable person... she's... unpredictable. Antisocial, too. She doesn't like going out. She lives in her head – or maybe even in another dimension. Part and parcel of being an artist, I suppose.

'But, going back to your initial question, I was kind of worried that, with me away, she wouldn't go out at all. So, when she told me about Grace, I was pleased. I thought she'd be all right. She told me Grace was a doctor, for God's sake. I couldn't argue with that. I was actually quite jealous. The older I get, the more I like to reconnect with people from my past and wallow in memories. I pictured them with a bottle of wine, getting out the old photos, reminiscing. I hoped she'd carry on with her painting and not get too distracted partying.'

'You had no reason to suspect anything, then?'

'No. As I said, why would I?'

Eighteen

Rohan wouldn't let me go to the airport with him.

'You know what you're like in crowds,' he said, 'and this is Heathrow we're talking about.' He shook his head and laughed, the idea of me at the airport preposterous. 'Anyway, I'd worry about you getting back home without me.' He pulled me to him then and squeezed me. 'I'll get a taxi and we can say goodbye at home. It's the best way, and you know it.'

I accepted the hug in silence and nothing more was said, but the thought of Rohan's departure had grown like a tumour in the back of my mind, a shadow on an X-ray, silent and threatening, and now it was almost here. I sat on our bed, my spine propped uncomfortably against the headboard, my legs stretching down the duvet, while Rohan packed his last few things. It was barely past dawn and the light from the bedside lamp pooled yellow. Alfie circled the room, unsettled by the early activity as much as by the suitcases. The cab was due any second.

'Passport? Boarding pass? Wallet? Credit card?' I asked, and Rohan nodded absently, his eyes taking in the sight of me alone on the bed, but his mind already leaving the house, me, our life.

'Glasses? Contact lenses?' I added, just to remind him that he and I were both still here, together for the last time for a good few weeks.

'Right,' he said as if I hadn't spoken, and he closed the lid of his suitcase, pulled the zip around and spun the combination lock. 'Done. I bet I've forgotten something, but – *pff.*'

'I'm sure they have shops in New York,' I said, and tried to smile but the effort was too much and tears oozed out from under my eyelashes. I turned away and tried to wipe them without being seen.

'Aww. Don't cry.' Rohan kissed the top of my head. 'I love you so much.'

'Don't go.' My words were barely audible. It was too late: the scale had tipped; the process begun. Tears leaked and I wiped them with my palms. Rohan sat down next to me on the bed and put his arm around me. I leaned into his body, wishing, wishing, wishing that I could go back in time and change everything.

'I'm sorry,' Rohan said. 'You know I have no choice. I wouldn't do it if I didn't have to. I'll be back before you know it.'

'I know. I love you too.' My face was hot and wet. It was like crying at school with the whole class watching.

'We can talk every day if you like. FaceTime. Or Zoom. Whatever you want.' Rohan kissed my hair again and got up with a sigh. 'My cab'll be here in a minute.'

He dragged his bag off the bed and let it land on the floor with a thud that surely bruised the house. 'You know it's not too late to join me.' He shrugged on his jacket. 'Any time at all. I'll pick you up. Even if it's just for a week.'

I watched him through my tears. He looked handsome, more so than usual. With a tug of jealousy, I imagined him chatting to a lone woman next to him on the plane. He could be quite the charmer while I was… well, I was stuck at home.

'Are you coming down?' he said, pulling his bag to the door with one hand, his cabin bag held aloft in the other.

I blew my nose and heaved myself off the bed and followed him as he clattered down the stairs, one bag scraping against the wallpaper, the other knocking against the balustrades. I winced. Outside, his cab hooted. At the door, Rohan turned and hugged me.

'Stay safe,' he said. 'Order everything online. Get it all delivered. Use Mum if you need to. She's desperate to be useful. Oh, and don't forget to get the tree cut.'

I breathed in the smell of him, the warm, familiar scent of his skin and the fresh tang of his cologne, and wished I was the type of woman who'd relish an adventure like the one he was offering; I wished I was the type of woman who'd jump at the chance to go to New York. Grace would, but… I squeezed my husband a little tighter, my head on his chest, but already his energy was moving through the door; his mind moving on to the airport, the trip, New York City. His lips found mine.

''Bye, darling. Have fun with Grace.'

'Thanks,' I said, and reluctantly I released him with the sense that I was letting not just him, but everything go.

Rohan carried his cases down the path, and I watched as he opened the boot of the taxi, put the bags in one after the other, then climbed in next to the driver. The window buzzed down, he waved, and the car pulled away. I watched until its brake lights came on at the top of Albert Road, the indicator flicking left. As it turned, I raised my hand and waved, but the passenger window was already closed and all I could see was a reflection of the trees that lined the road, like skeletons on the glass.

I closed the front door and turned to face the hall, listening to the sound of its stillness. The house seemed to shift within itself, tightening its walls around me, constricting like a corset, readjusting itself to the diminished energy it now enclosed. The air pressure felt heavier; a weight pushing down on my bones. I couldn't picture Grace here. Grace in the house. Tonight. My insides were jelly.

'It's just us now,' I said to break the silence and, on cue, Alfie appeared on the stairs, his tail a twitching question mark, his claws clicking. He curled around my ankles and I bent to give him a stroke. 'I'm at the hospice today, but Grace's coming tonight,' I told him. 'You'll like her. She's more fun than I am.'

Alfie continued twisting around my ankles, pushing against me as I tickled his head. He was very much my cat, although it had been Rohan who'd picked him out. I wondered if Alfie still remembered the day he'd arrived home in a grey plastic pet carrier, which Rohan had plonked on the hall floor right where the two of us now stood.

'Abi! Come and see what I've got!' Rohan had called. It had been about a year after we'd married.

'What on earth?' I'd asked, emerging from the kitchen and realizing with a thud in my solar plexus that my husband had brought home an animal.

'You need to love something besides me,' Rohan had said with a sheepish smile on his face. 'It's too much pressure.'

From inside the carrier came a mew. A series of mews.

'Aren't you going to open it?' Rohan said.

'Are you serious?'

'He's from the rescue centre,' Rohan said. 'Though how anyone could abandon him I've no idea. He's about a year old, they think. Vaccinated and neutered. Go on, take a look.'

I'd knelt down in front of the carrier, unfastened the door and come face to face with a small silver tabby cat with clear green eyes. He stepped forward and, without hesitation, rubbed his cheek on my hand, then on my knee, then all over me. Warming to the idea of a cat, I stroked his back – his fur soft and surprisingly thin; underneath the fur, his body had been smaller than it seemed. The cat's back arched up to meet my hand, his spine pushing against my palm. His movements around my legs left a swathe of silver cat hair on the black of my jogging pants. I wore paler colours now.

Rohan's smile had cracked his face. 'I think he likes you,' he'd said. 'What do you think? Is there room in your heart for both of us?' He'd given me a boyish smile. 'But seriously, if you don't want him, I'll…'

I'd scooped up the cat and cuddled his little body against me. His purrs had vibrated against my chest.

'He's lovely,' I'd said.

'Phew.' Rohan had mock-wiped his brow.

'What's his name?'

'At the shelter they called him Catty McCatface, but I'm sure he'll go with whatever you want.'

'Alphonsus,' I said. 'Alfie.'

'Good. It's good for you to have something to look after while I'm out all day,' Rohan had said with a nod. 'It's good practice for when the baby comes.'

Now, Alfie and I looked at each other.

'Are you going to help me check Grace's room?' I asked him. 'We've got to make sure everything's ready for her.'

I straightened up and looked at the hallway, imagining how Grace would see it when she stepped through the front door this evening. What would she think of 'the old heap', as Rohan liked to call the house? Given what we'd started with, I was proud of what we'd achieved before we'd run out of both cash and energy.

'It's enough for now, babe,' Rohan had said, his arms encircling me as we waltzed a lap of the new kitchen, the new digital radio turned up loud. 'Let's just rest for a bit,' and, fed up of dust and builders and the constant downward drag of the credit-card bill, I'd agreed – but now I wondered: was it enough? Our house still stood out on Albert Road among all the nicely maintained homes; it never quite managed to shake off the air of decrepitness I'd felt when I'd first seen it, despite how much we did.

'Come on, Alfie,' I said, hurrying up the stairs to try and disperse the feeling I had that I was disturbing something. The hairs on the back of my neck prickled as if I were being watched. I paused on the landing, then turned quickly. Alfie was behind me, his back arched and his eyes huge and unblinking. The tip of his tail swished left and right.

'Oh, you feel it, too?' I said just to break the silence, but what was it? The air? The house? The fact that Rohan had gone, his departure taking something unidentifiable with him; or the house compensating now it was just the two of us? I felt as if I were cleaving through something invisible; thick and heavy, like water. A draught pushed down the stairs, wrapping itself around me like cobwebs.

'Cold, isn't it?' I said, rubbing my arms. I must have left a window open upstairs. The heat of the summer was now no more than a distant memory. 'You're all right,' I told Alfie. 'You've got fur.'

I pushed open the spare-room door slightly too forcefully causing it to bang into the wall and Alfie jumped like a coiled spring. Inside, the room smirked back at me too innocently:

a naughty child behaving for its teacher. I stared at the rocking chair, half expecting to see it move as if it had just been vacated, but it remained resolutely still. Alfie crouched pounce-ready at the door, his ears flat and tail swishing like a carpet sweeper. I filled my lungs and exhaled slowly. The air, even colder in here than on the landing, still bore an echo of the rose-fragranced Shake n' Vac I'd used on the carpet.

God, I had to get a grip. It was just a room, and I was pleased with what I'd done. After poring over design magazines, frying my brain with too many options, I'd decided to keep the original bedstead, wardrobe and desk – the ones that had been here when we'd bought the house. There was nothing wrong with them, and they fitted the room perfectly.

The new bedding was a lavender that I knew Grace would like, and the rocking chair was dove-grey. I'd wiped down the wallpaper and the furniture, had the faded curtains dry-cleaned and, with the window thrown open so fresh air could lick every surface of the room, I'd vacuumed every crevice vigorously, sucking up dead spiders and flies and the super-sized ladybirds of that scorching summer, now crispy in death, along with a decade or more of dust, trying not to think about the people whose skin flakes were disappearing into the vacuum cleaner. With rubber gloves up to my elbows and a hankie tied over my nose and mouth, I'd cleaned out the fireplace and replaced the ashes with a bunch of dried flowers in a jug. In the wardrobe, I'd hung one of my winter coats in case Grace didn't own one after her years in Australia. But was that too much? Did I look too keen?

'What do you think, Alfie?' I asked, but he was no longer there. I pulled the coat out of the wardrobe and threw it onto the bed. Wasn't one of the problems before that I was *too* keen? Too accommodating?

90

But looking at the room now, I had another idea. I dashed up to the attic and knelt in front of the old boxes the previous owners had left. Rohan had said they contained toys. Maybe there was something I could put on the bed for Grace. She'd always liked stuffed toys, her bed at uni always adorned with a teddy or two. I blew at the dust and started pulling things out of the box. Random toys: a skipping rope, a bag of cars, some Lego, and then, at the bottom, a small, wooden cot painted lavender and white and, lying inside it under a stiff, flowery duvet, a faded brown teddy bear with threadbare patches on its chest and paws. I pulled it out and gave it a sniff. A bit musty but nothing an airing wouldn't solve.

'Would you like to come downstairs?' I asked the bear, waggling him as I talked, causing the bells in his ears to jangle.

'Thought you'd never ask,' I said in a gruff, bear voice.

I shoved the toys back in the box and, downstairs, I placed Bear on the pillow of the bed and stepped back. Nice. Homely. Welcoming.

I sat down on the bed and looked at the room from Grace's perspective. It wasn't big, but it was fresh, clean and cosy, and it was free. When I thought back to our student digs, I was sure this would be fine. We'd been happy in those days, hadn't we? To begin with, at least.

Nineteen

It was largely thanks to Grace that I ended up with a boyfriend. I was never man-mad; never one of those students who used her time at university to work her way through the male cohort. Neither was I like Grace, hellbent on finding my one-and-only. While I was studying, the other students didn't interest me with their silly psychodramas, amateur drinking and snapchat, so I went about my business quietly getting on with my work, staying resolutely single throughout my degree and it was only after I graduated that Tom appeared in my life. He was older than me; an artist who taught at a nearby school; a free spirit with longish, curly dark hair, and a goatee and moustache – which was a look I never thought I'd go for – and an appealing gravitas that came from having experienced, I got the impression, the underbelly of life.

I was juggling two jobs at the time. I'd managed to get a part-time internship at a nearby gallery and was looking for a 'proper' job when I'd mentioned to Grace that the art supply shop I used was looking for staff. She'd pushed me to apply for that too, saying, with a bit of a look, that it would do me good 'on every level'. I didn't love the job, but it just about paid the rent, offered a good discount on art supplies and kept me 'out of trouble', as Grace put it.

At the shop, there was a bell on the door, and I often glanced over when it tinkled. The clientele was a mixed bunch: grimy students from the university and the odd artist, but chiefly urban mums buying supplies for their kids – sketchbooks, paints, brushes, watercolour pencils, canvases.

Anyway, that day, the bell tinkled, I looked up and there he was: Tom. Not that I knew his name at the time, but what I did know was that right there, shaking rain out of his hair like a dog, was the person I was meant to be with for the rest of my life. It may be a cliché but time slowed and I grasped onto a shelf to stop myself from crumpling to the floor. Love at first sight? Who believes in it? But, as this man entered the shop, there was a pull, like gravity, running from me to him and I felt, rather than saw, the two of us together forever: laughing, loving, parenting, growing old. And while this movie of our life together carouselled through my mind – while fireworks went off in my soul – this person, this man – Tom – just carried on acting as if nothing had happened. He was new to the area, he told my colleague. He needed supplies. He was overjoyed there was an art shop so close to home. We'd better get used to his ugly face, he joked, because we'd be seeing a lot of it.

I tried to keep my feelings to myself to begin with, watching covertly as he shopped, letting the other staff attend to him while I waited for the avalanche of feelings I had to die but, when, after weeks, they didn't – when I found myself lying awake at night fantasising about my life with Tom and I couldn't contain it any longer – I confided in Grace.

'You dark horse!' she said. 'How long has this been going on? All this time and you haven't even said hello?'

'What shall I do?' I fretted at the tassels of the cushion I was hugging on my lap. 'How do I let him know I'm interested? He doesn't even know I exist.'

'Have you talked to him?' she asked, and I shook my head. 'Well, that's the first step. Say hello! God, Abs. It's not that difficult. He's a human being, not an alien, and in the shop you have the perfect excuse. When he next comes in, I want you to be the one who serves him. Okay?'

And so she coached me through it: what to say, how to be, and, eventually, how to ask him out. On her advice, I suggested, in a voice tight with nerves, a coffee to discuss an exhibition at Tate Modern.

'Sure,' he shrugged, peering at me with those nut-brown eyes as if for the first time. And Grace was right, of course: that coffee segued into a visit to Tate Modern, and then to a lunch, drinks, more drinks, and dinner. Before long, we were 'dating' as Grace so quaintly put it, but Tom didn't like to call it that. He was a Buddhist and didn't like to be tied down.

'*Upadhi dukkhassa mūlanti*,' he'd say, holding his hands up, if I tried to push him into any type of commitment. 'Attachment is the root of suffering. Let's just exist in the moment. In the end, only three things matter: how much you loved, how gently you lived, and how gracefully you let go of things not meant for you,' and so I learned not to ask too many questions about what he did when we were apart, and we co-existed alongside each other very well.

I didn't deserve Tom, of course, but I cared about him. A lot.

Twenty

I dashed into the hospice a hair past eight that morning, the painting of Bruce tucked in my bag. I was pleased with it – as pet portraits went, it was one of my best.

It was my job at the hospice to make sure the patients had enough water, to clear away any old cups, and make hot drinks for anyone that wanted them. That early in the morning, there were just a couple of visitors – it didn't usually get busier till later, once the school day finished. It was only then, from about four-thirty, that you'd start to see the procession of worn mums and dads bringing their kids, scruffy from school, to see ailing grandparents for what could well be the last time.

'Morning!' I said to Moira, the head nurse who was, for once, actually standing still behind the desk. She was a powerhouse in the hospice, the engine of the place, with a heart so big I often wondered how it fit inside the whip-thin body that encased it. She was also a mother to four kids under six; we were all familiar with their impish smiles because she had their photo in a frame on the desk.

'Can I leave this here for Mrs Keyson to pick up?' I said. 'It's a painting I did of Mr K's dog. You know: Bruce.' We all knew about Mr K's Bruce.

'Aww, that's so kind of you Abi,' Moira said, tilting her head and smiling. 'He'll love that.' She paused. 'But you can give it to her yourself. She's in there now.' She nodded towards Mr K's room.

'Oh? She's not usually in on a Tuesday?'

She shook her head again. 'He's not good.' Pause. 'We gave her a call.'

'Oh,' I said, my insides falling inside me. I held onto the counter for a moment. 'Let me just pop it in there, then I'll do the waters if that's okay?'

'Of course.'

Mr K's room was the last on the right. I listened for a moment, then knocked softly and popped my head around the door. Mrs K sat beside the bed and she looked up, a weary smile breaking over her face as she saw me. Perhaps because her husband was in such a bad way, I'd imagined Mrs K to be diaphanous and brittle with age but she could have passed for twenty years younger than the late septuagenarian I knew she was — even today, with her face hollow with worry.

'Abigail. Hello,' she said.

'Hey. How is he?'

She shook her head. 'Not so good. I don't know...' She closed her eyes briefly then we both looked at Mr K. He was half propped up in bed, his eyes closed. His paper-white face was almost indistinguishable from his white hair, his collarbones protruded above the neckline of his T-shirt, and his arms — already bamboo sticks — were thinner than they'd been the previous week. The shape of his body under the blankets resembled that of a young child.

'How long have you been here?' I asked.

'Most of the night.'

'Do you want a break? I can sit with him for a bit?'

She shook her head. 'No. I need to be here.'

'Okay. Well, I'm here all day if you need me.'

Mrs Keyson nodded. 'Thank you.'

I fished in my bag. 'I finished the painting. Do you want to give it to him?' I said, passing it to Mrs K.

'Oh, thank you. It's perfect,' she said, her hand over her mouth as she took in the picture. 'He'll love it. You've really "got" him. That's beautiful. Thank you.' She turned to her husband. 'Lennie, Abigail's here. She's done a painting of Brucie for you. So he can be here with you all the time, too. Look – she's done such a good job. It's just like him, isn't it? Lennie, dear, can you hear me?'

I wasn't sure if Mr K was resting, asleep, or even unconscious. His breathing was so slow it gave me the panicky feeling of wanting to draw air into my own lungs but, as we watched, his eyes opened and he grunted.

'Aww, there you are, love,' said Mrs K. 'Look, Abigail's here and she's done a painting of Brucie for you,' she said again.

I gave Mr K a little wave and watched as his eyes roamed over the picture that Mrs K was holding out for him. Then he closed his eyes with an exhale of breath, as if it was all too much effort. His lips, I'm sure, curved upwards.

'It's wonderful, isn't it?' said Mrs K. 'I knew you'd like it. Now, where shall I put it? Somewhere where you can see it.'

'Mrs K,' I said softly, 'I'm going to go and do the drinks. I'll be back in a bit to see how you're doing. Can I get you anything? A coffee?'

'Oh that would be lovely, dear, thank you, but no rush. Do the others first.'

'Okay.'

I slipped out of the room, closing the door quietly behind me. A nurse caught my eye and raised her eyebrows in question.

'Not yet,' I said.

I wasn't in the room when Mr Keyson died later that afternoon, but I saw a nurse go in and I was waiting outside when she came back out. She shook her head, just two shakes, left and right, and tears sprung to my eyes, my throat tight. Even though it was expected, I couldn't help but think it was too soon.

'It was peaceful,' said the nurse. 'She was there. Do you want to go in? I think she'd like that.'

'Sure.'

I dabbed at my eyes, took a deep breath, then slipped quietly into the room. Mrs K was sitting with her head bowed next to her husband, and I saw at once that the essence of him had gone, his body just a shell on the bed. I looked upwards as I always do at these times, imagining his soul flying happy and free. Mrs K glanced up as I entered. Her eyes were red-rimmed.

'Oh Abigail, he's gone,' she said. 'It's over.' A sob ran through her.

'I'm so sorry.' I went to give her a hug and she stood up and grasped hold of me for a minute before turning back to her husband.

'No, it's… it's good. He was in pain,' she said. 'He's at peace now. He hated being sick.' Her voice was tremulous.

'I'm glad you were there,' I said, squeezing her hand. 'It will have given him a lot of comfort to know you were there.'

'Do you think so?' she asked. 'Do you think he knew?'

'He knew. He absolutely knew. He waited for you to come. He knew you were there, and he was at peace.'

'Thank you. That means a lot.'

I bowed my head. It was my job. Helping dying patients to pass without fear, and giving comfort to the bereaved after their loved ones were gone was exactly why I was there.

'And thank you for everything,' she said. 'You volunteers, you're angels who walk the Earth.'

Transcript of interview with Mr Rohan Allerton, husband of Abigail Allerton: 20 December 2019

'Tell me a little about Abigail's volunteer work at the hospice. What motivates her to do it? Does she enjoy it?'

'Yes, she enjoys it. This might sound odd, but it means a lot to her to make sure people are in a good place when they die. She takes it really seriously. I mean, to me, it sounds awful, but she always comes back in a good mood. I tease her about why she wants to spend her days with dying people but… [shrugs] It gets her out of the house. I already mentioned that she doesn't much like going out so, if she didn't do that, she'd stay at home her entire life. Sometimes I think I shouldn't have suggested the website for the pet portraits. It makes it too easy for her to stay at home.'

[Rustles papers] 'Has she ever been diagnosed as agoraphobic?'

'Not that I know of, but if you gave her choice between going out and staying in, I know which she'd pick. Actually, is there, like, a scale for agoraphobia, you know, like there is for autism? Because, if there is, she'd definitely be somewhere on it. Anyway, she likes the hospice work. She was always really conscientious.

Never used to miss her day. She had responsibilities and she took them seriously. I know it sounds a bit depressing, spending time with people who're just waiting to die, but she's good at it. It makes her happy. If that doesn't sound weird.'

Twenty-one

Given her flight arrival time, I'd calculated that Grace would make it to the house around six. I got home from the hospice around four thirty, showered, changed and sat in the kitchen with a glass of wine as I let the reality of Mr Keyson's passing sink in. Around me the house settled into itself, too, as if it was also thinking about mortality. The clock beat out its interminable rhythm, each reverberating tick marking a countdown that took me ever closer to my own death.

What would Grace think about the fact that I was married? I wondered. I'd met Rohan just after she'd left for Australia, when he'd turned up out of the blue at my exhibition, smiling and smartly dressed. A sometime art investor and a friend of the gallery director, Francesca, he turned out to be a big fan of the violent landscape paintings into which I'd poured my soul. He loved the cruel way in which I'd slashed the canvases with angry reds, yellows, purples and blacks; he loved the birds I'd portrayed as monsters, dribbling red from jaws that hung open as they slid through an oily sky; he admired the devastation I'd imposed onto the classic beauty of the English countryside. It was, however, the gentle tone of his voice as he spoke to Francesca that first made me turn towards him: the man in the expensive navy suit.

'Hello there. You appear to have lost an earring,' he said, raising an eyebrow at my statement lone earring. 'I love your work. You're very talented.'

I blushed and fiddled with my bare earlobe, wondering whether to explain the solo earring or just let it go. Even then I saw the world through a sheet of glass. I watched life, always one degree removed from the bittiness of existence; always unsure what to say; always living in Grace's shadow. Yet, somehow, with his words and his gentle tone of voice, Rohan managed to break through.

And, as it was, he hadn't been entirely honest with me that night. He bought a couple of my paintings and, in the polite chat that followed, commissioned me to paint another: a portrait of him for his parents. It was only later, much later, when my defences had dropped and I'd allowed him to press his lips on mine, the thick hair of the glossy beard of which he was so proud tickling my cheeks, that he'd admitted he'd never been interested in the portrait; he'd only wanted an excuse to see me again.

I wondered if Grace would approve of my new life. And what would her own be like now? Would she have a boyfriend; a partner? Was there someone she'd left in Australia? I reached for my phone and opened Instagram. I hadn't checked it for years, but her personal account had always been under the name GraceTheAce, a name I'd given her as she powered through her coursework. The account came up and my heart lurched as the screen filled with colourful images. They were surprisingly arty, and there was a likeness to each of them; something indefinable that bound them – a tone, perhaps – that I wouldn't have expected coming from someone as scientific as her.

But her feed didn't give much away. The images were almost entirely of scenery, telling me only that she'd spent some time in remote coastal areas as well as in cities. There was a horse, a helicopter, a Jeep, several small boats. I pulled up a map and tracked the posts she'd labelled, tracing her route north up the coast from Sydney into Queensland, then further up, past Brisbane and the Sunshine Coast to Port Douglas. There were pictures there of rainforest: of lush green foliage, of the curling roots of ancient trees and crystal-clear pools of water dappled by sun and then, suddenly, there was a figure – a woman – on a vast expanse of beach.

Behind the person, the sea was indigo blue, with rolls of white surf frothing and hissing as they hit the sand. There was no one else on the beach. Not a soul. The woman was smiling, laughing maybe, but it was hard to tell much more since she was so far away – a tiny figure in the centre of the huge beach. She was wearing white shorts and a red vest – that I could see – and her feet were bare. One arm was raised, her elbow jabbing out like a pennant as she held onto a large straw hat that shaded her face. Dark hair coursed out from under the hat, a few bits dancing to one side, whipped by a wind that blew off the sea. In her other hand, the woman dangled a pair of sandals, as if she'd taken them off to run on the sand.

I expanded the image on my phone as far as I could, trying to get a better look at her face – looking for the familiar features: was it Grace? Or a friend of hers? – but the image pixelated as it expanded, causing me to shrink her back down for clarity. I half closed my eyes and gazed at the image. It was the right body-shape for Grace, and the hair also looked right. I was pretty sure it was her. I wondered who'd taken the picture; whether they'd then run to catch up with her on the beach. Whether they were laughing with her.

*

As six o'clock drew close, I climbed up the stairs and locked the door of the attic, then I went back downstairs, where I dithered, waiting for the sound of the taxi. In the hall, I settled on the bottom stair, my muscles stiffening every time I heard a car slow for the curve in the road outside.

It had been an oppressive day, the air so heavy I was grateful to the house for protecting me from it; for keeping the weight of all that *atmosphere* off my head. Even so, I leaned forward on the step and cradled the back of my head with my hands. As the evening drew in, the light took on a yellow tinge; I'd seen on the news that there was dust in the air from the Sahara, blown to us on a high, southerly wind – now, as the angle of the sun changed, the dust somehow filtered the light. The hallway looked liverish, sick. From somewhere came the sound of a woman singing a silly nursery rhyme and the ripple of a toddler's infectious laughter.

When I finally heard the sound of a car draw to a halt – doors banging – and the sound of someone dragging a case along the path, I jumped up, dazed, my bottom numb from the hard stair. Outside, I heard Grace curse as her bag got stuck in the cracks of the path, then grunt as she lifted it, yet her presence still came as a surprise, as if somewhere deep down I'd suspected she might not turn up at all.

I stiffened as she rang the doorbell, and then hesitated behind the door for a few moments before I sprung the lock, breathing fast, acutely aware that I was separated from Grace for the first time in four years by nothing more than a piece of wood. Outside, I could feel the pulse of her energy; on the inside of the house, my own energy reached towards her – fingers grasping at the air, clawing at her – just as it had that first day she'd appeared at my door at university. My breath came in shudders; after all the anticipation, all the planning, the preparation and the waiting, she was finally here.

I took a deep breath and opened the door.

'Abi!' Grace said, and we took each other in, our eyes trying not to show their greed for details. She looked slightly heavier than she'd been four years ago; bags under her eyes were concealed but obviously there; her freckles now hidden under foundation; her cheekbones accentuated with blusher. What differences did she see in me now I was older and married? Could she see that I was stronger? Was I stronger?

'Hey, Grace,' I said, shy like a schoolgirl. 'Come in,' and she stepped inside, then held open her arms to me. The hug was awkward, and she stepped back quickly as I drank in the sight of her, the smell of her, the substance of her; this person whom I'd successfully banished from my thoughts for the past four years.

'Thanks for letting me stay,' she said. Then she smiled. 'As if you had a choice.'

Twenty-two

Grace moved her bags over the threshold and closed the door behind her. She looked at me again and smiled.

'Nice earring.'

I put my hand to it self-consciously. 'It's my lucky charm. I wear it when I'm painting.'

'Still?' Grace gave a little laugh and looked more closely at me. I noticed the crow's feet that feathered from the sides of her eyes as she smiled.

'You look well,' she said. 'Married life must suit you.' Her tone was slightly barbed, or was I imagining it? I held her gaze and she looked away first. 'Nice place,' she said. 'Can I have a tour? I'm dying to see it.'

I started to move but she was faster than me, already off down the hallway, her head turning left and right as she took in my home, her fingers trailing across the new paints and papers, as if she were feeling for what lay beneath. I followed in her wake, trying to see the house as she would. She'd always loved interiors.

'So you bought this house?' she asked, nodding. Approval, I thought.

'Yes. We've done quite a lot of work.' *A lot of work, actually.*

She stopped at the old grandfather clock.

'Nice.'

I followed Grace into the kitchen, where she stopped abruptly and did a double-take, her brow furrowed.

'Wow.'

And I kicked myself at once: why had we gone for white gloss and chrome? Of course we could have done something less flashy, more in keeping with the history of the house: soft wood, stone, warmer colours that better reflected the Victorian architecture. But Grace didn't wait for an explanation; she swung around and headed into the open-plan living area, which we'd created by breaking down the wall separating the old sitting room from the boxy old dining room that had been barely larger than an eight-seater dining set. Gone were the previous owners' gaudy sofas, replaced with two big, squashy leather pieces bought in the John Lewis sale.

'Oh,' she said, looking around. 'Interesting.'

'It's much more practical than it was,' I said. I was pleased with the new space. 'The dining room was small. You could barely fit people in as well as the furniture.'

'Do you do much entertaining?' Grace asked, her head tilted sideways, but she knew the answer to that. We both knew the answer to that, so I gave a little self-deprecating laugh to show I knew she was joking.

'Shall we go up?' she said. 'I'm dying to see the rest.'

'Be my guest,' I said, waving her on since we'd already established she was leading this tour. I picked up her bags and followed, dumping them on the upstairs landing as she pushed open the door to the master bedroom.

'Nice,' she said, and I was glad we hadn't done too much to the room – just updated the decor.

'So this is where it all happens.' Grace faced me. 'I can't believe you're married. The mistress of the house. No doubt soon to be the mother of the house, too.'

'I always thought it would be you first,' I said.

'Me too, but…' Grace shrugged and looked down for a moment and I could see the hurt behind her eyes. It wasn't right that I had all this and she did not.

'So where do you paint?' Grace asked when she looked up again.

'In the attic.'

She backed out of the room and found the little door.

'Up here? Can I see?' she asked and, before I could say anything, she'd lifted the latch and scampered up the stairs. I lurched after her, my hand out to stop her but she reached the attic door before I did. She pushed it, then rattled the handle and turned to me.

'It's locked?'

'Yes. Work in progress.' I bit my lip.

Grace tilted her head sideways. 'Can I see?'

I took a deep breath. Stronger now. 'Come and see your room.'

We stared at each other for a moment, me wondering how far she'd push me, but she let it go, for now. She came back down the stairs and I kicked open the door to the spare room.

'After you.'

Grace walked in with her hand over her eyes then removed it dramatically and looked around. Butterflies tickled my ribs. Had I done the right thing to keep the old furniture? Was it tatty or quaint? She took in every aspect of the room: the wallpaper, the fireplace, the dresser, chair, the wardrobe, the bed, the teddy bear. She touched the curtains, pulling out the fabric so she could examine it with a nod; then she laid her palm flat on the wardrobe and then the desk, as if her fingers could feel a pulse in the wood.

She sat on the bed and gave an experimental bounce, then picked up Bear and gave him a kiss.

'He's cute,' she said.

'He came with the house.'

'Nice.' She sat the bear on her lap. 'So how come this room escaped the "modernization"?'

'Ran out of money,' I said.

Grace smiled. 'I'm glad. I love it.'

I smiled back at her. 'Good.' I looked at my watch. 'So, look, I'm making some dinner – it'll be ready about eight. Shall I leave you to get unpacked and – well, come down when you're ready.'

'Sounds like a plan,' Grace said, looking at me, and I took one more look at her as if to assure myself that it really was her after all these years; that it really was Grace, older, but still Grace, sitting on the bed in my spare room. It was, and the contented little smile that licked at her mouth told me that she was exactly where she wanted to be.

Twenty-three

Grace came down just before eight.

'You know what?' she said, entering the kitchen. 'After all that travelling, it's good to be home.'

As I smiled at the compliment, Grace pulled out a chair and Alfie sprang back with a hiss, his ears pressed back. Grace pulled a face. I laughed, embarrassed; Alfie was usually so easy-going.

'Don't you like cats?'

'No. But it's mutual. As you can see.' She glared at Alfie and he slunk out of the kitchen, the hair along his spine standing up on end. 'Wow, I can't get over this kitchen,' Grace said, giving her head a theatrical shake. 'It looks like a spaceship. I keep expecting to look out of the window and see the International Space Station floating past.'

We both looked out of the window at the red-brick hulk of next-door's wall.

'It was my compromise with Rohan,' I said. 'He wanted a new-build with a shiny new kitchen; I wanted this house… for obvious reasons…' I shrugged, hoping my reasons for wanting a decrepit Victorian house were as obvious to her as they were to me. 'The least I could do was let him have his gleaming kitchen.'

Grace raised one shoulder in a lazy shrug; of course, she never needed to compromise with anyone.

'Can I get you a drink? Prosecco? I thought we could celebrate.' I bustled over to the fridge.

Grace let out a long breath. 'Do you have anything soft? It's just…' she put her hand to her chest in a gesture that came across as pious, 'I rarely drink these days.'

'Oh, okay – yes, yes I do.' I scrabbled inside the fridge. 'I've got… oh.' I looked at her. 'I'm sure I've got some tonic water somewhere. Or there's tap water.'

'Tonic, if you have it. Water if you don't.' Grace smiled.

In the cupboard was one can of tonic, quite possibly out of date. I poured it for Grace, plated up some olives then opened the Prosecco anyway.

'Cheers. Welcome back.' I chinked my glass against hers. 'So how was Australia? Tell me everything.'

'Oh my God. It's been amazing. Oz is incredible, and I had the best time – but…' She shrugged as if England had the greater pull.

'Where did you go? What did you do?'

She sighed. 'I worked for a couple of years in Sydney, and we spent all our holidays travelling.'

If she saw me flinch when she said 'we', she didn't show it.

'God, we saw so much: Adelaide, Melbourne, Hobart, Canberra. We even made it over to Perth. Can you believe it took five hours to fly there? It's such a huge country. I don't think I really appreciated it till I went.' She exhaled. 'We went to Uluru, too – saw that at sunrise. Then I quit my job and drove up the east coast, stopping at all the interesting places. Byron Bay.' She laughed to herself. 'That was fun. Brisbane. The Sunshine Coast. Fraser Island.' I noticed the switch from 'we' to 'I'.

'Then I got bored driving and flew up to Cairns,' Grace continued. 'I spent some time in Port Douglas, and saw the rainforest, the Great Barrier Reef. Things that I'd only ever seen on TV. It was amazing. And what about you? What have you been up to?' She looked around, as if my life had been contained within the walls of the house while she'd been out adventuring. 'Well, you got married, I guess. To be honest, I never thought you'd actually meet anyone. Or at least let anyone get close. Such a prickly thing you are. Used to be.'

I looked down at the table and smiled. 'He's called Rohan. He came to my exhibition – four years ago?' The one she'd helped me arrange but then... all that *stuff* had happened, and she left before it opened.

'So he's into art?' she said, and I was grateful to her for glossing over the fight; the cold email she'd sent telling me she was leaving. So that's how we'd play it: as if nothing had happened. But who was forgiving whom?

'Yeah. He's really supportive. In fact, he's been pushing me because I actually have another exhibition coming up and I haven't painted anything yet.'

'You've got another exhibition? How come?'

'You mean, without you?' I asked, arching my eyebrow and giving a little laugh. 'Maybe I'm good.'

'You are good. Of course you are. That's not what I meant at all.' She stopped abruptly. 'But you were saying you haven't painted anything yet?'

'Well, not *anything*. I haven't painted anything *significant* for a while now. I do some volunteering, actually.'

I traced the grain of the table with my finger and waited.

'Oh?' she said. 'What sort of volunteering?'

So I told her about the hospice; what I did there. 'I love having the chance to try and make a person's last weeks, days or hours, the best they can be,' I said. 'Sometimes it just means being there, holding a hand, or listening. Sometimes I sit in silence and that's all that's needed but, if the patient has a bit longer, I try to find out if there's anything worrying them and help to resolve whatever that is.'

'In what sort of way?' Grace asked.

'Tying up loose ends mainly: I make phone calls; I contact family and find lost friends. I make connections – anything to give the patients peace before they die. I've just painted a portrait of a dog for a guy who was missing his dog, though—' my voice broke, 'we lost him today.' I paused while I gathered myself, then carried on. 'I can't bear the thought of anyone dying with unfinished business.' I didn't tell her that my volunteer work tended to spill over into my life as I sleuthed away on the computer at home – something Rohan was always chiding me for. 'The fact that I've done my best makes it more bearable for me when the patients I've grown close to do finally pass,' I said, 'because that's basically how it ends for all of them. But it brings me a lot of peace.'

Grace shrugged. 'Whatever floats your boat. So, the painting?' she said. 'You said you were painting again?'

'Oh yes! Well, suddenly I got inspired and I've done two in the last few weeks!' I laughed, still full of the wonder of having good paint on a canvas. 'I think it's going to be okay. It's going to be a series.'

Grace nodded. 'Landscapes again?'

'No. Portraits.'

She tilted her head. 'I can't wait to see them.'

Would I really be able to show her? Did I dare? I got up to

check the oven. 'I've done a roast chicken, by the way,' I said, 'I hope you're hungry,' and Grace pulled a face.

'Ah,' she said. 'I should have told you. Eek. Awkward.' She winced.

'What?' I said, oven gloves on.

'I don't eat meat anymore. Haven't for a long time. I'm a pescatarian.'

'Really?' I laughed. She had to be joking, *of course* she was joking, but she was shaking her head, her hand over her mouth and suddenly I was back in our student digs on her twentieth birthday. For a nanosecond, the old hurt flared, raw and angry, but I shoved it back down. I should have asked. Any decent hostess would have asked.

Grace and I had moved out of Halls for our second year, both of us overjoyed at the thought of having more privacy. Sharing a bathroom and kitchen was a torture I could no longer endure, so I'd found a student accommodation building that allowed me to rent a decent studio with facilities and a whole load of extras like WiFi and laundry. Grace was able to take a single room in the same block – given I cooked for her most of the time, there seemed no point in her wasting money on a kitchen, and the arrangement worked well: my studio was just about large enough for us both to eat and relax in but she had her own space for sleeping.

We'd been living there for a couple of months when she turned twenty. Things were still good then, both of us relishing the freedom of having a little of our own space after the cramped university Halls. I still felt I owed her after she helped me turn my life around and I'd be lying if I said I didn't like the quiet domesticity of cooking for her in my own place. Honestly, I think she liked it too.

Turning twenty sounded like a big deal to us back then: it was the beginning of a new decade; the first one since hitting double figures what seemed a lifetime ago and, maybe I brought it on myself, but I felt that the responsibility to make Grace's birthday special sat squarely on my shoulders. She'd often mentioned the lengths to which her parents had gone for her past birthdays and I didn't want her to be disappointed just because they weren't there. I'd set my alarm for an hour before I knew she'd come over for breakfast and smothered the studio with birthday banners and balloons. Then I'd gone back to bed and waited for her to knock.

'Oh my God!' she'd exclaimed on seeing the decorations, her hand clamped over her mouth. 'You did all this for me?'

'Happy birthday,' I said, smiling and shy. 'You'll have to wait till tonight for your present, but let me make you a coffee.'

She tapped away at her phone while she drank her coffee, birthday messages pinging in, then it was time for lectures and she was gone. I didn't have much money after paying the rent, but my gift to her was going to be a surprise – a special, home-cooked dinner, just like her mum would have given her: a roast, with all the trimmings.

After my own lectures, I went to the supermarket and hauled back my supplies. While she was still out, I made a soup, then I stuffed the chicken and parboiled the potatoes. I glazed the carrots and trimmed the beans, then I prepared two of Grace's favourite chocolate melting-middle puddings to serve with ice cream. When it was time, I put the roast in the oven, added the potatoes and carrots and dithered about making everything look 'just so'.

I didn't have a dining table, so I dragged my desk into the centre of the room and set it as best I could and then I sat back and waited for her to come home. When she didn't turn up at her usual time, I called her. Multiple times. I turned off the oven and opened the Prosecco. When I'd finished the bottle and the chicken started to dry out, I went to her room. From the lifts, I heard the pulse of music, the laughing, the shouts. I didn't need to go to her door to know she was having a party. A party she hadn't invited me to.

It was my fault, really. I should have told her what I'd planned. How was she to know?

'God, I'm so sorry,' Grace said, squashing up her face. 'I just don't. The meat industry. The planet.' She fake-gagged, her eyes rolled up and her tongue stuck out. 'I just can't do it anymore. Look, don't worry about me. I'm sure you've got something I can have – I'm easy to please, some pasta or something, or beans on toast – or maybe just the vegetables, but, please, you've gone to all this trouble, you eat the chicken. Don't let me stop you.'

And so I carved the chicken and heaped Grace's plate with roast potatoes and green beans – no gravy – and we sat and faced each other at the table. I looked at her plate.

'It doesn't look very interesting. And this was supposed to be a celebration,' I said, standing quickly and spinning around so she couldn't see the gleam of tears in my eyes. 'Let me order you a pizza. There's some arty place around here that does vegan pizzas. I think you can even have a cauliflower base if you're gluten-free too? They deliver really quickly, or I can run out and get it. It's not far.' I pulled open the drawer that housed our takeaway menus and pulled out a handful.

'Really?' Grace perked up then looked back at her plate. 'But no, this is fine. Sit back down. We can have the fancy pizzas another night. You've gone to all this effort. The least I can do is eat it. And I'm sure you've done dessert, right?'

'Chocolate fondant,' I said. 'Are you sure?'

'Yes, absolutely.' She forked a dry potato and put it resolutely in her mouth. 'Yummy,' she said. 'You always did do a great roast potato.'

I'd drunk the whole bottle of Prosecco and half a bottle of red wine by the time we finished dessert; I could feel the flush in my cheeks, the giddiness of the hit. Grace was telling me at length about the jobs she'd held in Australia – the places she'd travelled, the people she'd met – but I wasn't really listening: I was distracted by the Australian twang that softened the edges of her words; the inflection that rose slightly at the end of each sentence as she talked. She really liked the sound of her own voice. Always had. I shoved my chair back, piled the dishes in the sink and squirted washing-up liquid over them.

Grace interrupted her soliloquy. 'Don't do that now. I want to see your work.'

I fell still, my back to her, the breath wheezing out of me like an old bagpipe as I squeezed my eyes shut.

'Come on, Abs,' she cajoled. 'It's me. I was the first person ever to see your art, remember? That very first painting?'

I turned to her, only half my lips smiling. 'How could I forget?'

I hadn't intended to show Grace my work at university. Art was my therapy; the landscape an intimacy between me and the canvas. I kept it hidden and I told Grace never to look. But one night, way later than I ever expected her to knock, she burst through the door while my canvas was exposed and I froze, heart hammering. There was nowhere to turn; nothing to do but let her see it.

Grace also stopped in her tracks. She tried to hide her reaction, but I saw her stiffen and swallow. Her gasp was barely audible, but it was there. As the door clicked shut behind her, she opened her mouth.

'Wow,' she breathed. She took a step closer, unable to tear her eyes from the canvas. Her mouth fell open as she looked from me to it, examining the horror of the scene. 'Really, wow. Oh my God, Abs. This is unreal.'

And then she found more words and, all the while she spoke, she was giving me this look – a look like she couldn't believe that little old Abigail, the stuffy Management student, had painted something so raw, so compelling. So *horrific*.

She shook her head. 'This is it, Abs. This really is your thing. Shit. You're amazing. I've never seen stuff like this. It's incredible.'

But then everything changed as the doctor in her had taken over. She knelt down in front of me as I sat on the bed, and took my hands gently in hers.

'Abs, where this came from, do you want to talk about it?' she said, her eyes fixing onto mine, trying to see into my soul – and I could have told her. I could have told her that it came from the same place as did my nightmares, my grief, my shame, and my constant wish to die. And, for a glorious, heady moment I teetered on the brink of confiding in her – in saying the words out loud that might relieve the pressure inside me; words that could release me. I teetered on the brink of a world where I no longer carried this secret. Yes, for a moment, I fantasized about telling her, but to do so would change everything.

'I can't,' I said.

Grace let my hands drop and shook her head. 'What goes on in that mind of yours?'

I looked away, squeezing tears behind my eyelids. If she chose to see, she'd have an idea, because it was right there on the canvas. That's what went on in my head. Relentlessly. Twenty-four/seven. I'd painted the contents of my head and it had been an epiphany: the feeling of relief was as if I'd been bursting to go to the bathroom and then I finally had. *That* sort of release. It had, temporarily, eased the pressure inside my head, and I had the same feeling now while I was painting the portrait. I knew that when I was up there in the attic, I wasn't myself: I was channelling something that came from another dimension – it came through me and out onto the canvas – and I knew it had to come out because, if it stayed inside me, it would rot me from the inside out.

'You know, you were lucky to have me as a friend at uni,' Grace continued, her smile languid. 'I think I can talk about this now as enough time's passed, but you do know that, if it wasn't for me, you'd have become a raging alcoholic, don't you? Do you remember how much you used to drink?' She raised an eyebrow and I thought with shame of the empty bottles in the recycling bin out the back.

'Jesus, Abs,' Grace said. 'You could drink any guy under the table. I often came home and found you passed out on the sofa. I'd take you to bed and lie you on your side so you didn't choke on your tongue. Many times, I slept on your tiny sofa because I was worried about you drowning in your own vomit.' She drummed her nails on the table. 'Also, without me, you'd be dead.'

She looked at me and I lowered my gaze as a hot flush swept through me. Grace was the only person who knew about that. There was too much to say, and I couldn't say any of it.

'But anyway, I digress,' Grace said after a pause. 'If it weren't for me pushing you that night, you'd never have painted anything. Do you remember that? When I said, "Why don't you just paint – if it's what you want to do so much?" I don't know why you'd never thought about it.' She laughed. 'So, yeah, if it wasn't for me, you'd probably never even have had that exhibition. You'd be managing some blue-chip business somewhere. You'd be some suited and booted company-bot, unsatisfied and bitter. You probably wouldn't even have met the "wonderful" Rohan, so you've got me to thank, for that, too.' She laughed and pointed her finger at me. 'I'm right, and you know it!'

She doesn't mean to be so... *hard*, I told myself. But she had a point. Everything she said was right. Out of everyone, it was she who deserved to see my work.

'Okay,' I said, and Grace's eyes snapped back to me, as if she hadn't actually expected me to say yes. She stood up and held out her hand.

'Key, please.'

Silently I took it from my jeans pocket and handed it to her and, equally wordlessly, she turned and left the kitchen but, as I heard the stairs creak under her feet, dread flooded my body, ice-cold and suffocating. I launched myself after her.

'Grace! Stop! It's not ready! Come back!'

'Too late,' she sang, and I heard the lock click. I dashed into the attic after her. The two finished portraits were on easels, angled away from the door to best catch the light. I thought Grace would go straight over but she stopped abruptly on the threshold of the studio, her open mouth reminding me of that time she first saw my painting.

'This is where you paint?' she exclaimed. She moved further in, turning this way and that as she absorbed the size and space of the room. She took in the flowers stencilled on the walls then went over to the boxes shoved into the corner.

'Are these yours? They look old.' She poked a finger at the dusty cardboard.

'They were here when we bought the house,' I said.

'What's in them?'

'Old stuff. Clothes. Dolls.'

'Oh, how interesting. I'd love to look through them.'

'Be my guest.'

'I will. But first, the famous paintings.'

I watched as she went over and studied the canvases. What would she think?

In the second picure, the girl was older, around twelve, I'd say, on the cusp of puberty. And she was still happy: her skin was clear, her eyes still bright, but there was an edge of seriousness about her now, her clothing more subdued, her smile more self-possessed; a hint of what might be to come. She looked steadily out of the canvas at us, almost quizzically, as if we'd disturbed her from studying, or reading or thinking. The background, too, was muted – it wasn't as obvious as a colour change, more a lack of light – an omission rather than an addition – but the sense that came from the canvas was one of oppression; of a cloud, of a shadow hanging – of a threat. I wondered if Grace would pick up on that, but, no, as she took in the paintings, her hand was over her mouth and she was laughing. I looked at her, confused.

'I knew it!' she snorted. 'Of all the things in the world you could paint, I just knew you'd pick me!'

Twenty-four

Later that night, I sat in bed pretending to read until I heard Grace close her bedroom door, then I shut my own door. The evening hadn't gone as I'd hoped. I was angry with myself about the chicken, and Grace's reaction to my paintings hadn't been what I was expecting. I'd thought she would be flattered that I was painting her – 'grateful' might be a stretch too far – but it never occurred to me that she would assume she'd be the subject. I'd forgotten how hurtful she could be. How she would stamp all over my feelings as if she owned me; as if she had no idea how badly her words could wound.

The evening had been just how it used to be.

By the middle of my final year at university, I'd come to dread the sound of Grace's footsteps in the corridor; the sound of her perky knock on my door. I fantasized about hiding in my room and not opening the door. I'd realized that I liked being on my own; I liked my own 'quirky' (her words), 'alcoholic' (seriously?) company. I was increasingly finding Grace to be entitled and arrogant, always expecting me to be there for her; always expecting groceries to have been bought, and food cooked; always making snide comments. Maybe I'd created a rod for my own back with the cooking, but it was a situation I didn't feel I could easily back out of. Every time I thought about *not* preparing dinner for her, I'd pictured her coming home after a long day learning how to save people's lives and saying in that chirpy way she had, 'What's for dinner?' and I ended up cooking enough for her anyway – I mean, God, it wasn't such an effort to throw in a bit more, was it? I went around in circles: resenting it, then telling myself it wasn't a big deal. Though clearly it was. Maybe the problem was with me, not her. I was a soft touch. I should have put my foot down a long time ago.

Still, I couldn't break away from her. So, for much of that third and final year at uni, I'd been biding my time, waiting for my chance to get a place on my own. Grace still had two years to go on her course but I was going to be working. I'd have a salary and could afford something a bit better. I pictured myself in a light and airy one-bed: alone, painting in silence; 'passing out on the couch', as Grace put it, without anyone to notice and, as the end of the year had approached, I'd done my own flat-hunting in secret and pushed Grace towards getting a place with her medic friends.

I talked up how much better it would be for her to stay with people on the same course; to be with people who were still students; people who were experiencing the same things as her. She'd need to be able to talk about what she was going through with people who understood, I said. She'd be doing attachments in hospital and clinics by then, working all hours and being absolutely shattered. I'd be working myself, but nothing like the hours she'd be putting in. I wouldn't be a great support to her, I told her.

She smiled, and asked to see my flat. Oh, I'm such a fool. My heart sank as we walked along the street and I realized how central my new place was to everywhere she needed to be. She always had a good aesthetic sense and I saw how her eyes lit up when I stopped outside the white stucco-fronted building. With each flat privately owned, it was well maintained and smart from the outside. There were even window boxes with flowers.

Inside, the flat was like the Tardis: way more space than you'd imagine, and the owner had done everything possible to it to make it look light and fresh. There was a bedroom, a nice bathroom all done up in white, a separate living room and a new-looking open-plan kitchen that had an extra space attached: a dining nook, I imagined, but I was planning to use it for painting. The light was good despite the place being half underground – the living-room window ran the entire length of the room and was at head height, so you could see people's feet walking past. I'd never lived in a basement before and it gave me a safe, womb-like feeling, like I was buried and hidden away, but still able to see out and watch the world.

'It's only the basement,' I told Grace. 'Don't get too excited,' but I could tell from her energy, even as we walked down the steps to the front door, that I'd made a mistake letting her come. Inside, she rushed about examining everything like an overexcited dog.

'Oh my God,' she said, looking at the dining nook. 'There's enough space here for a sofa as well as a small dining table, so you could use the living room as a second bedroom...' She jiggled with excitement. 'You could have the big room! I don't mind being in the small one! What do you think?'

I'd laughed, thinking she was joking, but it turned out she wasn't. Had she misread the situation, or had she deliberately manipulated me? Deep down, I still felt I owed her, and she knew it. I was still grateful to her for being my friend; for helping me get on track with my art. Without really realizing what I was doing, I'd nodded, and Grace had flung herself at me, hugging onto me like a limpet, weeping her gratitude. Then she'd flung her arms out and spun in a circle on the living-room floor, as if it was her place already, and I'd ended up with her living with me, rent-free, for two more years.

The flat should have been my retreat; my safe haven. It couldn't have been further from it.

Would the same happen again now?

I closed my eyes. No. I was stronger now. Things could be different. I'd chosen to invite her to stay – the decision had been mine. And, at the moment, with Rohan away, it suited me to have the company. But I could be prepared. I could have a plan. In practical terms, I'd take her to estate agent's and help her look for somewhere – yes – but I also wanted her to treat me as an equal. I needed to find some techniques; ways to handle her.

I closed my eyes and tried to look objectively at the situation. I was never able to stand up to Grace, and I never had been. She belittled me, walked all over me and ignored my wishes, and I let her. Was this bullying? Was I enabling it?

Feeling like a traitor, I reached for the iPad, opened a new tab and typed in 'emotional bullying' then 'bullying in female friendships'.

Verbal abuse such as name-calling; threatening or intimidating behaviour; constant criticism; controlling or manipulating. Eye-rolling. Smirking.

Hmm. I clicked through a link and ended up on another page.

Your friend can make you feel like dirt or like you're the best and only person in the room. She makes you work for her friendship and, when you get it, it feels incredible.

That sounded familiar.

There was a click on the landing: Grace's door opening. I slid the iPad quickly under the duvet just before she knocked on my door and popped her head round without waiting for me to reply. Her hair was down, hanging loosely around her shoulders and her faced was cleansed and shiny with moisturizer.

'Hey. I saw your light was still on. Look, I was thinking about those boxes in the attic. I'd love to look through them?'

'Sure... I'll bring them down tomorrow.'

'Great. But there's no time like the present!' She beamed at me. 'Just chuck me the key and I'll get them.'

I sighed. I didn't want her alone in the attic with my artwork. 'No, it's fine. I'll get them.'

So Grace went back to her room and I padded up the stairs and hauled the boxes down, locking the attic after me. Grace watched from the rocking chair as I plonked them on the floor in front of her. I straightened up and looked at my hands.

'I'm filthy,' I said, but she was on her knees, pulling at the peeling tape of one of the boxes I hadn't opened.

'So exciting,' she said. 'It's like *Cash in the Attic*!'

'I really doubt there's anything valuable in there.'

'You never know. One man's junk is another man's treasure, and all that.'

Grace pulled out a blonde doll in a pink nylon dress and peered back into the box. She looked around the room and smiled. 'Just think, she probably used to live right here.' She held up the doll as if showing it the room, then spoke in a baby voice. 'Hello, do you remember this room? Did you used to live here? Is it nice to be back?'

The hairs on the back of my neck stood on end. 'You're nuts,' I said, backing out of the room, 'and I'm going to bed.'

'Okay! Sleep well!' Grace didn't even look up from the box. ''Night.'

I closed my bedroom door behind me, slid back into bed and got the iPad out again. I closed my eyes for a moment before finding my place, back on the emotional bullying page.

The behaviour is hidden, often wrapped in a package seen as somewhat harmless or just a 'girl thing'... attempts to defend oneself leads to an escalation of the aggression.

I shivered and pulled the duvet tighter around me. The air in my room was freezing.

Transcript of interview with Mr Rohan Allerton, husband of Abigail Allerton: 20 December 2019

'How did Abigail seem to you, when she spoke about Grace? Was it in a positive way?'

'Yes. She said they were best friends at uni. That they lived together on campus and off campus for five years... I got the feeling that Grace used to "look after" Abi, much like how I do these days. As I said, when she's painting, she's almost in another "realm". She's not entirely there, so to speak. She needs someone with her.'

'And she seemed happy when she told you that Grace was coming to stay?'

'Yes, I think so. It didn't occur to me that she might not be happy about it. Why would it? I mean, you wouldn't invite someone to stay with you if you weren't happy about it, would you? You'd just say, "Sorry, we don't have the space." Anyway, the timing worked out really well with me having to go away. We were both relieved, I think. It was the perfect solution.'

'Did she give any intimation as to how things were between them when Grace left for... umm... [shuffles papers]... Australia?'

'No. No, she didn't. I assumed they were friends.'

Twenty-five

I set my alarm for seven thirty, thinking I might catch Grace before she went into town to do any necessary admin before starting work the next day: setting up a bank account, changing money. As I made my way downstairs, I paused outside her room and listened, but all I could hear was the house itself, its walls almost ticking off the time as the seconds went by; its rooms yawning caverns of emptiness. Downstairs there was a scrabble of claws and Alfie miaowed, his tail swishing as he looked up the stairs at me.

'*Breakfast!*' he yowled. '*Now!*' so I ran down the stairs to sort him out before he woke Grace.

I was still waiting at the kitchen table with a coffee at nine o'clock when the doorbell rang. I stiffened. Nobody ever came to the door, unexpectedly: no friends, no neighbours, only deliveries, and I expected those. I waited, but it rang again, so I crept to the door, keeping myself below the level of the windows and peered through the peephole Rohan had installed for me. The tiny circle was filled with the unmistakeable bounce of my mother-in-law's hair. My heart beat hard in my chest – did I open the door, or not? – but then the letterbox burst open and Meena's voice shouted through:

'Abigail! Yoo-hoo! It's me! Oh! There you are!' This as her hand thrust through the letterbox and jabbed me in the hip.

Shit. I arranged a smile on my face and opened the door halfway.

'Hello,' I said, and I waited as Meena straightened herself out. She patted at her hair even though it was, as ever, perfect. She was wrapped up in a black coat that served only to make her look more glamorous.

'Hello, Abigail,' she said, and I noticed she was holding a paper bag. 'I just dropped by to see how you are. Now that you're alone.'

'I'm fine, thanks.'

But Meena smiled and tilted her head sideways as she got to the main purpose of her visit: 'So, have you heard from Rohan?'

'No,' I said, 'but I wasn't expecting to. Not so early on.' I waited but she didn't go. 'I'll let you know when I do?' I said.

Meena took a step towards the door so I opened it wider and closed it behind her. We stood awkwardly in the hallway.

'I brought chocolate brioche,' she said, offering me the paper bag. 'It's still warm. Maybe we could have breakfast and call him together? You look like you could do with a nice hot *chai*.'

I looked nervously up the stairs, as if Grace might appear at any moment. Meena's gaze followed mine.

'I don't think that's a good idea,' I said, my voice a loud whisper. 'With the time difference...'

'But I'm sure you could so with some company, anyway,' Meena said. 'Alone in this house.' She shuddered theatrically and edged toward the kitchen.

'I'm fine,' I said. 'I'm painting. Anyway, I'm not alone.'

That stopped her. 'Has something happened?' The words exploded out of her like fireworks, her eyes saucers. She'd have loved nothing more than for me to have seen or felt evidence of a spiritual visitation; to have good reason to 'cleanse' the space; to bring the troupe of aunties around to do whatever they did to release trapped spirits. I knew because it was her favourite topic. If you let her, my mother-in-law would go on and on about the secrets that old houses possessed; the spirits. 'Energy never dies' was Meena's mantra. Needless to say, she and Clive lived in a new-build.

I gave a little side-eye. 'God, no! My friend Grace is staying. From university. She came last night.'

'Oh,' said Meena, with a sag of the shoulders. She nodded slowly and looked back up the stairs as if Grace might miraculously appear. 'Rohan must have mentioned it, but I forgot. How long is she staying?'

'Until she finds her feet, or Rohan gets back,' I said. 'But the main thing is, you don't need worry about me. I have company.' I smiled.

'What does she do? Your friend?'

'She's a doctor.'

Meena nodded approvingly. 'Okay, okay,' she said, opening the front door. 'I was just worried about you, that's all.' She gave a little laugh and a waggle of her head. 'But if you're not alone…'

'I'm not alone. But thanks for checking. 'Bye, now. I'll call you.'

'Here, enjoy this with your friend.' She thrust the bag at me and I closed the door and stood with my back against it.

'Who was that?' Grace's voice rang down the stairs.

'Just my mother-in-law!' I shouted back.

'Checking up on you?' Grace appeared on the landing, still in her pyjamas, hair all over the place. 'What, doesn't she trust you without the wonderful Rohan? Anyway, sorry I'm so late. That blasted cat of yours was yowling outside my room half the night.'

*

She found a wholefood market on the internet.

'It's only a few miles away,' she said. 'Do you mind if I stock up on a few basics?'

'Be my guest.' I leaned against the kitchen counter. The morning had brought me positivity. I was stronger now. I knew what I was dealing with. I could cope with Grace.

'Okay,' she said. 'Great. Let me grab a coffee and I'll shower then we can go.'

'Don't be daft. You can order online,' I laughed, but Grace gave me a look.

'I don't trust some teenager on minimum wage not to do something idiotic like substitute quinoa with lentils,' she said, widening her eyes at the thought. 'Besides, I want to choose my food myself. It's part of the pleasure of eating. Come on, it'll be fun. Unless you're painting?'

'No. It's fine,' I said, looking out at the rain. 'I'll call a cab.'

The wholefood market was fiddly to get to, involving a complex one-way system. The driver agreed to wait, driving round the block if he got moved on, while we shopped.

'If I've learned one thing in life, it's that you really are what you eat,' Grace said as she walked around the shop, picking things up and examining them. A bundle of fresh kale ('for chips, and to add into smoothies'), high-protein pasta, chickpea puffs, cold-pressed juices, red and brown rice, cocoa nibs, apple cider vinegar with mother ('it's important'), line-caught salmon ('never farmed,' said Grace) and cotton bags of organic fruit and veg all went into the trolley. It didn't look a lot but it came to as much as I usually spent on a couple of weeks' shop for Rohan, Alfie and me.

'You should always buy the best you can afford,' Grace said. 'It's investment in yourself.' She fished about in her bag then paled as she looked at me.

'Shit, I don't have any British money,' she said. 'I only have a few Aussie dollars. I didn't change any at the airport because the rate was so bad. Oh my God. I'll put it back.' She turned to the cashier. 'Or can you keep it all till I've been to a bank?'

I thought of the cab circling. 'It's okay,' I said and pulled out my purse. 'I'll get this. It's the least I can do after the chicken last night.' I laughed to show I wasn't hurt.

'Thanks, Abs,' Grace said. 'If you're sure it's okay, I'll pay you back when I'm on top of things. I'll square it up with you. Thanks a mill.'

Transcript of interview with Mr Rohan Allerton, husband of Abigail Allerton: 20 December 2019

'Had you asked any family or friends to check up on Abigail while you were away?'

[Laughs] 'Obviously my mum. I'd given her a key, just in case, though I hadn't told Abs that. Mum likes to be involved; to be "useful" so it didn't surprise me when she said she'd popped round the day after I left. I'm surprised she left it that long! [laughs] And, yeah, she told me that Abs opened the door smelling of alcohol, so I just assumed that she and Grace had had a great old time catching up the night before. Why would I think anything else?'

Twenty-six

I worked much of the day, lost in my third portrait. In this one, Grace would be a little older; slimmer, too, the bone structure of her face beginning to show through now she'd shed the puppy fat of the earlier picture. This portrait was easier for me to paint than the previous two had been: an image of her face at eighteen was ingrained on my soul.

I worked solidly, almost in a trance as I recalled the qualities of Grace's face back then: the freckles that danced across her nose after her summer holiday to Thailand; the messy tendril of hair that she shoved impatiently behind her ear when it escaped her ponytail; the shadow that fell at her temples and in the hollow below her cheekbones; the spark of sun glinting on her earrings. It was only when I had to get up to switch on the light that I realized how late it was. I'd come to a natural break in my work, much of the base acrylic laid, so I cleaned my brushes and went downstairs, flicking on lights as I went. Light already spilled from under Grace's door. I knocked and waited.

'Grace? Are you there?'

I knocked again, then opened the door slowly. 'Hello? Grace?' but the room was empty bar the scent of her perfume. I flicked off the light and pulled the door to as I continued on my way downstairs.

In the kitchen, I googled 'kale chips' and made them as nibbles before a dinner of roast salmon and stir-fried veg. For dessert, I'd sliced a load of fruit – well, she wanted healthy. We ate at eight.

'This is really good,' Grace said with her mouth full as we ate off plates balanced on our knees. We were catching up on the latest series of *Cold Feet* – a series we'd last watched back when we lived together. Grace pointed with her knife to the screen. 'I don't know why that guy can't just get a job in a supermarket. I would if I were him. Anything to get an income.'

'Yeah, I know, right,' I said. 'Speaking of jobs, tell me all about yours.'

'Ah, right, well I'm going to be a GP in an Urgent Care Emergency Department,' Grace said, and that sounded interesting, so I paused the show.

'Like, critical care stuff? Road accidents, stabbings and…?'

'Yes, I guess.' She shrugged. 'Whatever comes through the door. But there'll also be walk-ins – probably a lot of those. You know: chest pains, strokes, falls, broken bones.'

'Interesting.'

'Yeah. No two days the same.'

'And you get to save lives.'

Grace gave me a funny look. 'Well, yes. That's why I went into medicine. But you can save a life in the GP's office as well, by diagnosing something like high blood pressure and treating it; or by getting someone to change their habits to beat diabetes. It doesn't all have to be blood and guts to be life-saving.'

'I guess,' I said, nodding. 'How many lives do you think you've saved already? In your career to date, I mean?' I asked.

Grace laughed. 'I couldn't say.'

'I mean, like, hundreds? Thousands?'

'Well, in an indirect way – like I said just now – thousands for sure. Maybe tens of thousands.'

'Wow,' I said. 'I can't imagine how that must feel. All my work does is decorate the houses of rich people.'

Grace gave a little laugh. 'Well, I don't really think about it. It's not something I focus on. I'm always just dealing with the next thing that comes along, and doing my best to treat that, or solve it. Anyway, I like this job because I *think* they're quite flexible on hours – at least that's what they told me – I think I'm allowed to work up to ten sessions a week, but there's a possibility I could do it part-time, which would be brilliant because there are other things I want to do too. Volunteer work.'

'Oh really?' For a moment I had the crazy idea she might join me at the hospice. I saw the two of us going in together, working together as a team, taking care of the patients – but Grace was a doctor: why would she be making cups of tea and changing the water glasses with me?

'I'm looking at a volunteer post in which I'm trying to connect underprivileged communities with the right healthcare. You know, acting as a sort of go-between.'

'That sounds right up your street.'

'Well, I've a lot to learn having been away so long, but I'll get there. I feel so strongly about people being able to access healthcare.'

'You always have,' I said. 'It's so worthy.'

She smiled. 'You shouldn't take it so personally when people say art is… "self-indulgent", or just for the rich. Art is for everyone. Plenty of people get enjoyment from it.' She gave a little laugh. 'We can't all be doctors!'

I flinched and took a deep swig of my wine. 'I work at the hospice as well…'

'Well then,' said Grace. 'You're doing your bit. Hopefully it makes you feel less guilty about spending your days farting about with a paintbrush.' Another little laugh.

I opened my mouth to remind her about Mr Keyson, about how I'd gone out of my way to paint his dog for him before he died, and how happy that had made both Mrs K and me but I knew she'd patronize me with another of those empty smiles, and that would take away from the beauty, the altruism, of the gesture. Thankfully my phone rang and I pounced on it: as I'd hoped, it was Rohan.

'Sorry,' I said to Grace, and connected the call. 'Hey,' I said, and Rohan's voice came on the line as clear as if he were in the next room.

'Hey, how are you?'

'Good, thanks. How about you? How's New York?'

'God, it's so busy! This is the first chance I've had to call – I've got a quick break for lunch. I can see why they needed me here. I haven't had a moment to myself since I landed. It's all been, "meet this person; meet that person".'

'It's good to be busy. Where are you staying?'

'I'm in a company flat in the financial district, close to the office in Lower Manhattan.'

'Sounds very you,' I said. Grace shifted in her chair and looked pointedly at me and then at the television. I slipped out of the room.

'It's a luxury high-rise,' Rohan was saying, 'the antithesis of our house, obv, but I think you'd like it.'

'Hmm.'

'It's got these amazing floor-to-ceiling windows that face Brooklyn Bridge. If you were here, you'd sit there all day just staring at the view – I know I would if I had the chance. You'd paint it, for sure – and, get this! Even the bathroom has windows that overlook the East River. I look out at that when I go for a shit!'

'Charming!'

There was a swimming pool, too, he told me, and a load of sporting facilities, a roof terrace and even a private cinema.

'Not that I'll get to use it. But you know what? It's actually really nice to be in an apartment. I love being high up – I really like the bird's-eye view of the city.'

'And you finally got to live somewhere brand new, too,' I said. Rohan laughed. 'Yep. Mum would be proud.'

'Speaking of which,' I said, 'she came over this morning…'

'Oh really?' he said, his voice cautious. 'What did she want?'

'Checking I was okay on my own…'

'Aka checking up on you!' Rohan said, with a little laugh because we both knew it was true. 'But Grace's with you, isn't she? Did she arrive okay? How's that going?'

'Oh… good,' I said, looking back towards the living-room door, trying to judge whether or not she could hear me. There was a burst of laughter from inside the room – she must have put *Cold Feet* back on.

'Yeah, it's nice to see her,' I said carefully. 'She's changed a bit.'

'Well – it's been four years, to be fair, and she'll have had a lot of new experiences in Oz.'

'I know, but…'

'In what way?' he said, and out came the story of the roast chicken and the fancy organic, pescatarian diet.

'She could have told you before you went to all that trouble,' Rohan said. 'How difficult would that have been?'

I sighed. 'Well, you know what? I think she's right. I took her to a wholefood shop and we stocked up on all this heathy stuff.' I paused. 'I mean, you really are what you eat. You should always buy the best you can afford. It's investment in yourself.'

'If you say so,' said Rohan. 'But you're never going to wean me off a good fry-up, so don't even try.'

I laughed. 'As if I would.'

We chatted a bit more, then hung up. Back in the living room, the congealed remains of my dinner sat on the coffee table.

'You should have told him to call back later,' Grace said, nodding at the food. 'Now your dinner's ruined. It's not good to jump to his every beck and call. Keep him on his toes.'

'Yeah, but...' I shrugged, the irony not lost on me that, while she might dispense relationship advice, I was the one with a husband.

'He wouldn't have been able to call back till after work,' I said, 'and they're five hours behind... I probably wouldn't have got to talk to him till at least this time tomorrow.'

'And the problem with that is what?' Grace shook her head dismissively, and that old familiar feeling I used to get came flooding back: the feeling that she didn't want me to have anyone else in my life. The feeling that, once again, I'd somehow let her down.

Twenty-seven

You shouldn't take it so personally when people say art is... 'self-indulgent'. You shouldn't feel guilty spending your days farting about with a paintbrush.

I needed to be stronger. I needed to arm myself against Grace. That much was apparent, and the key to that lay in understanding what our friendship was. After she went to bed, I opened up the iPad and, feeling like an absolute traitor, I searched 'toxic friends' once more.

Your friend blurts out criticism with a self-righteous attitude. Yes. Your friend tells you that you need to change. Yep. You're walking on eggshells. Dear God, yes. You're riding an emotional rollercoaster with your friend at the controls. Totally! I scrolled and clicked through to other websites: *Women's Health* magazine, *Psychology Today*, *reddit*. They all told the same story.

You feel used. You're giving more than you're getting. The inconsistency and lack of predictability leaves you doubting everything.

I pressed my hand to my mouth, my throat thick with emotion. This was it. This was our friendship to a tee. How had I not seen it before?

On *Huffington Post*, I found 'Warning Signs of a Toxic Friend':

> They're covetous – they feel bitter when you acquire things they don't have.

Those looks she gave me when I mentioned Rohan; and the little digs about being married; about the house.

> Toxic friends are freeloaders – they take advantage of your generosity and give nothing in return. They can stay at your house for months or years without chipping in for groceries or even offering a thank you.

I couldn't have made it up.

> They're self-centred. Their life is a drama. They talk too much. They're judgemental, big-headed, stubborn; they're picky, needy and difficult to please.

And then, a sentence that forced a shudder through me:

> They're resentful: they never give up their ruthless nature. If they believe you have wronged them, they won't forget until their mean-spirited wrath is launched on you.

I snapped the iPad shut and went upstairs to paint.

I wasn't ready yet to use the negative emotions I'd just triggered – just as my relationship with Grace had changed from the day I'd been grateful to have her as a friend to the day I'd finally, dramatically, thrown her out of the flat; the portraits, too, would darken. But, for now, on the third picture, I was still in the happy phase – the innocent phase – and I needed to focus on all that had been good in our friendship.

We had lots in common. During the first week of university, we'd discovered that Grace also used to live not far from where I was brought up, in Kent. Her family had moved away when she was ten but they still visited from time to time, and she knew the same places that I did. Incredulously, we'd listed the places we used to go; all the castles that children got taken to in the summer holidays. Leeds Castle, Hever Castle, Chiddingstone and Bodiam. Maidstone, Rochester, Canterbury, Dover. She, too, had played in Knole Park, been to Howletts Zoo and got lost at Groombridge Place. Over the years, we'd both been subjected to the same 'edifying' experiences and days out. We even worked out that we'd both bought chips at the same chippy in the same tiny village.

'What are the odds?' Grace had gasped, making me feel special to have this link, this bond, with her. 'Just imagine if you're in the background of one of my photos!' and we'd looked at each other, eyes wide and mouths hanging open at the thought, then scrolled frantically through the pictures on our phones, expanding screens and passing them backwards and forwards to each other.

'Could this be you?'

'I had a dress like that!'

'Nah. I never wore my hair like that!'

When that drew a blank, we flipped the pages of my photo

albums, going further back in time, desperate to find a link – some sign that our meeting was written in our destiny – and then we hit the jackpot. There was one picture, of me on a rope bridge in the woods at Groombridge, in which she thought she could identify herself. Pointing a finger to the smudge of a girl in the background, she'd said, 'I had a T-shirt like that. And those shorts. We have a photo of me at home in those clothes in that place. My hair looked like that. Oh my God, oh my God, oh my God, I think it's me!' She'd got onto her laptop and pulled up images of herself from that same day that she stored online and, indeed, the outfit seemed to match. 'There, look! We first saw each other when we were ten years old! Little did we know!'

The memory made me smile. Although I didn't keep up with photos these days, I still had the albums Dad had made for me up here in the attic. I pulled out the album, turned to that page and looked now at the grainy figure standing by the little zipwire in the woods.

'Who knew?' I said to the picture. 'Who knew where it'd all end up?'

Suddenly, the sound of a laugh rippled through the house, tearing me from my reverie. I froze, heart thudding, but the silence dragged long enough to make me wonder if I'd imagined it. Then, just as I began to relax, there was another peal of girlish laughter followed by another thick silence. I crept down the attic stairs to Grace's room and knocked softly on the door. The smell of her perfume flooded the landing.

'Grace?' I waited. 'Grace? Are you awake?'

Once again, a line of light ran along the bottom of the door. I knocked harder. 'Grace?' then I tried the handle: locked. Maybe she was watching something on her phone with headphones on.

Twenty-eight

By the time I woke the next morning, Grace had left for work. I knew she'd gone, even as I lay motionless under the duvet allowing consciousness to slide its way slowly through me. The quietness that surrounded me had a depth to it, a richness that was punctuated only by the occasional scrabble of claws as Alfie chased demons in the hall. When I finally dragged myself downstairs, he scampered ahead of me towards the kitchen, his tail twitching in that way that means, '*Follow me!*' Miaowing loudly, he led me straight to his food bowls. Grace hadn't fed him on her way out; she hadn't even topped up his biscuit bowl.

'Oh, baby, I'm sorry,' I said bending to tickle his head. 'She doesn't have pets. She doesn't know.'

He twined about my legs, purring and chirruping as I removed the dirty bowls and replaced them with fresh food and water, then I pottered about in the kitchen, cleaning up the mess from last night. Grace, it seemed, hadn't had breakfast – not unless she'd washed up her utensils and put them in the cupboards, which seemed unlikely since last night's dinner plates were still dirty in the sink. I'd just sprayed the counters and was wiping them down when the doorbell rang. I froze. Surely not Meena again?

The doorbell rang again, impatient and jarring, so I rushed

over and opened the door just in time to see the back of a delivery man walking down the path.

'I'm here!' I called.

'Grace Shaw?'

I missed a beat. 'Yes. She lives here.'

There were three parcels, soft, like clothes, but heavier than I'd have imagined, and they flopped in my arms as I took them up to Grace's room. I stopped at the door, feeling as if to go in would be to trespass, but then I pushed it open with my shoulder and inhaled the unfamiliar scent that lingered in the air – a different deodorant to mine, maybe, and the heavy floral perfume. The bed was half made, the covers neatly folded back and the pillow dented.

Grace's suitcase stood in the corner. There was a glass of water on the bedside table, alongside other bits and bobs: lip salve, a hair tie, perfume, tissues and a book, the cover of which was curling at the corners. I nodded my approval: it was *Rebecca* by Daphne du Maurier. One of my favourites.

But what caught my eye more than anything was the line of toys arranged along the windowsill. Dumping the parcels on the bed, I went over and picked them up one by one. A Cabbage Patch doll with chubby cheeks. A grubby lavender-and-white spotted dog with long, floppy ears and a missing eye. The blonde doll from the box in the attic, a squishy-bodied baby doll with a thumb that fit in its mouth, an open Jack-in-the-Box that gave me the creeps, and a couple of Barbies. Thirteen eyes regarded the room as if they knew it better than I did; as if they belonged there and I did not. I wasn't sure I'd like them watching me while I slept, especially the Jack-in-the-Box. Still, it was Grace's space now, not mine.

I turned to leave, but then hesitated. What if she wanted to wear her new clothes tomorrow? She wouldn't mind if I opened them, would she? She might appreciate that I'd hung them. Turning back, I carefully slit open the packaging and held up her purchases one-by-one: she'd ordered a suit, three blouses and a pair of work shoes. A new work wardrobe. Nice.

I opened the wardrobe to hang them and gasped.

The cupboard was full, packed with clothes that gave off a damp, musty smell. I flicked through them: little toddler dresses, dresses for an older girl. Trousers, jeans, blouses, cardigans – even a little blazer for an eight-year-old. They must be from the boxes in the attic. What was Grace playing at? I shuddered and laid her new clothes out on the bed, then left the room with those thirteen eyes boring into the back of my head.

Twenty-nine

It was inevitable, I suppose, that Grace would meet Tom.
Perhaps she felt protective given it was she who'd advised
me on how to approach him in the first place, but she wanted
to know everything about my relationship with him: where we
went, what we did, what we talked about, what he drank, what
he smoked, what we watched on TV, what he was like in bed.
Whenever I got home from spending time with him, she'd be
there on the sofa, eyes shining, waiting for the latest instalment.
It was almost as if she were living the relationship vicariously
through me – but something – instinct maybe? Or selfishness?
– pushed me to keep them apart for as long as I naturally could,
despite her curiosity.

But once we'd been 'hooking up' for some time, she started
asking when she was going to meet him. She pushed and pushed
until, one day, against my better judgement, I invited him to meet
me at ours before we went out for a bite to eat. Grace buzzed around
like a mosquito before he got there, primping, straightening and
tidying the living room.

'Stop it,' I told her. 'It's only Tom.'

'I can't wait to see what he looks like in the flesh,' she said,
fluffing up the sofa cushions. 'If he's as nice as you make out. No

one can be that perfect,' and then there was a knock at the door and suddenly he was standing there, incongruous, on our doorstep.

He held out a bottle of wine, and Grace appeared behind me, standing with the posture of a model, shoulders straight, chest out, hip popped.

'Hello, there!' she laughed, grabbing the bottle. 'I'm Grace. Is that for us? You shouldn't have!'

She sashayed into the kitchen to get a bottle opener while I invited Tom inside. Grace's hair hung loosely down her back. She tossed it about as she opened the wine showily and poured it into our best glasses. She was wearing shorts. Micro-shorts that barely covered the curve of her buttocks, and she had bare feet, legs that went on forever and a tan from summer, but Tom didn't seem to notice any of this. He sat with his hand on my knee and awkwardly drank his wine, then he stood and said, 'Let's go,' so it seemed I'd got away with it.

But you know that feeling you get when you're watching a movie and you know something bad's going to happen and you're just waiting for it to happen, kind of dreading it and expecting it at the same time? That sense of impending doom? That's how I felt after that weird little get-together – and I wasn't wrong. Looking back, I should have realized that Grace wouldn't like me being in a relationship. That she would never let me have something that she wanted for herself.

That she'd never let me be happy.

As my relationship with Tom continued, Grace changed. By that time, she was on her fifth-year specialty rotations and our lives were going in different directions, yet it seemed that, even though she was allowed boyfriends, I was not.

At first it came out as little barbed comments.

'You're seeing him *again*?' Heavy sighs. Eye-rolls when I mentioned his name. Smirks that weren't altogether pleasant; jokes about child-snatchers, as if seven years was such a huge age gap.

She didn't like it that I wasn't always there for her. She didn't like it when she found my room door locked on the rare occasions Tom came back for the night.

'I want you to myself!' she joked.

And then the rumours started. Stories about Tom that she'd overheard – stories about him perhaps not being faithful. Grace, shy and apologetic, her lips in a judgemental pout patting the sofa next to her: 'Come and sit down, Abs. There's something I have to tell you. I hate to be the one…' but she'd seen him in a pub in town with a younger girl – much younger – maybe even one of his pupils.

'They looked cosy, Abs,' she said, reaching for my hand. 'I'm only telling you because I care. I'd want to know if it were me.' She'd peered into my eyes and I'd tried to read her expression: concern? Or *schadenfreude*?

I'd asked Tom and he'd denied it. I believed him, but the crack was there, the seed planted, and Grace was very good at watering seeds.

'You deserve better,' she said. 'You shouldn't let him treat you like this. He walks all over you. The age gap warps the power ratio.'

Tom hadn't believed that I was breaking up with him.

I did it in a busy café, cups of coffee in front of both of us, a smile on Tom's face to begin with as we faced each other across a table for two. But then I'd told him.

'Abi,' he'd said, the hurt pooling in his eyes as he stroked a lock of hair from my face. 'What happened? I thought we were good.'

We were. I closed my eyes, unwilling to see the concern on his face. We *were* good.

'Was it something I did?'

I squeezed my eyes tighter to stop the tears from spilling, and shook my head. I know what Grace said, but I didn't believe it; didn't believe there was anything but a reasonable explanation – if he in fact had been seen out with a younger woman.

'I just think it's for the best.'

'The best for who?' His voice rose. 'Abi? *For who?* Because this is not something that I want. Not at all.'

It's not you; it's me. Such a cliché I couldn't say it, although it was the truth.

'I just...' I turned my face away. 'Tom, please.'

'Look, I know we don't talk about the future, but I'd imagined us together long term. Really long term. I know I don't believe in marriage and diamond rings, but, in as much as I believe anything, you're The One.' A pause. Words I'd longed to hear, but not now, not like this. 'I've actually never felt like this before.'

'Stop it.'

'I need you to know that. I need you to know that wherever this is coming from, it's not a feeling I that echo.'

I swallowed a sob and refused to look at him. His fingers played with the bracelet on my wrist, then stroked the top of my hand. I pulled it away.

'If you tell me it's what you want, I'll walk away now,' he said. 'I'd never hassle you. But look me in the eye and tell me it's what you want. Because I don't believe you. Abi, look at me.'

He put a hand to my cheek and tried to turn my face. His

fingers, long and slim, felt warm on my cheek. My eyes, full of tears, looked up at his beautiful face for the briefest second, then fell back down to the table. Inside my chest, there was a physical ache.

'It's what I want,' I whispered.

Grace laughed when I told her I'd done it.

'So we're quits,' she smiled. 'We don't need men. I'll stick with you forever.'

It sounded like a threat.

Thirty

I painted all day. The next thing I knew, Grace was banging on the studio door.

'Abs! Are you in there? I'm home! Do you want a drink?'

I sat back on my stool and dragged my focus away from the canvas. I'd been deeply involved in the details of this portrait. Although I had lights trained on the canvas, the room around them was dark. Through the black windows I could see the orange glow of the streetlights. When I painted, it was as if I were in a trance.

'Abs!' Grace yelled, knocking again on the door, more urgently this time. 'Wakey, wakey! Are you in there?'

That sent a jolt through me. 'Sorry! Just cleaning up!' I shouted. 'Why don't you pour us something and I'll be down in a sec?'

'Can I come in?'

'Later! When it's finished!' I called. I was going to have to tell her that I didn't want her to see the pictures until the series was complete. The portraits, I'd realized, would tell a story as Grace grew older, and I didn't want any comments from her to affect the way I portrayed her.

'I'd love a vodka, though!' I shouted. 'I'm just cleaning my brushes and I'll be down!'

'Okay,' she said, disappointment hanging in her voice, but

I heard her steps retreat down the stairs. I turned the finished portraits so they couldn't be seen if she even glanced inside the room, then I stood back and looked at my day's work.

Grace's face was slimmer in this one; the puppy fat gone, the lines of her face more angular. Although she didn't wear much make-up, I'd curled and thickened her lashes with mascara, made her lips gleam with a little rosy gloss, and groomed her eyebrows. Other than that, her skin was bare, with the gleam of porcelain about it. Light reflected off the tops of her cheekbones and down her perfect, straight nose, and there was a smattering of freckles across her cheeks, faint under her tan, which gave the impression of a summer spent in the sunshine. In her lobes, her earrings glimmered.

I reached out and traced my finger across her cheek on the canvas.

'Yes, perfect,' I said softly, then I cleaned my brushes and headed down.

'I thought we could have a girls' night in,' Grace said. 'You know, paint our nails, do a face mask, listen to some music. You used to love doing that.' She laughed, and not in a nice way. 'It was all you ever wanted to do.'

I smiled, a little blindsided, and Grace smiled back. She'd changed out of whatever it was she'd worn to work and was sitting at the kitchen table with a drink and a saucer of vegetable chips and now she raised her glass to me. 'Cheers, by the way.'

I raised mine back. 'Cheers. To your first day. How was it?'

Grace popped a chip in her mouth and crunched. 'Yeah. Good,' she said. 'No major dramas.'

'Well, I guess that's good,' I said. 'Easy start. Did the people seem nice?'

'Yeah.'

I waited for her to elaborate but she said nothing more. In the end, I spoke. 'Did you find the clothes you'd ordered? I hope you didn't mind that I opened them.'

She shrugged. 'Yeah. No worries.'

'I was going to hang them, but…'

She gave a little *pff* of a laugh. 'The wardrobe was full?'

'Yes! Why did you do that? They stink! And the toys? How can you sleep with that Jack-in-the-Box watching you?'

She shrugged and popped a chip in her mouth. 'I just felt that they might like to be there. They probably used to be there. It's their home. What right did I have to keep them squashed up in a box?'

'They're old clothes. They don't care. They've probably got moths in them. And they make the wardrobe smell. We should throw them away.'

'Chill out, Brussel sprout! It's no big deal, is it? I think it's kinda cute.'

'Well… if you don't mind your clothes smelling musty…'

'Exactly. It's my issue.' She took another chip. 'So, I'm starving. What's for dinner?'

Anger jabbed at me. 'I haven't had a chance to make anything yet.'

'Oh, I'm easy.' Grace raised an eyebrow. 'I'm sure you can rustle together some nibbles – maybe some smoked salmon and some olives or something? It'll be just like the old times.'

'Wasn't it Quavers in those days?' I said.

'Well, we're grown up now.' She smiled and I could almost taste the *faux* cheese flavour of the Quavers on my tongue as I remembered the nights we'd spent doing exactly that at university. 'Who needs food?' we used to say in the early days. 'Who needs food when you've got vodka?'

Maybe I was trying to make a point, but I refused to cook anything, so we settled in the living room with some drinks – another elderflower cordial for her and vodka for me – and some of the fancy snacks she'd bought at the organic store, and I got the nail polish while Grace put on some music. She was applying the top coat on my nails when my phone rang.

'Husband?' Grace asked with one eyebrow raised. I nodded. 'Leave it, or you'll smudge your nails,' she said, flapping a magazine to create a breeze. The phone rang again a minute later, and then again.

'Maybe something's wrong,' I said, as the anxiety troops started to assemble in my chest with a familiar surge of tightness. I took a deep breath, and then another, to push it back down.

'I doubt it,' said Grace. 'Do you ever not pick up?'

'Sometimes... if I'm painting.'

'But not otherwise?'

'No.' Another deep breath. Anxiety spiralling.

'Because you're the perfect Stepford Wife, of course.'

I looked at Grace, stung by her words, but she gave a little laugh.

'Just kidding. Anyway, these will be ready in a minute so you can gossip with your husband all you like.'

I tapped a nail to my tooth. 'I think if I'm careful...'

The phone rang again. 'Oh God, now it's Mili. My sister-in-law. I'm going to have to take it.'

So I connected the call. Mili dived straight in.

'Where are you?'

'At home?' I said slowly, as if it were obvious.

'Oh shit,' she said. 'I'd hoped you were on your way.'

'On my way where?' I goggled my eyes at Grace and she widened hers back then shook her head and drew her finger back and forth miming 'no, no, no.'

'To dinner with Mum and Dad?'

It took a moment for the penny to drop. Of course, it was the monthly catch-up dinner and Rohan and I had agreed with his parents that I'd go.

'Shit, sorry, Mils. I've been painting all day and I completely forgot.'

'Can you jump in a taxi now?' she asked. 'Mum's saying she won't order till you're here.' She paused and lowered her tone. 'You know what she's like.'

I did – I could just picture Meena sitting at the table like the Queen, looking at her watch and stating that she would wait for her daughter-in-law. She loved to play the martyr.

'You could be here in twenty minutes,' Mili said hopefully. 'There's not much traffic.'

'Oh, but… God, it's just that I have a friend here,' I said. 'We're all set up to stay home tonight.'

'Bring your friend,' said Mili. 'Just get here.'

I put my hand over the phone. 'Do you want to come to dinner with my in-laws?' I asked Grace. 'They're really nice.'

Grace snorted a laugh and put her hands up, palms facing me. 'Computer says no. You're on your own.'

I took a deep breath and returned to the call. 'Mils, I'm so sorry but we've eaten and I'm in my pyjamas. I'm absolutely shattered. It really took it out of me today. It was quite emotional… this new portrait series? I lost track of time and everything and now I'm out of battery and I just need to go to bed. Would you mind explaining that to your mum? Please?'

Mili didn't reply.

'Mili? Are you there?'

'Looks, Abs, don't take this the wrong way, but are you all right?' she said. 'We spoke about this at dinner just before Rohan left. You said it was in your diary.'

'It is! I just didn't look at my diary. That's all.'

'Are you sure?'

'Yes! I'm sorry. It just slipped my mind what with Grace arriving and Rohan leaving, and the painting and everything...'

I left the sentence hanging but Mili didn't reply and I worried that I'd slurred. I did suddenly feel a little fuzzy-headed. Could Mili hear the vodka in my voice? Was she wondering if I was drunk? I'd had a couple of vodkas in the afternoon as well as the two I'd now had with Grace. And they'd probably been doubles. If not triples. Grace poured a generous measure. Mentally I totted up the units; I had high tolerance but it was quite possible that I sounded a bit tipsy.

But whatever Mili was thinking, she kept it to herself. She sighed down the phone. 'So you're not coming? I've got to go in and tell her that?'

''Fraid so.'

'You know you're never going to hear the end of this, don't you?'

'Yep.'

'And you're fine with that? It's going to be family history: "the time that Abigail forgot".'

'I know,' I said. 'I'll take it. But thanks, Mils. Really. And, sorry.'

Thirty-one

As Grace's first weekend with me approached, I asked her if there was anything in particular she wanted to do. She closed her eyes and breathed in deeply as she thought about it, then snapped them open as a smile crept over her face.

'I'd like to go to the theatre.'

'Oh. Okay. Anything in particular you'd like to see? Comedy? Thriller? Watford Palace is bound to have something coming up.'

But Grace laughed. 'Watford Palace? That sounds like a football club. I want to see a musical. One of those all-singing, all-dancing West End shows,' Grace said. 'You know, with a cast of hundreds and a live orchestra. I've never, ever been to one – can you believe it? I was thinking *Matilda*, *Phantom*, *Les Mis*. Something like that?'

'Oh. Oh, I see. Okay. Well...' I shrugged and Grace peered at me.

'Are you still scared of crowds? Don't worry. I'll look after you. We'll be fine.'

'Okay,' I said, not wanting to admit that she'd hit the nail on the head. Even Rohan knew I didn't 'do' city centres. 'I'll have a look online and see what's available.'

I put tickets to the matinée of *Phantom of the Opera* on my credit card, and Grace and I rattled into the West End on the Tube on Saturday morning. She dozed next to me while I kept a lid on my anxiety by repeating 'happy place, happy place, happy place' to myself. I shut my eyes and visualized the attic with the sun pouring in through the open window, a fresh easel set up, and all my paints and brushes waiting for me. I imagined the smell of the paints and the new canvas, and focused on breathing deeply and evenly. I let myself fall almost into a trance, as I pushed away the thought that I was in a tin can speeding through a tunnel under the ground. When we surfaced at Charing Cross, I gasped in the filthy city air like a dying fish on the deck of a trawler.

'Let's walk through Covent Garden!' Grace said. 'I love this part of town. It's so *alive*!'

That was certainly one word for it. The piazza was thrumming with people and a street act had drawn a large crowd. I kept my head down and my arm linked through Grace's as we skirted around the edge of the crowd, trying not to stumble on the cobbles. Every now and again the crowd roared with laughter or burst into applause. The street artist was shouting through a megaphone and the noise sucked the energy out of me, leaving me jumpy and ragged. Grace, I could see, was in her element.

'God, I've missed this so much!' she laughed, letting go of me and spinning around to take in the people, the shopfronts – the busyness – of the scene. 'I could sit and people-watch here all day! It's so interesting! I mean, look at those two. Look what they're wearing! I've never seen anything like it. You can tell I've been in the Outback too long, can't you?'

She stopped dead and grabbed both my hands. 'Oh my God.

I've just thought! We could try to have lunch at Brown's. I used to love Brown's! I haven't been there for years! Come on!' She pulled me down a side street. 'If I remember right, it's not far!'

And she was right: Brown's was lovely, and the theatre blew me away and, with Grace at my side, I began to think that maybe I could 'do' Central London after all, if I was careful, if I was with someone. But, as we threaded our way back to Charing Cross after the show, we saw, up ahead of us, a knot of people gathered on the pavement. As we drew closer, I saw that some of them had their hands over their mouths; others had their phones pressed to their ears; a couple were shaking their heads. A man was kneeling on the ground near the back of a bus, which I realized now was unnaturally still, the engine off and the driver pacing helplessly nearby, his hands tearing through his hair. The traffic lights moved robotically through their cycle but the traffic didn't move. Shock echoed in the air.

'Something's happened.' Grace peered forward, straining towards the scene. Dread pushed upwards from my stomach; my hands suddenly cold and clammy inside my gloves.

'It looks serious,' I said. 'Maybe we should…'

'I don't see an ambulance. No paramedics,' Grace interrupted. Her tone was brisk. Professional. 'Whatever it is, it must have just happened. They might need me.' She broke into a run.

'Grace…' I said. My legs were weak and my breathing shallow. Heat flooded my face and I swallowed. Already I'd clocked the distant wail of sirens. We should turn back, I wanted to tell her: go a different way; let the emergency services deal with whatever it was that had happened, but this is what Grace did. This was her thing. I followed as she hurried towards the scene.

'I'm a doctor! Let me through!' Grace shouted, twisting

her way through the onlookers. At the kerb, she paused for a second and took in the scene then, within moments, she threw her handbag down and was on her knees close to the rear wheels of the bus.

I shouldn't have looked. It was my mistake. I should have turned and walked the other way. I should have sat in a pub or stood in a shop; I should have done anything but look. I saw the bicycle bent out of shape. I saw the leg protruding out from under the bus. A woman's leg, bent at an unnatural angle and deathly still, the trainer on the foot a shocking pink that stood out against the black of the tarmac. I saw the look on the faces of those standing watching.

Then suddenly the air was rent with sirens. A paramedic motorbike roared up, followed by two police cars. The air pulsated with sound. The buildings, the people, the wet road, everything lit with the flash of blue lights. In slow motion, I watched Grace stand up and I saw her mouth move as she spoke to the paramedic, her hand pulling at her hair. A policeman jumped out of one of the cars and herded people away from the bus with his arms spread wide while another marked off the scene with tape, and then it came: the panic spiralled up inside me, pressing down on my heart.

I clutched at my throat and gasped in a breath but the panic was a wave I was unable to suppress. It crushed my chest, and my mouth opened wide as I struggled to suck in air. An ambulance cleaved its way through the stopped traffic and, from the corner of my vision, I saw Grace walk slowly back towards me, her face white and her features tight. She shook her head as she saw me, then the world started to close in: darkness crept in from every angle, and I swayed. The blue lights flicked on and off, on and off. I tugged at Grace's arm, unable to speak, unable to tell her.

'Very sad,' she said, and that was the last thing I heard as the world span around me and I sank to my knees.

'Grace,' I gasped. 'Grace!'

Thirty-two

When I woke on Sunday morning, my head was still echoing with the trauma of the accident, my grief for the dead woman I'd never known a palpable thing. How old was she? What did she do? Did she have a boyfriend, a husband, children? My thoughts went down the rabbit hole of her life as I pictured where she might have been going, what she was doing; how she came to be at that junction at that time; how she felt when the bus surged way too close to her; the jolt of terror when it brushed her, pushed her, knocked her down and dragged her under. I lay in bed and felt not just for her, but for her family and her friends; and for the shock of her co-workers arriving at work tomorrow to find out that their colleague was dead.

It was a negative train of thought and I wrestled myself away from it, heaved myself out of bed, wrapped my dressing gown around me and went gingerly downstairs, where I made a coffee and drank it looking out at the garden. In contrast to the stillness of the woman's leg yesterday – an image I couldn't get out of my mind – the garden was full of life; movement. The wind ripped leaves from the oak tree, sending them scurrying across the lawn like rats. The pink roof of the old Wendy House was completely covered in the brown mulch of dead leaves. All I could see of it was the faint gleam of the broken glass in the window and, behind that – a shadow? A movement? I squinted, craning my head towards the window but then the wind gusted harder and the whole tree creaked and swayed. For a terrifying moment I pictured it toppling towards the house, its claw-like branches reaching out for Grace and me.

'What are you looking at?' I spun around to see Grace in the doorway. She, too, was wrapped in a gown, her feet poked into a pair of my slippers. She had her glasses on; her hair in a messy bun.

'The oak tree. Rohan said I should have it removed. I think it's rotten inside. I completely forgot to find someone.'

'What a shame. It's a beautiful tree.'

'He's worried it'll fall on the house.'

'Then we'll both die together.' Grace smiled. 'Anyway – morning. How are you feeling?' Her face creased with concern. 'That was quite a "thing" you had yesterday. Do you remember getting home?'

I shook my head, although there were fragments: a taxi, Grace's arm around me, the blur of lights, rain on a windscreen.

'Do you get them often, these panic attacks?'

I blew air out through my mouth. 'I used to. But no, not so much these days. I try to control them.'

Grace nodded.

'It happens sometimes. In crowds,' I said. 'It's why I don't tend to go into Central London.'

Grace smiled. 'Well, no harm done.' She paused. 'It was worth it, though, wasn't it? I thought the show was fantastic.'

'I can't stop thinking about the woman.'

Grace sighed. 'I think it would have been pretty instant. That's something, I suppose.'

'I hope so. I hope she didn't know what happened.'

We lapsed into silence. I could barely remember *Phantom* – it was as if I'd watched it in a previous life. I sighed. 'I haven't been into the West End for ages. I can't believe that happened the one time I went. Maybe I'll leave it a while before I go back.'

Grace opened the fridge and surveyed its contents.

'Ah,' she said, with her back to me. 'I was thinking about that… you know what they say: you gotta get right back on that horse.'

'What?'

'Well, if you stay stuck out here in the suburbs, you're never going to get over it. Are you? It's going to become a phobia and before you know it you'll become a recluse. A cat lady flicking at the lace curtains.' She gave a little laugh. 'The way to deal with it is to submerge yourself in the thing that scares you, until you learn there's nothing to be scared of.'

'You want me to go back into London?'

'Well…' Grace said carefully as she spooned Greek yoghurt into her bowl. 'Not specifically. I was thinking about 32b. I always remember it.'

My heart thumped. 'Really?'

'Yes! Don't you? So what do you say? Should we go back and take a look at the old pad, for old times' sake? We can take a cab if you like.' Her tone softened. 'It'll be fine.'

My hands clenched under the kitchen table, the nails digging into my palms. It wasn't the journey that bothered me.

'Really? You want to go back?' I said.

'Well, we did spend two years living there.' Grace stared out of the kitchen window for a moment and chuckled. 'God, I'll never forget those steps. That feeling I got going down them.' She closed her eyes then nodded. 'Yeah. I'd like to see where it all… played out.'

She said the last two words slowly as if she'd chosen them carefully, and I guess she really had, because 'played out' covered a lot of situations, many of them unpleasant. I pushed my chair back and stood.

'Sure. What time do you want to go?'

Grace waved her yoghurt spoon at me. 'Just give me a chance to eat this and get ready. So, maybe, like, forty minutes? Does that work?'

Thirty-three

Grace didn't tell me that she'd got together with Tom. Neither did he. They left it for me to find out myself one night in the March of Grace's final year. I'd woken, thirsty, around two in the morning and padded to the kitchen of the basement flat. I was used to Grace bringing men home and, unless they were drunk and rowdy, it never bothered me. They were always gone in the morning. That particular night, I stood at the sink drinking water from the tap when I heard a giggle come from her room. Then, like a slap in the face, a murmur in a male voice with the exact same timbre as Tom's. I froze, ice in my veins, wondering if I wanted confirmation, yet already knowing in my heart what I was hearing. I tiptoed to Grace's door and pressed my ear silently to the wood, straining.

It couldn't be him. She wouldn't.

The sound of rustling bed sheets was followed by more giggles; more murmurs. I stood there, heart galloping as I struggled not to comprehend what I could patently hear, but then Tom had moaned, and it was unmistakeably him, and, in the end, it was not from Grace, but from the rhythm of the bed springs that I'd found out the truth.

It was my fault. I should have realized that Grace was a threat. That she took whatever she wanted from me.

*

The cab dropped us at the end of the road we used to live in. Grace strode in front of me, her head swivelling right and left as she took in the buildings, shops and landmarks she remembered. My breath came faster as I rushed to keep up.

'Oh my God! This place is still here!' she exclaimed, standing outside the small souvenir shop that sold everything from London trinkets to snacks, ready meals, alcohol and cleaning products. 'I don't think I've ever paid as much for vodka as I did buying it from this shop late on a Friday night. I'm sure his prices had a sliding scale.' She shook her head and walked on and then, there it was: the black railings, the steps down to the front door, and the half windows that formed the top of the living room peeping up at the street. We stood on the pavement and looked at the windows. They were frosted now; it was difficult to see inside. Somehow it all looked smaller, older, seedier than it did in my memory, despite the fact the building's façade had clearly had some sort of paintwork done.

'I wonder if it's still a rental place,' I said. 'Hey! What are you doing?'

Grace was already halfway down the steps.

'Come back!' I said. 'That's trespassing.'

'Not if we knock,' she said, looking back at me. 'Come on. Don't tell me you're not curious?'

And so I joined her at the bottom of the steps and it was my hand that pressed the doorbell. It was me who spoke to the woman who answered, a small baby clutched in one arm.

'Hello,' I said, already regretting disturbing her. Dark circles were etched on her face and her skin was pale. She looked as if she was trying to rock the baby to sleep. 'I'm so sorry to bother you but I'm looking for a friend who used to live here… I moved away and, I mean, I know it's random, but I was just passing for the first time in ages and I wondered if there was a chance she still lived here?'

As I spoke, Grace and I peered around her like meerkats, as if our mystical friend might suddenly appear out of the bedroom. The woman sighed as if one more unexpected glitch was exactly the kind of thing she expected in life.

'Her name was Grace Shaw?' I said. Over the woman's shoulder and through an open door I could see that the separate living room that had served as my bedroom and studio was once again being used as a living area, while the small open-plan area outside the kitchen, which we'd used as our main living space, now housed only a dining table. It all looked so much smaller than I remembered; like a toy version. The kitchen where I'd spent so much time cooking for Grace was cluttered with baby paraphernalia.

The woman screwed up her face as she tried to remember someone called Grace. Her hand patted rhythmically on the baby's back and she shifted her weight from foot to foot in that dance new mums all seem to do.

'Grace? Nah.' She shook her head. 'We bought it from a Pakistani couple. Tall guy. Quiet. I don't remember the wife's name. Lianne? Liyana? Leela? Something like that. Definitely not Grace.'

'Oh you bought it?' I nodded my interest, buying more time. 'Recently, or…?'

'About a year ago, give or take a duck's fart.'

I edged closer to the door and inhaled. I picked up the smell of coffee and toast but was it my imagination or, underneath that, could I still detect that hint of – what was it? A sort of dank smell we could never shift. The smell of subterranean living that had permeated our clothes at the time, yet which I never noticed until I left the flat. The woman's face was blank, uninterested.

'And it wasn't tenanted when you bought it?' I asked desperately. 'Grace rented it, I think. But maybe she'd moved on by then?'

The woman nodded. 'I guess.' In her eyes, the conversation was finished. I looked toward the bedroom door; the door outside which I'd stood that night and listened to Grace fucking Tom and the thud in my abdomen was visceral: muscle memory. I wondered if Grace, next to me, was remembering the same thing. On the woman's shoulder, the baby's eyes were closed, its head finally flopped down in sleep.

'Sorry, I need to put him down,' she said, stepping backwards, ready to close the door.

'Ah, well, thank you anyway,' I said, understanding that this was all we were going to get. 'It was worth a try.'

The door clicked closed. Back on the street, out of sight of the windows, Grace high-fived me.

'That was brilliant!' she said. 'Asking for me when I was standing right there. Can you imagine if she'd actually known who I was? Then what would you have said?'

'Well, she obviously didn't.'

We walked in silence for a minute or two and I wondered if seeing the old place – smelling the old smell – had brought the memories flooding back to Grace as it had to me. We reached the Tube station and my steps slowed and stopped. I felt short-changed, the visit an anti-climax.

'Now what?' I said, my mouth full of words left unsaid.

'We could get some lunch?' Grace suggested with a shrug, so

we wandered toward a café and took a table. We ordered, then Grace slumped back in her plastic seat.

'So what did you think?'

'It looked different.'

'Yeah, I thought so, too. It looked so much smaller today. Maybe all the furniture they had in there.'

'Maybe.'

'It was a big flat for the two of us. We did well!'

I let it go; the fact that it was 'my' flat that she'd gate-crashed; that it was I who'd paid the all the rent on a flat I'd chosen for one.

'Speaking of flats,' I said, 'have you thought any more about looking for your own place?'

'Not really.' Grace smiled, the gleaming white of her teeth just showing through her lips. 'Are you sure your husband doesn't want to stay in New York a bit longer? Like, six months and really get ahead with his career? I wouldn't mind! Then it could be just us.' She gave me a full-beam smile, but I laughed. Not this time. I wasn't falling for her tricks again.

'God, no. I want him back as soon as possible.'

She shook her head as if I were a lost cause. 'Why did you get married, Abs? I don't understand why women shackle themselves to a man.'

'Ironic coming from the girl who had the wedding folder. Remember? All the details? The dress, the apple pie, the children? Two girls, wasn't it?'

She had the decency to laugh. 'Yeah. That was then. I knew no better.'

We lapsed into silence while the waiter brought my wine. I took a sip and looked at Grace across the table. She was checking her phone, giving little smiles and private laughs at the screen as she did so, and I thought: *is that it?* Is that all that's going to be said? I was going to do it. I had to.

'Happy days,' I said, even though they weren't. Not for me, anyway.

'Yeah.' Grace didn't look up.

I took another swig of wine, then dived in.

'How's Tom?' The words exploded out of me, unplanned, then hovered there over the table like blimps as the scar she'd etched onto my heart throbbed. 'Do you still see him?'

Grace laughed then. 'Tom?' She scrunched up her face as if she barely remembered who he was. 'Oh God. No. We broke up – wow – years ago.'

'I thought he was a "keeper",' I said, my voice brittle. 'That's what you said on Facebook.'

Grace laughed dismissively and I waited for something else – an explanation, an apology – but she just smiled to herself and carried on tapping and swiping her phone until the food came.

Transcript of interview with Mr Rohan Allerton, husband of Abigail Allerton: 20 December 2019

'So, would you say things started to go wrong properly once you'd departed for New York?'

'I guess so. I suppose the first sign that things weren't going so smoothly was when Abi missed the dinner with my family. It's just not the done thing and everyone knows that. You don't miss those dinners. [pauses] But she said she was painting, and I know how she gets when she's in that "zone" so I kind of understood. Or maybe she was going out with Grace and didn't want to admit it. But, yeah, looking back, that was probably the first sign.'

'And did you do anything about it?'

'I feel terrible now for not paying more attention, but what could I do about it? I was on the other side of the Atlantic. I messaged her. I gave her a bit of a hard time about it, but that was it. I'm her husband, not her keeper. She knew she'd stuffed up. I didn't need to add to that.'

Thirty-four

M aybe it was the visit to the old flat and all the memories that stirred up, but I couldn't sleep that night. Eventually I gave up trying and went up to the attic to paint. I was on the fourth portrait now, and Grace was, again, older but I was experimenting with a different style for this one: I was distorting the face a little, blurring it, as if she were looking up at me from under moving water. I didn't want it to look as if she were drowning; she was very much alive. Rather, I wanted to make her look as if she were trapped in this other dimension; this subaquatic world of dark greens and hazy turquoise, of weeds and light diffused through opaque water; as if the current were carrying her, her face drifting this way and that like the underwater weeds of a river, her hair streaming all round her, leaving you wondering if she'd escape, or if she'd drift away forever, getting smaller and smaller.

I painted in bursts, thinking and painting, smudging the colours onto the canvas using my fingers as much as the brushes, smearing my DNA with the paint. By the time the buttercup yellow of the morning light slid through the slats of the attic blinds, changing the tone of all I'd achieved in the night, the painting was largely done and, despite the fact that Grace would have left for work,

I realized – with a stiffening of the hairs on my neck and that jolt of sixth-sense awareness we all sometimes get – that the house was not empty.

I crept down the attic stairs, silent as a ghost, my feet noiseless on the carpet. I stopped on the landing and listened to the walls, to the ceiling, to the bricks and the wood that made up the frame of the place that protected me. What or who was it hiding? There was no sign of Alfie but, even so, I sensed the inhale-exhale of breath; I sensed life. I crept into the bedroom and took a shoe from the wardrobe. With that in my hand, I slipped down the stairs, every fibre of my being listening and then I heard it: footsteps, clear as a bell, from the kitchen, and then the unmistakeable tone of my mother-in-law's voice.

'Nah, *beta*,' she said, 'it doesn't look as if she's been in here this morning.'

I pushed open the door and faced her, shoe still in my hand. 'Meena?'

She twirled to face me, her scarf swinging with the movement, her eyes large as she looked me up and down. 'Abigail! You *are* here! Why you didn't answer the door? I've been ringing and ringing! Rohan told me to come in and check you are all right! We've been worried about you…' she trailed off as she looked me up and down. She spoke quickly into the phone, 'She's here. I'll call you back,' and clicked off the call. 'Are you all right? What happened?'

I shook my head, my eyes squinting against the bright sunshine of the kitchen. With the sun coming through that window it must have been up a little while. 'Nothing. I was in the attic.'

Meena swept her hand towards me. 'But… what?'

'What?' I said looking down at the nightshirt and robe I'd worn all night. 'It's paint,' I said, realizing she was looking at the stains on the front. 'What are you doing in the house?'

I was suddenly aware of my lack of sleep, and the floor swayed under my feet giving the feeling I was walking the deck of a rolling ship. I put a hand to the counter to steady myself. My mouth, I realized now, was parched. Meena pointed her nose into the air, sniffed and frowned, her brow furrowed.

'Have you been smoking?'

'No?' But I could smell the stale fug of cigarettes too. 'It must have been Grace. I'll have a word.'

'Please do. It's not healthy. Anyway, as I said,' Meena continued, 'I was ringing the doorbell so many times and you didn't reply, so Ronu suggested I let myself in. To check you were okay.' She had the dignity to flush – faintly, but I saw it. No one had told me she had a key. Her eyes slid to an expensive-looking bouquet of flowers propped up on the table. 'And to give you these.'

I looked at them, reluctant to admit their beauty and let her score a point.

'What are they for?' I said.

'Your birthday. Today?'

'Oh, I… thank you.' Shit. My birthday already? Sweat broke out all over me and I swayed. I could feel the dampness rank under my arms and I hoped Meena couldn't smell that, too. My heart stamped out one of those flurries it did when I stopped drinking after a heavy night: *clip-clippety-thump. Clippety-thump.*

'I need water,' I said, grabbing a dirty glass from the counter and filling it from the tap. I drank greedily and nausea washed over me. I put the glass down and held the sink top for a moment until it subsided. I rubbed a hand across my forehead and it came away wet.

'I'm sorry,' I said when I'd gathered myself. The only way to deal with Meena was to bow down. 'I was up all night painting. I couldn't sleep. I'm sorry I didn't hear the door.'

Meena tutted. 'And what's with your cat miaowing?' She tilted her head. 'He sounds frantic. Is he okay?'

We both looked up the stairs from where I now noticed panicky miaows were coming.

'I don't know. It's unlike him. He usually comes to see visitors…'

We both went up to the landing. The miaows were coming from the bathroom. As we got closer, I could hear the sound of claws scratching at the door. As I opened it, Alfie rocketed out and my nostrils flared. In the bath, three shiny brown slugs of excrement lay in a yellow-green puddle. Meena's jaw clenched and she turned abruptly.

'Looks like he got locked in,' I said. 'Poor baby. He must have been there all night. I don't know how that happened.'

I did, though. I could picture exactly how it happened. Grace.

Alfie circled the hall, mewing and mewing, shouting at me; his miaow catching and extending like an accusation: *I was locked up! Where were you?* I followed as he led the way downstairs, tail twitching, then I changed his water and squeezed a sachet of wet food into a saucer, all the while trying not to gag at the smell. Alfie started eating before the dish even touched the floor.

When I was done sorting out Alfie, I stole a glance at Meena. Her face was serious.

'Abigail, sit down,' she said, pulling out a chair for me and my legs folded gratefully. Meena looked at me and I held her eyes until mine burned and I squirmed. 'Tell me,' she said, looking at me as if she could see the organs and sinews, the flesh and blood inside me. 'What's going on?'

'What do you mean, "what's going on"?' I said.

'I mean exactly that. Drinking. Smoking. Locking up the cat. Not hearing the door. What's going on with you, Abigail?'

I closed my eyes. Meena wouldn't go until she was satisfied. I had to play along. 'I'm sorry. My friend Grace's staying. I'll tell her not to smoke in the house. We've stayed up a few nights talking.' I looked at the empty bottles on the counter. 'Alfie must have got locked in the bathroom by accident. As for me, I'm painting a series for a gallery exhibition,' I said slowly. 'That's what's going on. I'm sorry I forget things and don't hear the door.' I gave her a weak smile.

Meena sighed. 'This isn't about the dinner you missed. I haven't come here to tell you off.' She sighed again and pushed her hair back. 'I'm worried about you.' Her eyes moved to the empty vodka and wine bottles I'd chucked into a box on the floor – I hadn't got around to recycling them yet. I hadn't taken the rubbish out either. Now I noticed, the bin was overflowing, with cigarette packets poking out from a lid that wouldn't close, and piles of dirty glasses and food-encrusted dishes lay not only in the sink but on the draining board as well, along with some olives, well past their prime.

'Grace's here,' I said. 'It's not just me.'

Meena's lips were a flat line. 'Is everything all right with your friend?'

'Of course.'

'What then, Abigail? I sense something isn't right.' She closed her eyes, her palms facing up on the table and breathed in and out as if she were a medium, trying to feel something that patently wasn't there.

'Everything's good,' I said. 'I'm just busy. And tired.'

We stared at each other and then she picked up her phone. 'Tell you what, why don't you tell your husband that because he's been beside himself trying to call you today to wish you a happy birthday.'

'Really? I didn't see any missed calls,' but as I said it, I realized that my phone was here on the kitchen counter, and had been all night.

'Eight times he tried,' Meena said, pressing a button on her phone. 'Plus the messages. Here, speak to him.' She thrust her phone at me and I put it to my ear.

'Abi?' Rohan's voice came down the line, strained and thin. 'Thank God. What happened? Are you all right?'

'I'm fine!' I got up and paced the kitchen, uncomfortable with Meena listening to the call but aware that I had to take it in front of her. 'I'm so sorry I missed your calls. I was painting and my phone was in the kitchen. What time is it there?'

'Just gone four thirty in the morning.'

'Shit. I'm really sorry... have you...' *Been up all night?* was what I needed to ask, but I didn't want to know I'd caused him a sleepless night. 'I've done some amazing work,' I said. 'I can't wait to show you.'

'I'm looking forward to it, Abs. I've been counting the days till I see you.' A pause. 'You must be really into your painting.' I was still sweating, my hand clammy on the phone.

'I've been consumed by it,' I said. 'I barely know what day it is.' It felt as if my voice was coming from somewhere else; someone else speaking. 'I've been so busy. I've pretty much finished the fourth painting. I was up all night.'

'I'm glad you're being productive,' Rohan said. 'I was really worried you wouldn't have anything for the exhibition.'

'Well, I will now. I'm aiming for nine or maybe ten in the series and, if I can keep on at this pace, they should be done in time.'

'Fantastic.' His voice was warm. 'But please, baby, keep your phone with you and just send me a text if you're busy. I understand. I get it. But I never want another night like last night. Okay?' He wished me a happy birthday, asked if I was doing something with Grace later, and I hung up the call a few minutes later.

Meena was sitting at the table, staring into space.

'I think it's the house,' she said randomly, drumming her fingers on the table. 'I've always said there's something about this house. A spirit, maybe.'

She looked up at the ceiling as if she could see the wisps of ghosts traversing the plaster; ectoplasm stuck to the window panes and I stifled a sigh of impatience, wanting nothing more than painkillers and my bed.

'Don't you feel it, Abigail?' she said. I didn't say anything, and Meena carried on. 'Maybe you don't. But my family, from my mother's side, we were always sensitive to these things.'

I shrugged. Rohan had taught me not to indulge Meena's spiritual-slash-fanciful side, not because he didn't believe in it, but because once Meena got an idea about something, she snowballed, and I could see where this was going.

'Do you remember when Mili was pregnant?' Meena asked and I closed my eyes to hide an eye-roll: *dear God, here we go again.* We all knew the story she was about to tell: it was family lore, along with the time when she left a newsagent's moments before it was held up by armed robbers. 'She hadn't done the pregnancy test,' Meena said, 'but I guessed she was expecting because I felt the extra aura in the room.'

She touched her hand to her chest. 'I can feel something again now,' she said. 'I always told Rohan not to buy an old house, but he wouldn't listen, would he? Hmm? You never know what's happened in a house like this. All the people who lived here. All the people died right here, within these walls.' She shuddered. 'Under this roof. All that energy.' She stared into the middle distance again, as if she could see through time.

'Energy never dies,' she said to the kitchen, and her voice took on a trance-like tone, as if she were speaking to spirits themselves. 'It might change form, but it never dies. Sometimes it gets trapped.' She turned and looked meaningfully at me. 'You sit here all day, alone, painting, Abigail. You open your brain, your heart and your soul to forces we can't see or understand. You receive instruction from another plane. And this is how it works – this is how the good paintings come to you...' My hackles rose at that. Did my mother-in-law really think I had zero talent without the input of some extra-terrestrial energy? 'But sometimes things you don't want will come in, too.'

Meena's nail fretted at the surface of the table, the oak distressed by a designer rather than years of use, and she sucked in her cheeks. I picked up my water and took another sip to hide my impatience. I would never admit it to her, but I felt the energy, too. I felt the shell of the house pulsing with it: it was the energy that had made me want to buy the house in the first place. I knew that the house wanted me here. It had chosen me – but I would rather pull out my own fingernails than tell Meena that.

'I have a very strong feeling about this place,' Meena continued. 'There's unhappiness here. Something bad.'

I knew her well enough to know what she was picturing: something dark and brooding that skirted the house, breathing on us all, wisping its way around us and inside us like a macabre fog; something too ethereal to put into words. If I wasn't careful, she'd be here before I knew it with a group of friends burning sage and chanting, and I didn't even have Rohan here to stop her. I snapped to attention.

'No. That's ridiculous. I don't feel it at all. Look!' I pointed at the ultra-modern kitchen, at the new floors. 'It's all new. Nothing old is here anymore. Any spirits are long gone.'

But Meena got up and started opening the cupboards. For a moment I thought she was actually looking for ghosts behind the cereal bowls.

'Where's your salt? Proper sea salt, not this table salt.' She flicked her fingers as if sprinkling salt on food.

'What do you want salt for?'

'There's something wrong with the energy in this house and I'm going to fix it.'

Really, I could do without this right now. 'With salt?'

'Yes, and lemons. It might help. If not, we will think again. Now, do you have lemons?'

'Help yourself,' I said, pointing lamely to the fruit bowl where a couple of dull lemons sagged.

Meena bustled about, finding a knife and the chopping board. She cut the lemons, arranged them in saucers and sprinkled salt on them.

'Right, I'm going to leave these around the house. Please don't move them. I'm also going to sprinkle some salt around the doors and windows. I learned this from my mother – Ronu's *nannima* – she did it every time we stayed in a hotel or overnight anywhere, she'd scatter salt in the corners of the room and at the windows and doors and we were never troubled by spirits.'

My chin was resting on my hands. It seemed to ease the pounding in my head. My eyes were heavy. 'What?'

Meena sighed. 'There are many things in this life that we don't understand, Abigail, but trust me on this.' She cocked her head. 'Anyway, shouldn't you be at the hospice today? I thought you went every Tuesday?'

Shit.

Thirty-five

By the time I got to the hospice, I was over an hour late for my shift. I'd spent the journey there alternating between hope – *I was painting! She'll understand!* – and dread, unsure which was the more realistic option but the moment I pushed through the door and saw Moira look up from the drinks cart that I should have been pushing from room to room and shake her head, I knew which way things would go. Still, I tried. Throwing my coat behind the nurses' station, I went to take the cart from her.

'I'm so sorry, Moira. I...'

She cut me off. 'In the office, Abigail,' she said, so I slunk over to the small room at the far end of the ground floor. There, I ran my hands through my hair. In my rush to get Meena out of the house and get here, I hadn't showered, neither had I bothered with make-up. Sitting waiting, I turned the selfie camera on my phone onto my face to check my appearance and recoiled from what I saw: dark circles under my eyes, lank hair, sallow skin, the beginning of jowls. *It's just the angle. It's the camera,* I told myself as I snapped back to the home screen and rubbed my finger across my front teeth, trying to polish off some of the fuzz that remained from a night – or more? – unbrushed. Moira didn't come for ages – she must be finishing the drinks before attending to me, and quite rightly. But I was so tired... I leaned my head back against the wall. I just needed another vodka. That'd sharpen me up.

'Abi.' Moira's voice was brisk, a call to attention as she brought a swirl of busy energy into the room. 'Wake up.'

My eyes snapped open and, as I focused, my hand went up to wipe the dribble I could feel gathered at the corner of my mouth. My body bolted forward to attention.

'Moira. I'm so sorry. I was painting and I was up all night. I lost track of the days.'

She stood there in front of me, her hands on her hips; she may be diminutive in stature but her entire body brimmed with authority.

'It's not good enough, Abigail. I'm sorry.' She glowered at me and I shrank before her. 'It's not the first time this has happened, is it? It's one excuse after the other with you these days, isn't it?'

I closed my eyes in acquiescence. Since Grace had arrived, I'd become slack.

'I don't know what's going on in your life,' Moira said, 'but you need to sort it out before you come back here. I need to be able to rely on my volunteers – to have them turn up when they're supposed to and do the jobs they're supposed to do. That's all I ask. This isn't a hobby, Abigail. It may be a volunteer position, but I need you to be professional in your conduct.'

I hung my head in shame.

'And turning up drunk, or smelling of alcohol? It's not on. It's simply not on, Abi.' Her voice rose here and I realized how angry she was. I'd thought she hadn't noticed. 'Imagine what the relatives think when they see their loved ones around someone who looks and smells like she slept rough.' Moira paused and stared at me until I squirmed, then she began again in a gentler tone. 'If you need help, I can recommend people. We can get you the help you need. Alcohol's a highly addictive substance. It's nothing to be ashamed of.' She opened the desk drawer and held out a leaflet: *Am I an alcoholic?*

'No, thank you. I... I'm not an alcoholic. I'm fine.' My voice was a whisper. Everything was so much effort this morning. 'I'm just painting for an exhibition. It takes over everything.'

Moira sighed. 'Well, that may be. I've no idea how the artistic mind works – but I've thought about this and discussed it with the powers-that-be and I'm sorry to have to ask you not to come back until you're able to guarantee your reliability and focus on the job in hand. I'm not saying never. I'm saying take a break, and get in touch once you have things under control again. You're a good volunteer and I don't want to lose you. But we can't continue like this. Does that sound reasonable?'

Tears sprung to my eyes and I squeezed my lips together to try and stop them from spilling out. 'Yes, yes it does. Thank you.'

Moira pushed a box of tissues towards me. 'All right. Well, stay in touch. Let me know how you're getting on. And if you need help, it's here.' She pushed the leaflet towards me again and, with that, she was gone, leaving me with a devastating sense of failure and loss.

It was a feeling I knew well.

Thirty-six

The decision to kill myself hadn't been one I'd made slowly. I'd simply woken up one morning a few weeks into the first term of university with the weight of the world on me and known I couldn't surface through it. I couldn't carry on anymore. It had been that simple. The decision on how to do it had taken far longer.

I'd lain in bed and looked at the window that morning and it had struck me how easy it would be to jump out of the window and never feel anything again. A few moments of fear as I fell, maybe, then the sweet release of oblivion. I'd lain there thinking about how the nightmares would finally stop, and how I wouldn't have to deal with anything anymore, and I'd got up and opened the window to see how wide it went. I'd peered down at the grey pavement below and imagined myself, splayed and broken on it, blood oozing from my head, and found the image morbidly pleasing.

But I was also practical. It would be no dress rehearsal; no cry for help. My room was only on the second floor: I'd have to go higher up, or maybe try to jump headfirst in order to make sure I did actually die. Were there methods for these things? It was oblivion I craved, not sympathy. Later, I googled 'best way to jump suicide'. I knew that the world would be a better place without me. It was as simple as that.

That morning – the morning I calmly searched the best way to jump – marked the beginning of a phase during which I'd find myself thinking about how to kill myself many times a day. I'd look at the buses passing on Marylebone Road or Oxford Street or wherever I was and think: *I just need to step out right now* – and then the moment would pass and I'd almost be washed with disappointment that I hadn't done it. Every failure served only to refuel the idea that I was worthless: that I didn't even have the guts to follow through. Same with the Tube, and with trains. A dithering moment of dazzling possibility, then the whoosh of the train and I'd missed my chance. A coward, that's what I was. Unworthy.

And then I might buy something and find myself looking at those warnings on plastic bags that say 'Danger of suffocation' and think: really? Is it that easy? Could you do it yourself? I had no access to a gun; couldn't picture myself using a knife. Slashing your wrists takes too long. I learned the word 'exsanguination'.

I continued to go to lectures and seminars; to smile at people. I continued to hand in assignments; to do my best. It didn't occur to me to tell anyone what I was thinking. It didn't occur to me to talk to Grace. To seek help. I was ashamed.

When it came to me, the answer was much simpler than I'd imagined. Pills.

I did my research; I found out what I could buy over the counter that would do the job and calculated how many I'd need. I became an expert at buying the tablets. I walked the streets, finding new pharmacies; places where they didn't know me; pharmacies with kind-faced staff who'd hand me more pills without suspicion. I'd explain that I'd hurt my back playing hockey. I'd hold my back, yawn and say I couldn't sleep at night and then I'd nod attentively while they gave me the usual warnings. My patter became slick. I almost believed I'd hurt my back: if I concentrated hard enough I could almost feel the pain. If only injuries inside your head, your heart, were so obvious; so easy to treat.

And, as I'd walked back to Halls that day – the last batch of little boxes burning a hole in my backpack – I remember I'd noticed everything: the pattern of the paving slabs, the drain covers, the dirty weeds fighting for life at the base of filthy brick walls. It had seemed as if the whole of London was covered with the soot of city life; everything was tarnished. The sun, which might have made things better by gilding the edges of the city, had tried, and failed, to break through the clouds, and I'd seen even that as a sign. There was no going back.

I'd decided to do it on a Wednesday. Hump day, late November. Grey sky, naked trees stiff like skeletons, rain sliding down the window of my room in Halls. I'd lain in bed listening to the sounds outside my window: the cars, the hoots, the sirens – always the sirens. In the corridor, doors had banged as people went off for breakfast, and I'd caught snatches of conversation, voices I'd come to recognize although I still couldn't match them to faces. The one with the American drawl; the Scottish one; the guy who shouted everything as if he were addressing a stadium.

Oh, shut the fuck up.

I'd stacked my books and folders neatly on the desk; tidied my room. I got up, made the bed, went for a shower, and dressed. I opened the window, then I sat at the desk and pressed the tablets out of their packets. I arranged them in lines of five, ready to take and, when they were all laid out like rows of soldiers, I picked up the first five tablets and was rattling them in my hand thinking that this was going to be relatively easy after all when the door burst open.

Grace paused only for a fraction of a second before leaping across the room like a martial arts ninja. She swept the tablets off my desk with her forearm, making them fly through the air and rain down all over the carpet.

'What are you *doing*?' she yelled. 'You fucking idiot! You selfish cow! How *dare* you?'

She slapped my hand hard – the one that still held five tablets.

'Let them go! How many have you taken? *How many?*'

'None,' I mumbled, and Grace prised open my hand, snatched the tablets and flung them across the room so hard they bounced off the wall. She grabbed one of the packets. 'You didn't take any? Are you sure?'

I shook my head miserably. A failure again.

We stared at each other. Grace had her hands on her hips and she shook her head at me in disgust, her nostrils flaring and her face squashed with anger. Two spots of colour had appeared on her cheeks.

'You have no idea!' she yelled, her voice hard with passion. 'You have *no idea* how lucky you are to be here. To be alive! To be healthy! To be here, studying for a degree. Some people never get that chance!'

I clamped my hands over my ears to dampen her words but still I could hear and, all the while she went on at me about getting through this together and making the most of my life, I stared at the floor, looking at the pills scattered on the carpet, feeling smaller and smaller. I tried to swallow but I couldn't. My face was hot and my throat thick with shame. Tears pricked at my eyes and my nose throbbed with the effort of holding them in. And still Grace's words rained down on me, hot and acrid, like lava, ramping up the self-disgust that built in my belly because, underneath everything, I knew what she was saying, and I knew that it was true: *I was selfish*.

Getting up to leave Moira's office, I remembered those desperate times in the first year – the utter blackness that had so nearly consumed me; the pointlessness of life that had swum through my veins; the emotions that had tried to destroy me – and recalled how Grace had pulled me through. Without really knowing how, and certainly not knowing why, it was Grace's tough love that had ultimately saved me.

'You need to make your life count,' she told me when the dust had settled, and I was back on track. 'Do something worthwhile with it.'

The thought that I'd let Grace down grew inside me as the Tube rattled me towards home, until it was a balloon that filled my insides, squashing my organs and choking me. I pressed my hand to my throat, swallowing again and again, to try and rid the feeling that I couldn't breathe but I knew there was only one way I could puncture that balloon and create the space to breathe: I needed to strip Grace of that power she had over me. I needed to bury the past.

Having someone save your life is a powerful thing, but there comes a point when you need to draw a line under it and move on. This was the mistake I'd made last time we lived together: I'd subsisted in Grace's shadow, always believing that I owed her; always believing that I should be grateful to her – but she not only knew that, she took advantage of it. She knew how I felt, and she took that feeling and walked all over it. She used me. She abused me. My life was a constant battle against the nagging feeling that I was letting Grace down but I was an adult now. Married. I had to move on.

Thirty-seven

Grace and I ate dinner at the kitchen table that night: I hadn't done a shop so it was toasted cheese sandwiches. I'd cut the mould off the cheese before Grace got home. And off the bread.

'Are you going to meet up with anyone else at any point?' I asked her as I ate hungrily, the bright red ketchup oozing out the back and sides of my sandwich like blood. Grace was still in her white work shirt; I told her she was playing Russian roulette to eat ketchup in a white shirt but she didn't seemed to care. 'I'm the only one you've seen since you've been back.'

'I wasn't planning on it.'

'But your other friends must be dying to see you? Luna, Steve?' I struggled to think of the names of the medics she used to hang around with.

She shrugged. 'Yeah. I guess.'

'Why don't you look them up and go for a long weekend or something? You've been working so hard.'

Grace put down her sandwich and looked at me. 'Are you trying to tell me something?'

I gave myself a silent pep talk: *be strong*. 'Rohan's coming back for the weekend soon,' I said as casually as I could. My palms were sweating. I really needed her to toe the line with this.

'Oh lovely!' Grace said. 'I can't wait to meet him.' I didn't reply. I just looked at her until she got it. 'Oh,' she said, slapping the table. 'You don't want me here – is that what this is about? The two lovebirds want some space? Am I right?'

Well, there is that, but I also don't want you stealing him.

I smiled. 'I hope you don't mind. I haven't seen him for weeks. You can meet him another time, once he's back for good.' I paused. 'I'm happy to help pay for your train ticket.'

Grace pouted while she looked back at me with her eyes narrowed, then she smiled. 'Sure,' she said. 'If it means that much to you, I'll get out of your hair when your hubbie comes home. Maybe I could go to a spa...'

Did she say it just to annoy me? To remind me? We'd gone together to a spa once when we were students – her idea, of course. It wasn't my thing at all so I'd flopped about, bored and out of place, in the plush white dressing gown as she'd ricocheted from facial to massage to pedicure to spa pool, then she shot back to London early, claiming work, and left me with the bill.

'Yes,' I said with a smile. 'Why don't you?'

Thirty-eight

Rohan was taking the red-eye out after work on the night of 30 October, and was due to land in the morning of 31 October: Hallowe'en. I stayed up all night painting yet, as the sun rose, my concentration faded and I paced the attic, brush in hand, unable to work. Grace was faffing about in her room and it worried me that she might suddenly change her mind and stay. The thought of her meeting Rohan – of her saying something snide – of her voicing her opinion of him at all – was too much to bear.

I looked down at the street from the attic window. It was a grey day, a day in which the slate of the sky leached the colour from everything. A handful of houses had made the effort to decorate for Hallowe'en, the hedges gradually disappearing beneath the tangle of white, shop-bought cobweb. On pathways and front walls, pumpkins had appeared, so roughly hacked at by the children of the houses that their toothy grins were more gruesome than perhaps intended: lopsided gashes in the flesh and eyes in places too horrific to be natural.

After an hour of looking at my canvas and failing to land a single brush stroke, I downed tools.

'Hey,' I said, knocking at Grace's door. 'Can I come in?'

'Sure.'

She was sitting on the bed, a small overnight bag open next to her. 'Checking I'm really going?' she asked with only half a smile.

I tutted. "Course not.' I stood with my back to the window so I didn't have to look at the creepy row of toys. 'Where are you off to?'

'Raw-food and health retreat.' She paused. 'Down in Kent. Near Canterbury.'

I swallowed. 'Nice. Got your yoga pants?'

She laughed. 'There is a lot of yoga. Meditation, too. Sound meditation and chanting. I've always wanted to try those.'

'Sounds good.' I looked at my watch, my heart chittering with anxiety. 'So, do you have a cab coming?'

'I'm taking the train.'

'Ah, okay.'

Grace looked around the room, then zipped up her bag. 'Right. I think I've got everything.'

'I'm sure they'll have anything you might have forgotten,' I said. 'As long as you have your wallet.'

She peered into her handbag. 'Yep. Got that.' She looked around the room again and exhaled loudly. 'Should I take Teddy? I've kind of grown fond of him.'

At that point I was happy for her to take the kitchen sink as long as she left. I picked up the bear. 'Here, take it.'

Grace opened her bag again and put the bear inside, pressing its ratty ears carefully under the zip. Finally, she picked the bag up off the bed and heaved it over her shoulder. 'Right, I'll be off out of your hair then.'

We clattered down the stairs and I opened the front door for her. She turned on the doorstep.

'Have a good time with hubbie. Maybe this'll be the weekend you make a baby.'

My smile was as fake as hers. 'Maybe.'

With Grace gone, I was itching to paint. I had five completed canvases lined up along the attic wall. After the aquatic effect of the fourth picture, things had taken a darker turn and it crossed my mind on many occasions that maybe there really was something in what Meena had said. Maybe an unseen energy was entering my body because I didn't know where the ideas, the feelings and the colours came from: when I worked, my eyes were half closed and my hands moved to a rhythm that came from the universe. It's not as if I *planned* what I was painting. It just came. When I opened my eyes and regarded the canvases properly, I was often surprised – stunned – at what I'd actually painted.

In the fifth portrait Grace was older again, perhaps in her thirties, though it was hard to tell because her features were so perverse. She had four eyes and three sets of lips, all of which were blurred as if she'd moved – struggled? convulsed? – while being captured for a photograph, and yet I'd somehow also managed to put a look of disdain on her face, her chin lifted and her eyes looking down with such contempt it made a shiver run up my spine.

But the thing that scared me most about this portrait – the thing I had no idea how I'd managed to paint – was the way I'd created the illusion that her face was trapped beneath something more solid than water. Yes, this version of Grace was trapped beneath the canvas itself; as if it were a barrier she couldn't pass. She was struggling, suffocating in a way that made me imagine that her unseen hands might be trying to claw their way through the fabric to let in some air. The colours blurred and merged; her deformed features distorted by the material that stopped her from surfacing, the three sets of blood-red lips slightly parted as she struggled to get a breath between them.

It was suffocating to look at and had been suffocating to paint, reminding me of that feeling I'd had on the Tube that a balloon was filling my insides, choking me. It was when this feeling became too much and I found myself gasping for air that I went over to the window and looked down at the street; at the bare branches of the oak trees reaching up to the grey sky, an invisible wind whipping the dead bodies of the leaves into eddies at the kerbside and buffeting the house; at the ghoulish decorations that brought horror to the street. On the roof, the extractor outlet banged with the stronger gusts: *knock, knock, knock.* The attic window wasn't double-glazed and, up close to the glass, I could feel the sharp coolness of the air as the panes rattled in their frames. I raised both my hands to the glass and pressed against it: the woman in the window. *Let me go.*

The sixth portrait was coming along frighteningly well. In it, Grace appeared to have escaped from behind the canvas, at least that quality of suffocation that I'd managed to infuse into number five was no longer there, but her beautiful face – because she was, without doubt, beautiful – was smashed, broken and pulled apart, the flesh distorted, deformed, melted, and bleeding out of itself, the skin dripping towards the edge of the canvas, the textures and colours of the paints I was using suggesting pain, horror and destruction. Stepping back to view my progress, I realized that although the image was undeniably *horrific*, it was going to be perfect. I'd been up all night and the walls of the attic seemed to pulse beyond the periphery of my sight as if the room itself were breathing and I were the heart of it – but I couldn't stop painting now. I put my brush once more to the canvas.

I don't know how much later it was when I finally laid down my brushes and came down the stairs – my mind on the coffee I so sorely needed – and suddenly there was Rohan, standing in the hall in his jeans and a sports jacket, and looking as surprised to see me as I was him. I hadn't realized he'd be home from the airport already; I hadn't heard the door. My body swayed as I held onto the bannister.

'Rohan?'

'Who else were you expecting?' he said, looking around with a laugh. 'Your lover?' He frowned and sniffed. 'Does he smoke? Or have you been…?' Both of his eyebrows shot up.

I tutted. 'No. It's Grace. I told her not to, but I think she sticks her head out of the window. It's not enough, is it?'

I took in the suitcase on the hall floor, the keys Rohan had put on the side table, and the pile of unopened post he had kicked away. Rohan moved to the bottom of the stairs, his eyes glued to me the whole time.

'How are you?'

'Fine.'

I walked down towards him, still dazed, still not quite part of the real world, still tired, in need of sleep. Rohan scooped me in his arms and squeezed me to him, breathing deeply with his face in my hair, then he kissed me long and hard on the mouth.

'I missed you, gorgeous wife,' he said as he pulled away and, in his beard, I picked up the scent of outside, of aircraft, of travel, of New York. His breath smelled stale but I imagined mine wasn't great either. I breathed into the palm of my hand and my nostrils flared.

'I missed you too. I'm sorry, I didn't hear the door,' I said. 'I was…' I pointed vaguely up.

'No problem. I have a key.' Rohan was laughing at me, but he held me by my shoulders and stared into my face. He touched the earring I wore in my right ear without comment, then traced my cheekbone with his thumb.

'You look tired,' he said. 'And you've lost weight. I can see it in your face.' His hand slid down my body, hesitating on my rib cage, then over my waist and hips, then he squeezed my bum playfully. 'You have.'

I shrugged. 'Maybe. I haven't weighed myself. Anyway, look, I was about to make some coffee...'

'I could murder a coffee. Let's go,' he said but, at the kitchen door, he stopped, and I walked straight into the back of him. He turned around. 'What's going on?' he said. 'What happened?'

I pushed past, my mind on the coffee. 'What do you mean, "what's going on?" Nothing "happened".' I got the coffee jug from the machine, moved some dishes to one side so I could rinse it out in the sink, and prepared to set it up for two.

'But, Abs. The mess.' He went over to the bin and wrinkled his nose. 'Don't you clear up after yourself? And where's Grace? Is she still staying?'

'She's gone to see some friends this weekend to give us some space.' I smiled, aiming for 'beguiling'.

Rohan grimaced. 'Oh, shame. I was hoping to meet her.' He looked around. 'Anyway, doesn't she do any housework either? It looks like a bomb went off in here.'

'Sorry, sorry,' I said, quickly gathering dishes and moving them to the counter near the sink. I bent under the sink and took out the surface spray and sprayed it on the counters, then found a cloth, wet it and started wiping. 'I'll sort it out. You unpack, and when you come back down it'll be good as new.'

'But Abs...' Rohan said. He bent down over Alfie's dish. 'Have you even fed him today?'

'I haven't been down. I was painting all night.'

Rohan picked up the food bowl and examined the crispy, blackened remnants of a meal we could both see was eaten long ago. 'When did you last give him wet food?'

I shook my head, a stab of shame piercing my heart. 'Yesterday?'

'Because this looks really old.'

'He's got dry food,' I said. 'And water.' And that was true. But something cold clasped at my heart: I hadn't seen Alfie for a while. Where was he? When had I last seen him? I tried to search my fuddled brain but it was like trying to make sense of candyfloss. Again, I was sweating, shaking slightly. Painting always took it out of me, but never as much as this series was doing. I was a dishrag. When the coffee was done, I poured us each a cup, feeling Rohan's eyes on me as I slipped a snatch of whisky into mine.

'What?' I said.

'Nothing.'

I pulled out a chair and sat at the table while Rohan adopted his customary position leaning back against the counter, his body open to the room.

'So – how's it going with Grace? Is it nice to have her staying?' he said.

'Yeah. She's working, so she's out every day, but, yeah.'

'What's her job?'

I explained about the GP work and the volunteering. 'As long as I've known her, it was always her plan to save lives; to help people,' I said.

'That's amazing,' Rohan said. 'But I'm glad it's just us now. I missed you.'

'Me too,' I said.

Rohan's eyes slid to the whisky bottle and then back to me. 'So the painting's going well?'

'Yes. I'm sorry the house is a bit of a tip. It's just… I've been really focused, and I have a lot on with Grace here. Double the work.'

'Doesn't she help out?'

'She does what she can. But, you know, she's out saving lives and I'm home so, yeah, the housework tends to fall on me… I don't mind. It's nice to have the company.'

I saw Rohan bristle. 'Sure. But, I mean, you could ask her to help? I'm sure she could – I don't know – empty the bins or *feed Alfie*,' he looked hard at me and I squirmed, 'if you asked her to?'

'I don't mind,' I said. 'I'm sorry about Alfie. It won't happen again.'

'So, can I see the paintings?' Rohan looked so eager it made me shy.

'Later?'

'Okay.' A silence fell. I watched Rohan's eyes roam the kitchen. Now I looked properly, I saw that things had become really bad. Why hadn't Grace said anything? She must think I'm such a slob. I resolved to get everything shipshape by the time she came back. Rohan broke the silence.

'Do we have any plans this weekend?'

I shrugged. It hadn't occurred to me to make any plans. 'What about your mum? She must surely have lined something up for your grand homecoming?'

Rohan coughed. 'Well, actually, she did mention a lunch tomorrow. You know what she's like. She said "kebabs and *biriyani*". Are you up for it?'

I closed my eyes and pinched the bridge of my nose. I'd have to be up for it. When Meena summoned, there was no choice.

'Sure,' I said flatly.

'Don't you want to come? I thought it would be nice for us all to get together.' There was an edge to Rohan's voice; an unspoken sentence: *since you missed the last dinner.*

I sighed. 'It's just that I'm on a roll painting and I don't really want to stop. And you know how those lunches go on. You know, all that family gossip and in-jokes and me sitting there pretending I know what you're talking about.' I paused. 'It's a good chance for you to tell them all about New York.'

'Don't you want to hear about New York?'

I felt as if Rohan and I were an engine misfiring, the two of us trying but failing to connect. Was it my fault? I was out of practice socially; lost in my head; knocked for six to have found him in the hallway.

'We can go out on our own tonight if you like,' he suggested. 'Date night?'

I laughed, but then I saw his face. 'Great,' I said. 'Good idea.'

Transcript of interview with Mr Rohan Allerton, husband of Abigail Allerton: 20 December 2019

'So, you said earlier that you first started noticing changes around the time the topic of your secondment to New York came up.'

'Yes. Well, in the weeks leading up to my departure.'

'And we've established that you felt there were adequate people around to help Abigail if she needed it, so you went off to New York without worrying. And then you came home after four weeks away. How was she then? Did you notice any changes in her?'

'Yes. The first thing I noticed was how much thinner and more tired she looked. She'd lost a lot of weight off her face, and her skin looked grey. She looked… gaunt.'

'Unwell?'

'I guess. But she'd been painting, and I get that she forgets about eating and sleeping when she's painting. She doesn't really go outdoors or anything. I guess I'd forgotten how pale she can be.'

'So, you weren't overly worried?'

[Sighs] 'I'm her husband. Of course I was concerned. But, as I said, I realized it was part of the "process" of creating her work, and I hoped that a few days spent with me keeping an eye on her would put her back on the right track. And don't forget that Grace was staying with her. She said she was a doctor. At the back of my mind it was always there that if things got bad, Grace would say something, or do something, or call me.'

'I see. And you mentioned earlier that Abigail hadn't been looking after the house, either? Was that unusual?'

'Yes, it was unusual. She's no domestic goddess but things are usually pretty nice at home. You know: clean. Tidy. I was surprised to see how bad things had got. But, as I said, she was painting.'

'I see. And anything else?'

'Well. There was what happened to the cat.'

Thirty-nine

We went to Mr Ho's.

'Unimaginative, I know,' Rohan said somewhat apologetically after he booked, 'but the food's good, and we can walk, so I can have a drink too.'

It was still blustery as we walked down towards the High Street, my hand small and cold inside the warmth of Rohan's big paw. He gave my hand a squeeze as our feet hit the pavement in rhythm: two of my small steps to each one of his. The last of the trick-or-treaters were out now – teenagers at this time. They moved in little gangs – nylon capes swirling around short skirts, black tights and platform heels; splashes of garish make-up – fake teeth, black eyes and dark red scars – as they zig-zagged to the decorated houses. I'd had a few vodkas at home and I had to hold consciously onto the thought that they were just costumes; that ghouls and vampires weren't circling us, hungry for blood. The streetlights bathed everything in yellow light and the wind buffeted our faces, whipping my hair into Medusa snakes.

'You should see the decorations in New York,' Rohan said. 'Makes this look laughable. God, for days now, the Upper East Side's been absolutely covered with some really ghastly stuff.

Ghouls and headless monsters and things that cackle and flash when you walk past. The Americans have got it down to a fine art.'

'Sounds awful,' I said.

Rohan inhaled deeply. 'But nothing beats the smell of a British autumn, does it, babe? Bonfires, fireworks and hot takeaway chips. Always takes me back to bonfire night as a kid. Can you smell it, too, or is it just because I've been away?'

'Yeah,' I said but, really, I felt the wind was hostile; against us, pushing us back, making our walk more difficult. It swirled around my nose and forced me to breathe it in. *Let me in*, it said, trying to get inside my body and I refused as long as I could, denying it access until I had to gasp.

'Do you remember that night we came here in August?' Rohan said once we'd taken our seats at our usual table and given our drinks order. Now he'd shed his coat, I saw he'd made an effort with his clothes, wearing a shirt I hadn't seen before in that navy that he knew I liked. His beard was neatly groomed and he smelled fresh and clean. Shame licked my insides as I touched my old sweater self-consciously.

I flicked through the menu, although I knew what I'd have. It wasn't a fancy restaurant, but I wished Mr Ho would change the tablecloths from the cloying pink that made it look so dated. It was like one of those ads that used to pop up at the cinema before the main film, crackling and old-fashioned.

'It was so hot that night,' Rohan said. 'Do you remember? It felt like the summer would go on and on.'

'Was that the night it rained?' I said. 'I remember thinking that thunder sounding like the world had split in half. Everyone jumped.' I shivered and Rohan took my hand across the table but then Mr Ho arrived with the drinks.

'Haven't seen you for a while,' he said. I was never sure if his abruptness was a language thing, or just his manner.

'I've been in New York,' Rohan said.

'New York? You find nice Chinese food there?'

Rohan laughed, his big, social laugh, and rubbed his hands together. 'Maybe. But never as good as here. How's the family?'

'All good,' said Mr Ho, clearly not willing to say more tonight. It was quite busy; several tables had been pushed together to accommodate a large and loud party of women in tiaras and feather boas – a hen night, or a birthday, maybe, since I couldn't see any of the usual hen paraphernalia.

I ordered a bottle of Chianti. Mr Ho opened it at the table, then poured me a splash to taste. I swirled it in the glass and breathed in its scent, before tasting it and nodding.

'It's good,' I said to Mr Ho, who gave me the slightest side-eye: *as if* he would serve bad wine. He poured me a glass and placed the bottle on the table.

'You want a straw with that?' he asked, and there was a heart-beat of a shocked silence before he burst out laughing. 'Joking! What can I get you to eat?' We ordered, and he left us.

'It seems like so long ago. So much has happened,' Rohan said and I looked at the familiar wedding ring on his left hand; pictured it in New York, seeing things and touching things I had no idea existed. 'I can't believe I've been in New York for a month already.'

'I know, right.'

'That was that night you told me Grace was coming,' Rohan said. 'So tell me how it's been. What's she like? Has she changed? Gone all Aussie? *G'day!* See you this *arvo*!' His accent was dire.

I shrugged. 'It's the same as it used to be, really. I guess we never really threw it about too much when we were at uni, so... yeah, similar.'

'But what's she like? As a person, I mean?'

'Hard-working. Driven.'

'Cute too?' Rohan laughed. 'It's hard to see her face on Instagram.'

'She doesn't really post pictures of herself,' I said, wrong-footed that he'd checked.

Rohan laughed. 'Jealous?' He leaned across the table and stroked my cheek. 'Don't be. I was only teasing.'

I took a swig of wine. Would she be his type?

Maybe.

'So what do you guys do in your spare time?' Rohan asked. He leaned over and stroked my cheek again. 'Sorry. I feel like I'm interviewing you! Have you been out anywhere?'

'We went to the old flat. There was a woman there. We could see a bit but we didn't get to go inside.'

'Amazing. How was it?'

'Older.'

He smiled. 'Now you're used to a house, I guess any student flat would look pretty crappy.'

'It wasn't a student flat as such,' I prickled.

'Whatevs.' He held up his hand, palm towards me. 'I never saw it. I'm not arguing about it.'

'So, anyway, yeah, we've been busy,' I said.

'She saving lives and you painting.'

'She may work in an emergency setting but she's still only a GP. It's not as if she's a paramedic or anything.' I huffed. 'Anyway, I don't think I can explain to you how wrapped up I've been in my painting. I only really see her in the evening. We have a few drinks and cobble something together for dinner, and we watch TV till we fall asleep. I often work most of the night, too, while she gets her beauty sleep.' Was that clear enough? *She's not that amazing.*

'Has she seen your work?'

I grimaced at the thought. 'She saw the first two but none since.'

'Why not?'

'I don't want her to see them till they're all done.'

'Fair enough. And you said they're not of anyone in particular? I'm intrigued.'

I squeezed my hands in my lap thinking of the dark clouds; of Grace's distorted underwater face; of her struggling where I'd locked her under the canvas; of her face ripped apart; and of the dark, dark places I expected to take her next.

'Yeah. They're just a woman.' My body twitched and my hand jerked up so I planted it on the wine glass and lifted it to my lips. 'It's a series,' I said carefully. 'The subject is young at the start, and then she grows up.'

'Okay,' Rohan said. 'Sounds good. What's the style?'

'I can't really explain it. But dark.'

Rohan nodded. 'I don't want to push you, but I'd really like to see what you've done.'

What was the harm as long as he didn't know it was Grace? 'Sure. Later.' I took a deep breath. 'So how's New York? What's it like?'

So Rohan started telling me about the apartment and his office and the people he worked with and the deli on the corner that made the most amazing sandwiches and how delicious the baloney was, and I tuned out. In my head I was thinking about the seventh portrait – a feeling was coming to me now and I was getting an idea of what it might be: a slideshow of images ran through my head, shifting and moving: colours, shapes, patterns and a sense in my chest of restriction, of panic and fear. Blood. There would also be blood.

'Abs? I said I think you'd like New York,' Rohan said, and I realized I hadn't been listening to a word he was saying. 'Why don't you come back with me? What do you think?'

I flattened my lips and shook my head. 'I can't... I'm sorry. I just need to finish what I'm doing.'

'You could paint there. As I said, I have amazing views from the apartment, and I'm so close to all the galleries. God, you should see how the river changes colour as the sun comes up. It's beautiful.'

I closed my eyes with a little laugh. He just didn't get it. I couldn't paint anywhere outside our house; outside my attic. The force for these paintings came from there, and Grace was a part of it. What would I paint in America? What would flow into my soul over there? A big blank.

'I'm not painting a river.' I picked a little at my food, pushing it about the plate.

'Are you okay? Are you tired? Do you want to go home?' Rohan asked when the silence had stretched too far. 'We can get this boxed up.'

'No, I'm fine.' I took a bite of food. 'It's fine.'

Rohan sighed and put his fork down. 'Abs, what's bothering you because... I can't get through to you. I've been so excited to come back and see you. I've been counting the days but it's as if you just don't care. This is supposed to be date night, for Christ's sake, but...' He shrugged and sat back in his seat. 'What's the point?'

'I'm sorry. I'm just...'

'Just what?'

I gave a little laugh. 'It's just… "date night". It's such a cliché. So parochial. Middle-aged. Grace would die laughing if she could see us doing this.'

'It's not so bad,' Rohan said. 'It gets us out together, and that's a good thing, right?'

'It's forced romance,' I scoffed. 'As if you can force romance. Like, everyone here probably sees us and thinks: oh, he's brought his wife here to get her "in the mood" – they'll have their perfunctory once-a-week marital shag when they get home. Grace wouldn't be seen dead on a date night,' I snorted. 'It's ridiculous when you think about it. Isn't it?'

Rohan was looking at me in a way I'd never seen before. 'I'll get this packed to go,' he said.

Forty

As if determined to prove Grace right, I made a move on Rohan when we got home. We'd walked down Albert Road in silence, the weight of his disappointment lying on me like a lead blanket. I was a failure, useless, a disappointment to my husband.

Inside the house, he went straight to the kitchen to put the food in the fridge while I took off my coat slowly in the hallway then, when he came back out, I slid my arms around his ribs, pushed myself up against him and kissed him, lightly at first but then harder, but he remained impassive, his lips rigidly closed under mine; his hands resolutely by his side.

I stepped back with a sigh of frustration; failed again. Pathetic. 'I'm really sorry about dinner.'

Rohan ran a hand through his hair and I saw now that he looked shattered, his eyes small, and ringed by dark circles, his skin feathered with fine lines and I remembered that, of course, he'd flown overnight from New York.

'We're both tired,' he said. 'You're right. We shouldn't have tried to "force romance" tonight. Let's just go to bed. Tomorrow's another day.'

'Okay,' I said. 'Agreed. Tomorrow's another day, and it will be better.' I pushed down the thought of the family lunch I'd have to endure. 'Thank you. And darling? I'm glad you're back.'

Rohan raised an eyebrow then turned to fetch himself a glass of water. 'Still doing your checks?' I nodded. 'I might not be awake by the time you come up, so good night,' he said and went on up the stairs while I pulled out a chair at the kitchen table and let my head fall into my hands. How had the date gone so wrong? I felt as if Rohan and I had been struggling all day for a way to reconnect; each of us scrabbling to strengthen the bonds that held us together; scrabbling but failing. I had the sense that the ties of our marriage were loosening; that they'd stretched until I was floating, barely tethered, in orbit around Rohan, lost, and failing to make contact.

It was easy to blame him for taking the job in New York, but was this actually my fault? He'd said how much he'd been looking forward to coming back and I could even picture him on the plane as it hurtled towards London, whisky in hand, knee jiggling with excitement. I could see him telling the check-in staff that he was flying back to see his wife whom he hadn't seen for way too long; I could see their indulgent smiles. Rohan wore his emotions like a dog: if he was happy, if he was excited, everyone knew it.

And, in contrast, I hadn't even realized what time he was due back, let alone heard him arrive. Any decent wife would have been waiting – my insides shrivelled with shame when I remembered how I'd waited on the stairs for Grace's arrival – or even gone to the airport to meet their husband. A part of me that I didn't want to acknowledge could picture Rohan scanning the Arrivals hall for the sight of me there to greet him; of my face lighting up when I saw him, tired and crumpled, for the first time in weeks.

But I was painting, I told myself. I mustn't forget that. I was deep inside my head, lost in the inner world in which I saw things on the canvas of my soul. Day-to-day things suffered. It was just how it was. I had to tell myself that because to consider the alternative – that Rohan and I had little to say to each other after just four weeks apart – was too awful to bear.

I looked despondently around my fabulous new 'show' kitchen – the kitchen that stuck out from the house like a sore thumb for its modernity and that looked – at the moment – in a worse state than any student kitchen. As I stared at the grease marks and splotches on the pristine counters, I knew exactly what I could do to make amends – at least, to show willing. I would clean, not just the kitchen but the whole house.

I started with the bins, emptying them all and bagging up the rubbish, and that alone gave me a sense of release, as if the rubbish itself had been weighing me down. I loaded and ran the dishwasher, washed all the things that wouldn't fit into it by hand. I cleaned the counters, emptied the fridge of everything that was stale or mouldy. I cleaned inside the fridge, taking out each shelf and wiping it; I cleaned the inside of the microwave and then I mopped the kitchen floor with bleach that cut through the stickiness I hadn't noticed till now. I squirted green stuff down the loos, wiped the sinks and mopped the bathroom floor, and then I gave the vacuum cleaner a run-around downstairs. Rohan was a deep sleeper – I knew it wouldn't bother him even without the jetlag.

And, all the while I worked, I imagined I could feel the house appreciating it, purring under my hands, breathing its thanks to me, but my mind was on Grace and how things spiralled out of control with her last time – the time she took Tom from me. I'd shown a chink in my armour and she'd wriggled her way in and taken what should have been mine. Rohan already thought she was cute; it stung that he thought she was 'amazing' for saving lives.

Painting just couldn't compete. It was solo and self-indulgent. It helped no one, not even those who bought my art at the galleries. They hung it on the wall and then what? They got so used to it they barely noticed it? They showed it off to their friends at dinner parties? And it's not as if I had the volunteer job to salve my conscience anymore.

Yeah, that.

By the time I was done with the house, I'd resolved, again, to be stronger with Grace. I sat at the table and drew up a housework rota. From now on, she would do her share. I was an adult. I was strong. There would be no chinks this time. Rota done, I opened the back door to put the rubbish out and screamed: lying there, dead in a pool of shiny black blood, was Alfie.

Forty-one

His head lay at an unnatural angle, his front paws were curled as if he'd been trying to run and his mouth yawned open in a silent scream. Across his beautiful silver neck, a tell-tale line of dark-red blood showed that his throat had been slit. I swallowed down the bile that rose into my own throat. There was no need to touch him: there was nothing I could do for him now.

'Alfie,' I murmured, as tears sprang from nowhere. 'My darling Alfie. My poor baby. I'm so sorry.'

Still, I bent to touch his side and stroked the softness of the fur that wasn't matted with blood. No purr met my hand. He didn't arch against me the way he always did. His body was stiff and cold, a stuffed toy; not my Alfie. I turned and dashed up the stairs to wake Rohan. He was fast asleep, snoring loudly.

'Ro,' I whispered. He didn't stir.

'Ro!' Louder this time, but still nothing. I touched his upper arm and he moved against it in his sleep, as if shaking off a fly.

'Darling!' Then, as my eyes adjusted to the dark, I saw his jar of melatonin capsules on the bedside. Of course. He'd have taken something for the jet lag. I'd have to deal with Alfie alone.

Back in the kitchen, I found an old towel and a pair of rubber gloves then, gingerly, I picked up the cat's body, and wrapped it in the towel, wishing with all my heart that Rohan were here to take control – to dig the hole and bury the cat; to say a few words with his arm around me; to give me a squeeze and tell me everything would be okay.

What had happened to Alfie? Who'd done this?

I found the spade in the garden shed, located a spot under the oak tree and started to dig a little grave. In the distance, a dog barked – someone else's pet, alive, warm and well, its heart still beating. The spade sliced through the soil; through earthworms and grass roots. How deep did this have to be anyway? I didn't want the squirrels digging Alfie up by accident. Soon I was sweating with exertion and I straightened up to unzip my jacket and wipe my forehead. The oak tree branches swayed and the clouds broke, giving me a racing glimpse of the moon. I dragged the towel containing Alfie's body to the hole and lowered it gently in. I had no flowers, but I closed my eyes and clasped my hands together.

'Rest in peace, darling Alfie. I love you.'

Then I shovelled the soil back over the body, using my feet to stamp it down once it was levelled. I'd make a cross or something from some sticks in the morning.

But who would kill a cat? So brutally? Yes, it was Hallowe'en and the neighbourhood kids were out and about more than usual. Yes, those kids were thinking about ghosts and ghouls and death and horror, but I doubted very much that they were responsible for this. In my mind there was only one suspect.

'Don't you like cats?'

'No. But it's mutual.'

Transcript of interview with Mr Rohan Allerton, husband of Abigail Allerton: 20 December 2019

'What did happen with the cat?'

'Oh God. It was awful. He was a gorgeous little thing. His throat was slit. Abi found him one night.' [sighs] 'He was her cat. She really loved him.'

'How did she take it?'

'She was calm. Just dealt with it.'

'Did you ever find out who did it?'

'No. At first I thought it was kids from the local neighbourhood. You know how it is. Group bravado, or a prank gone wrong. I don't know. But then Abi admitted, a long time later, that she thought it was Grace. Apparently, Alfie – the cat – used to miaow outside Grace's room at night, which really annoyed her. And then there was a time when Grace had locked the cat in the bathroom. [pauses] Apparently cats didn't like her.'

'Grace?'

'Yes. Grace.'

Forty-two

'Oh my God! Abi!' Rohan shook me, his hand clawing at my upper arm and I jerked awake, not sure where I was; I'd fallen into bed around half past two and slept like the dead. The country road of my usual nightmare was printed on my eyelids, the birds in my head were singing, the wildflowers were as bright as ever, but, when I opened my eyes, there was no disaster, no horror: just the curtains, our bedroom, and Rohan holding his phone as if he'd read that the world had ended. Inside my chest, a knot of grief: Alfie.

'What? What's up? What time is it?' I rubbed at my eyes.

'It's Mum,' Rohan said and my heart lurched. The only thing that could be worse than Meena interfering in my life would be Meena unable to interfere in my life. I couldn't imagine the drama, the chaos that an illness or – God forbid – her death would cause.

'What about her? Is she okay?'

'Yeah. She's fine.' I sagged with relief. 'But that lunch? Today? She wants to do it here.' Rohan moaned and ran his hand through his hair. Even I knew there was no possibility of us refusing. If Meena wanted to come over, Meena came over.

'Abs,' Rohan said. 'We have to clean the house, like, NOW!'

'It's okay,' I said. 'It's done. I stayed up last night and cleaned it to a state that even your mum will approve of.' I hesitated, ready to tell him about Alfie, but Rohan interrupted.

'Are you serious?'

'Yes! The only thing I didn't do was vacuum upstairs because I didn't want to wake you, but downstairs looks like a show home, even if I do say so myself.' *I even buried Alfie.*

Rohan reached out an arm and pulled me against him, covering my face in big, sloppy kisses. 'You star. You absolute star. I didn't hear a thing.'

'You were dead to the world. And I'm sorry about last night. What I said about date night. I didn't mean it. I like date night. I like going on dates with you.'

'I know. It's okay. We were both tired. I do love you, you know.'

'I love you too.'

He pulled me closer to him and I basked in the familiarity of the way our bodies fit together, and then the reality of what was going to happen later permeated my consciousness. I pulled back sharply.

'Hang on. So they're coming over, but who's cooking? Am I expected to pull lunch together?'

Rohan sniggered and kissed my nose. 'Oh, ye innocent. Can you imagine my mother not cooking?'

'So she's going to come to ours and take over the kitchen?'

'Sorry, baby,' said Rohan. 'You know how she is. And, umm, she's invited Mili, Jay and Sofia too.'

'Great,' I said without expression; with the Allerton Circus in town, I'd be lucky to get any painting done at all, let alone tell Rohan what happened to Alfie.

*

Meena and Clive arrived just before twelve. Rohan and I had been hovering for the previous half hour, unsettled like birds before a storm.

'Showtime,' he said, rubbing his hands together when we finally saw the car draw up and my in-laws spill out onto the pavement. The nip of vodka I'd had for Dutch courage was sour on my tongue.

'Ronu! *Beta!*' Meena said, making a beeline for Rohan and enveloping him in a hug before pushing him back to arm's length so she could drink him in from top to toe while I dithered in the background. Behind her, Clive picked his way up the path laden with Waitrose Bags for Life. His jeans were well ironed and his grey-and-white trainers were too retro to be cool. He'd missed a patch of stubble at the corner of his mouth when shaving, the salt-and-pepper bristles a contrast to the smooth pink skin of the rest of his face. I moved around Rohan and Meena to take the bags from my father-in-law.

'There's more,' he said, rolling his eyes towards the car and making his way back down the path. When everyone was inside the house, all the bags and tubs stashed in the kitchen, Meena turned her attention to me.

'You shouldn't do dieting, Abigail,' she said as she gave me 50 per cent of the hug Rohan had had, brushing her cheek against mine and wrapping me in the familiar smells of fenugreek, cumin, popped mustard seeds and deep-fat frying. She pinched my cheek with yellow fingertips that smelled of fresh onion and gave me the hope that she'd at least pre-prepared some of the lunch. My stomach rumbled. 'You're too thin. How are you? The salt worked?'

'I'm good, thanks,' I said but my reply was lost as Rohan said,

'Salt? What salt? Mum...?' He looked from Meena to me and back. I opened my mouth but Meena said, 'For the spirits, *beta*. Like *nannima* used to do. Remember? But, look, Mili will be here any minute. I need to get started. We'll talk about it later.'

She rubbed her hands together and led the way to the kitchen. Rohan looked at me and licked his lips; when it came to his mum's cooking, he was like one of Pavlov's dogs. Meena pointed to three large Tupperware tubs on the table.

'*Samosas, aloo vadas* and *pakoras*. These I cooked at home.'

Rohan ripped the lid off one of the boxes and stuffed a *samosa* into his mouth. 'Delicious.'

'Ronu! Plate! And put the chutneys into dishes!' Meena snapped. She was already tying on an apron and pulling out pans. As she clattered about, I swiped a *pakora* and then a *vada*. They were still warm, and better than anything you'd get from a restaurant.

'So, how are you, Abigail?' Meena said.

'Good.'

'Where's Dad gone?' Rohan asked.

'For a walk. His BP is a little raised – nothing to worry about. Doctor told him he should take some exercise every day so he's walking around the block. Does Abigail look thin to you, Ronu?'

I widened my eyes at Rohan and coughed to make the point that I was in fact present in the room.

'New York's great, thanks for asking,' Rohan said, winking at me. 'The work's hard, but I'm loving living in the city. Can I help you with anything?'

'Nay. Good, *beta*. Do you think she's okay? I mean, I've been worried. Look at her. So gaunt. Just skin and bone. Losing her memory, too.'

'The apartment's fantastic. It's got a pool and amazing views of the river.'

Meena turned to Rohan then, her hands on her hips. 'Ronu, why don't you want to talk about Abigail? Is there something you're both not telling me?' Hope flashed in her eyes. 'Is it morning sickness? Like that Kate Middleton when she had to go on bed rest?' Finally she turned to me. 'Is that why you're so thin? You're vomiting?'

'Mum,' Rohan said. 'Abi's not pregnant. If she were, you'd be the first to know. And it's not that I don't want to talk about her. It's just that there's nothing to say. She's working. Aren't you, darling?' I nodded. 'She has an exhibition coming up. She's an artist. It's not like working in an office. She gets consumed by her work. It takes her over. And yes, sometimes, she forgets about pedestrian things like eating and sleeping so, if she looks a little tired or a little thin, that'll be why. Right?' I nodded again. 'And it's fine,' Rohan said, 'because once she's finished, she'll have an amazing exhibition and then she'll get back on track.'

'I will,' I said, feeling as if I was making a promise to Meena.

'We just need to give her the space she needs to do her "thang",' Rohan said, sticking his tongue out and making peace signs like an ageing hippie. 'Okay?'

I nodded again and took another *pakora*, as if to prove the point that I wasn't on a diet. In the background, I heard the front door open, then the sound of Mili's voice talking to my father-in-law. *Thank God.*

'Do you think Abigail's got thinner?' Meena asked the moment Mili walked into the kitchen.

'Mother! Leave her alone!' Mili tutted as she gave me a hug. She was wrapped, as always, in a cloud of her signature Oud perfume. 'Yo, Brohan,' she said, hugging Rohan. 'Good to see you. Jay sends his apologies. He's taking Sofia to a birthday party.'

Clive came in then. No hugs from him. It wasn't his thing. He nodded at everyone and pulled out a chair at the kitchen table, and we all sat down, chatting and helping ourselves to snacks until Meena handed us dishes to carry through to the dining room. I thought I'd got through the worst of it then, but no.

Mili and I shared a bottle of white wine with lunch. It was nothing to me, but she drank slowly, clearly unused to daytime drinking. Before I knew it, the bottle was empty, and I was getting up to fetch another.

'So, tell me about the salt,' Rohan said to his mum, apropos of nothing. 'What brought that on – or am I better off not knowing?' He laughed. 'Can you pass the kebabs? These are delicious.'

Mili raised a hand and waved it while she finished her mouthful. 'Oh, it's a good one. You have to hear it.' Her voice implied she was highly amused by what was to come next. She paused to check everyone was listening. 'Mum thinks your house is haunted and – get this – that Abi's been possessed.'

I almost spluttered my wine: *me, possessed?* She hadn't said that to my face.

Rohan snorted. 'Oh, please. The only thing my wife has been possessed with is artistic inspiration.'

'Mum thinks it's a bad spirit! *Whoo-whoo!*' Mili said, waving her hands about. Clive concentrated on his food. Mili's cheeks were flushed and she was biting her lip as if trying not to laugh;

Meena rested her chin on her hand and looked steadily at Rohan. I squirmed.

'Don't you go pretending you don't know what I mean,' Meena said, waving a finger at Rohan. 'You know exactly what I think about old houses. Who knows what energy is trapped here? Oh, don't look at me like that, Rohan. You said yourself the cat would never go up to the attic. And Abigail's alone up there all day, her heart and mind open to the universe...'

Rohan rolled his eyes. 'I wish I'd never asked. Mum, you should write a Bollywood movie because, seriously, you have a brilliant imagination.'

'Well, maybe I will.' Meena folded her arms. 'There's always been a feel about this house. You know I told you that the first time I saw it.'

I looked at Clive for support but he raised a palm and shook his head: *keep me out of this.*

'Have you told Ronu what you want to do?' Mili asked. She sucked in her cheeks and played with the edging of the tablecloth – a picture of innocence – and Rohan glowered at his mother.

'What do you want to do? Aside from the salt that you've already thrown around my house.'

Meena had the grace to look a little embarrassed. 'Just some mustard seeds, *beta*, to ward off evil spirits.'

'*Whoo!* I'm a ghost! I'm scared of mustard seeds!' said Mili, flapping her arms.

'Seriously?' Rohan said to his mum. 'Do I need to get my key back off you?'

Meena wrung her hands together. 'Don't be like that.' She paused. 'I'd really like to cleanse the house's energy, too – just a simple thing, nothing whacky... Oh, Rohan, indulge your mother, please — it would make me feel better... I'm just worried about Abigail, that's all. With you away and her alone... especially if she might soon be expecting.' She paused; her mind having lit upon her other pet topic. Her head tilted sideways as she looked at Rohan. 'Speaking of which, did you call the Harley Street doctor?'

I started to clear the plates.

Transcript of interview with Mr Rohan Allerton, husband of Abigail Allerton: 20 December 2019

'You mentioned in passing that your mother is quite intuitive? Did she notice any changes in Abigail over this period? Any that she mentioned?'

'*Pff.* The same as me, I guess. That she looked pale and had lost weight.'

'I see. Did she have any thoughts on what could have caused this?'

[Sighs] 'My mother is very superstitious. We humour her, but we don't take her very seriously.' [pauses] 'She blamed the house.'

'The house?'

'Yes. It's an old house – Victorian. My mother was – is – convinced that energy remains in old houses unless you take steps to remove it. She felt that our house was full of negative energy and that this was quite possibly the cause of the problems Abi was having. Apparently it was worse because Abi was there alone, without me to protect her. Though God knows how I would have done that because I really don't see myself as someone who can ward off evil spirits.' [laughs]

'And what did you think of that theory?'

[Laughs] 'What do you think? I thought it was ridiculous.

Abi was just working really hard. She hardly ever went out, let alone did any exercise. She drank way too much alcohol. Of course that was going to have an effect on her.'

'And did that bother you?'

'Grace was there. And it was only a temporary phase. Only until she finished the paintings. Then everything would get back on track. So, of course I was concerned, but not overly. I'm not a worrier.'

Forty-three

Given the Allertons talked about me even when I was present, and especially given what had gone on at lunch, I had no qualms excusing myself the moment we'd finished dessert, claiming I had to work. Which I did. But the wine and rich food had had an effect, and my eyes were heavy. I cleared the mess off the small sofa in the attic, flopped down onto it and let my mind drift.

Within moments I was standing on a beach, not unlike the one I'd seen on Grace's Instagram, but, as I stood there breathing in the fresh sea air, absorbing the sight of the dunes and feeling the wind in my hair, I realized something was missing: I couldn't hear the swoosh and crash of the waves. I turned to face the ocean only to see that the water had been sucked out further than I could see, and that the sand I stood on was waterlogged; dark sand that was never usually exposed to the sun. It was littered with the carcasses of dying fish.

With a sense of dread in my stomach, I scanned the horizon for the first sight of the tsunami I knew must be coming. It wasn't too late to run to higher ground, but would I? Or would I stand still and face it? Let it slam into me, roar over me and decimate me? What would I do when faced with the tower of the wave?

*

Every day since I'd found out about Grace and Tom, I waited for them to tell me. But as the days ticked by, it became clear that she intended not only to take him, but not even to bother telling me, and something started to grow inside me: courage, maybe, as well as anger. Even now, the anger courses through me when I remember how she treated me; what disdain she had for me while living for free in my home. It was as if all the hurt and the frustration of the previous five years suddenly piled up: the barbed comments, the way she walked all over me, the passive-aggression dressed up as concern. The way she assumed I wanted her in my life; the way she assumed I should be grateful to her for saving my life all those years ago; the fact that she clearly thought I still owed her. Even a criminal does time and is then released, but it seemed I could never escape Grace. She was a ball and chain around my ankle, dragging me back, dragging me down.

I recalled now the thud of trepidation I'd begun to feel when I heard her shoes skip down those steps to our flat in the evenings; the cloying sense of suffocation as I heard her key turn in the lock. I'd tossed and turned at night, wrestling up the strength to claim my life back from her: Grace, my power source, my supporter, my friend, my master, my tormentor, my enemy.

It had taken a fortitude I hadn't known I had to ask her about Tom and, when I saw her hesitate – when I saw her face flicker as she considered lying – something exploded inside me. I could no longer contain myself.

'Get out! Get out of my flat and get out of my life!' I'd screamed at her because, in that moment, I actually wanted to kill her. I could picture myself with my hands around her neck, throttling her until her eyes bulged and her lips turned blue.

Grace's mouth fell open and then she'd smiled; a slow, sick

smile. It was far worse than I'd imagined, the hundred times I'd rehearsed it in my head.

'You're kicking me out?' she laughed, entitlement dripping off her like oil. 'As if you would! After all I've done for you?'

'So help me, God, get out now or I cannot be responsible for my actions,' I'd said stepping quietly toward the knife drawer, and that had rattled her.

She shoved her chair back, the legs scraping across the kitchen floor. I followed her to her bedroom door and watched as her arms windmilled things into a bag, grabbing wildly at anything within reach – my things included – then she stalked through the flat without looking back, and slammed the door behind her, leaving me standing, stunned, in the sudden silence. That was the last time I saw her until she came back from Australia.

I saw the Allertons leave as I looked down on the street from the attic window. Their family goodbyes took at least twenty minutes. It was something I never understood. Say goodbye, then go. But no. If you were an Allerton you said goodbye inside the house, then you all trooped outside together, weather permitting, and you had another chat, then you said goodbye again, had a hug, chatted a bit more, had another hug, then stood there waving the car off. Mili was the first to go, in a cab, while Clive waited in the driver's seat for Meena to let go of Rohan. As the blue Mercedes drove off, I turned back to my easel and it was only then I was able to start painting once more.

The light was fading when I finally put down my brush. I was almost finished with the sixth portrait and I knew in my bones that it was good – the best thing I'd painted so far. After I cleaned my brushes, I stepped back to take in the full horror of it and shuddered. It was perfect.

Forty-four

There was a spring in my step as I locked the attic door and went down in search of Rohan. All in all, I was pleased with the way I'd handled myself today. The lunch could so easily have gone wrong, especially with Meena seemingly hellbent on getting a rise from me. I was sure she didn't mean it maliciously – sure she didn't deliberately rile me – but even so...

I stopped on the landing. The door to Grace's room was ajar when I was sure it had been left closed. I was barefoot and made no sound as I approached, which is presumably why Rohan had no time to stop what he was doing. I stood in the doorway and watched in disbelief as he rifled through Grace's wardrobe, touching and feeling the garments. His hand passed over the musty children's clothes but stopped on one of Grace's new blouses. He pulled it out, examined it, brought it to his nose and sniffed it.

'What the hell are you doing?'

Rohan turned as if he'd been scalded, his face a picture of guilt as he froze, still holding the blouse.

'It's not what it looks like!' he said quickly. 'I'm not being a perv, I swear. It's just...'

'Just what? You go around sniffing other women's clothes?'

Anger came down on me like the rust-red curtains of a theatre:

thick, heavy and dark, spilling over everything, oozing into every crack inside me, sliding around my organs and firing up my heart. 'Going through her wardrobe! Sniffing her clothes! That's not normal!' I shouted. 'Not in any way is that normal! What the *fuck* are you playing at?'

Rohan's mouth was open but no words came.

'I can't think of a single reason why you're in this room, let alone looking through Grace's wardrobe!' I yelled. 'Get out! Now!'

'I just...' Rohan paled. 'And why is it full of kids' clothes anyway? And those toys? They're so creepy. Did Grace put them there?'

'Get. Out. Now. Get out!' I yelled when Rohan still didn't move. Then he quickly put the blouse back, closed the wardrobe and raised his hands in surrender, a soldier going over the top. I waited as he edged across the room and past me, then I pulled the door closed and followed him down the stairs.

'What were you doing in there?' My voice was icy. 'Don't you think our guest deserves her privacy?'

'Abs, it was nothing like that, I swear. I just found some things on the credit card statement that didn't add up and...'

'And what?'

'Well, I just... I don't know.' He sighed and ran his hand through his hair. 'Look. I saw some packaging in the bin from Hobbs and it was Hobbs on the credit card bill. I couldn't see anything that might match it in your wardrobe, so I thought I'd check hers...'

'And what did you find?'

'Well, she seemed to have new clothes from Hobbs, so...' he shrugged.

'Didn't you think to ask me?' I said. 'Instead of going through her wardrobe and sniffing her clothes?'

'You were painting…'

'Not anymore!' I shouted.

Rohan flung his hands up. 'I didn't know that, did I?' His voice dropped a tone. 'Please don't be unreasonable.'

'Me? Unreasonable? I think you're the one being unreasonable! Imagine if Grace knew you were going through her things! *Smelling* her clothes!'

'Look. Okay. I'm sorry. All right? I shouldn't have done it. I just wanted to know if they were new.' Rohan put his hands on his hips and his nostrils flared. I could see this was far from over. 'So, are you going to tell me what's going on with the kids' stuff? What the fuck's going on?'

'Nice dodge.'

'Okay,' Rohan said. 'How about why you bought clothes for Grace. Can you tell me that?'

I shrugged. 'She needed them. She didn't have any work clothes.'

'She's going to pay you back, I assume?'

'She hasn't a chance to save much money at the moment.'

'So… they're a gift? Is that what you're saying?'

'She's a friend. It was the least I could do to help her get back on her feet.'

Rohan took a deep breath and let it out as he pinched the bridge of his nose. 'Jesus, Abs. I know I earn a good salary, but I'm supporting both of us, paying the mortgage and the bills, flying to and from New York to see you, *and* trying to save for the future as well – for our children.'

I rolled my eyes. 'Oh, here comes the emotional blackmail.'

'Look, Abs,' Rohan said. 'All I'm saying is there's helping, and then there's giving someone free board and lodging, and buying them a new wardrobe. Grace's been here several weeks already. When's she going to start standing on her own two feet? Has she even looked for a flat yet? If you make it too cushy here, she's never going to want to leave.'

'You sound like you want her to leave,' I said. 'You disappear off to New York and then want my friend, *who's keeping me company*, to move out. Charming.'

Rohan threw his arms in the air. 'For God's sake! Don't be so ridiculous!' He picked up some of the mail that he'd stacked on the hall table. 'How long's she planning on staying? Have you asked her? Because this post is for her. She's having her mail sent here. That's not the action of someone who's planning to move out.'

'Where else is she supposed to send it? She doesn't have an address in the UK yet and her parents are dead, if you remember.'

Rohan stared at me. 'I'm just worried, that's all. She's staying here rent-free. She's not helping around the house. She's not con-tributing to the grocery bills, yet she's getting her mail delivered here and now you're buying her new clothes – not just any clothes, but from Hobbs! For God's sake, Abs.' He paced the hallway with his hands linked behind his head, then he turned to face me. 'Is everything okay with her here?'

I shrugged. 'Why wouldn't it be?'

'I just wonder. Because I'm getting the feeling she's using you. And I know how sweet and kind you can be. Sometimes people take advantage of you.' He put a hand in the air to stop me inter-rupting. 'You know it's true. So, do you actually like her being here? Because from what I see, I'm not so sure.'

'It's not as if I see so much of her,' I said. 'She's at work all day. But it's nice to have company. Of course it is.'

Rohan narrowed his eyes. 'You've changed, Abs. Since she's arrived, you've changed. And I don't like it. I don't like it one bit.'

My mouth fell open. 'Can I remind you that you're the one who's been away living it up in New York? Maybe it's you who's changed. Maybe I've always been like this.'

'And anyway,' Rohan continued as if I hadn't spoken, 'the least she could have done was to be here. I'm paying for her life at the moment — it would have been nice if she could have stayed to say hello.'

'Oh my God,' I said. 'You want her to grovel at your feet? Jesus, Rohan, take a look at yourself. What kind of God complex do you have? I told her to go. I wanted you all to myself this weekend.' Tears pricked at my eyes. 'Fat lot of good that's done. I needn't have bothered!' I turned and stormed back up the stairs.

'Abi!' Rohan shouted. 'Don't be so ridiculous! Come back here now!'

I didn't. And neither did he come after me.

Forty-five

I stormed up to the attic, my feet thumping extra hard on every stair, anger still buzzing in my head. How dare he swan off to New York and then complain about how I live my life while he's away? That was the thing about Rohan: yes, he was understanding, sensitive, in touch with his feminine side and all that stuff, but he was also arrogant, and that side of him was rigid. My husband – like his mother – was never wrong. Yes, it was Rohan's way or no way and, as long as I wanted what he did, things were fine. But when my view differed from his, things became bumpy. I might have my issues with Grace, but how dare he criticize her?

I thumped about in the bedroom, using my anger to tidy it. I picked up a dirty shirt, balled it up and flung it across the room with all my energy. It hit the wall with an unsatisfying flop.

'How dare you? You've never even met her!' I yelled.

I picked up more clothes, scrunched them into balls and flung them after the shirt, then I picked up Rohan's slipper and hurled it at the wall followed by the other one. 'It's all right for you, living in your fancy flat in New York but I'm not allowed to have a life of my own!' I yelled. 'You want me to put my life on hold because you're not here? Well, fuck that!'

There was a small knock at the door, then Rohan stuck his head around. 'Have you seen Alfie, by the way? I can't find him anywhere.'

'Piss off!' I yelled. His eyes widened but his head disappeared, and the door closed softly behind him. I continued venting my anger on the room until I was spent, then I threw myself down on the bed, hating myself because a thought had started to push its way into my head and I knew it was true: Grace wasn't even here and she was getting between us. Here Rohan was, home from New York for three nights just to see me, and all we'd done was fight. We'd had a miserable date night, and we'd fought today. It was as if Grace had become a thing between us, solid and unyielding, a barrier that was preventing Rohan and I from enjoying our weekend together. I knew where this would lead: if I wasn't careful, we would never be free of Grace. She was entwining herself into our lives like the roots of a tree that grow under, around and into the very foundation of the house, working their way inside via the pipes, blocking the water supply and cracking the walls.

If things were to be okay with Rohan, I needed to be stronger with her. I needed to push her out of my head and focus on my husband and on our weekend together, before it was completely ruined.

I slunk up to the attic and stared at my paintings lined up on the floor. They were shocking and horrific and incredible, all at the same time. I could feel in my heart that they were exceptional; that they would sell. Probably the whole set would go to one collector. Maybe there'd even be an auction. And, while I still had three or four more to do, I knew that if I didn't want to risk losing another man I loved because of Grace, I needed to do something about her. Rohan, as usual, was right. Grace *was* walking all over me.

Again.

Why was I even defending her?

I had to handle her better this time. I had to make sure that, when she went, she would never come back. If there was one thing I'd learned about my friendship with Grace, it was that it would never change. It was a rollercoaster ride: it went up, it went down, it went left and it went right, but it always ended up in the same place. The power was too skewed; the friendship poisonous. I'd reached out and given her a second chance and what was happening? The exact same as before.

I opened my laptop and searched 'how to deal with a toxic friendship'.

Guard your boundaries. Realize it's okay to go your separate ways. Don't wait for an apology – ha! Let yourself move on. Plan an exit strategy.

Good stuff, but how exactly? *Sit down and talk to them*, said one article. I pictured myself sitting with Grace having a civilized discussion over some nibbles about why I no longer wanted her in my life – and snorted out loud. Seriously? She was such a skilled manipulator; she would tie me in knots and throw my words back at me like a razor-sharp boomerang. I knew she would.

Write an email. No. Slowly make yourself less and less available – aka ghost her. But she was living in my house... cut ties abruptly, once and for all, and be prepared for retaliation.

Forty-six

I poked my head into the living room. Rohan was on the sofa, the remote in his hand as he flicked channels.

'Do you fancy giving date night another try?' I asked, giving him a smile.

He looked back at me, assessing my mood, I suppose, then his face softened. 'Come here,' he said, patting the sofa next to me. He opened out his arm so I could snuggle up next to him, breathing in all the smells I associated with everything good about my husband: the scent of his deodorant, of his aftershave, his skin, our laundry detergent. The scent of home. I wasn't going to let Grace take this away from me.

'I'm really sorry,' I said to his armpit. 'Again.'

He let the silence stretch, long enough for me to feel a jolt of doubt – maybe he wouldn't forgive me? – then he said, 'It's okay,' and gave me a squeeze. 'But I'm worried about you, Abs. When I said you'd lost weight I didn't mean in a good way.'

'Oh, here we go,' I said, stiffening. 'You and your mum...'

Rohan stroked my hand. 'Don't be defensive. I love you. I'm just worried about you, that's all. You look so hollow; so fragile.' He paused. 'What does Grace say? She's a doctor, right?'

I shrugged. 'She hasn't said anything.'

'She must notice how thin you are.'

'Not that she's said. But,' and I squeezed Rohan's hand, 'if you think I look thin, you know the answer to that: take me out and feed me.'

'So… date night? Again?' Rohan said with a small smile. 'Really? I thought you hated it. I thought Grace said it was "middle-aged" and "parochial"? I thought she would "die laughing" if she knew we went on date nights? Hmm?' He pressed his lips together trying not to laugh.

'Yeah… but…'

'How about we just "go out for dinner"?' he said. 'If you're in the mood for it. Because if you're not, we can get a takeaway and "Netflix 'n' Chill".' He licked his lips lasciviously and it made me laugh.

'Okay, dinner out it is,' I said.

We went to Ti Amo's. Just down the High Street from Mr Ho's, it was a good choice: it was where we'd eaten on the first night we'd moved into the house, when the dusty old living room was a sea of boxes and we couldn't be bothered to find the plates. We'd walked up the road with our arms around each other that night, giddy with the excitement of finally owning our own home, and in such a nice area, too. We'd clasped hands across the table and fed each other morsels of aged Parmesan cheese and *grissini* while we'd waited in the flickering candlelight for the food to come. We'd licked our lips and gloated about our good fortune to have found the house on Albert Road. We reminisced as we walked there tonight.

'I'm glad you remember that too,' Rohan said. 'Sometimes I wonder. I feel as if I'm the keeper of memories in this marriage, while you hurtle through life from day to day.'

'Excuse me, but I paint! What's that if not recording stuff on a canvas?'

Rohan tutted. 'That's not what I meant. Look, I know people say to live in the present, but you – God – you never look back; you're never interested in wallowing in memories with me or spending an evening going through photos.'

'That's because life's for living!' I said, and ran ahead of him to the door.

Ti Amo's was a bit of a cliché, with waiters dressed in Breton tops, red-checked tablecloths and candles that dripped wax down the sides of straw-clad Chianti bottles. The same skinny Polish waiter had worked there the entire time we'd known the place and, every time he repeated back our order, I had to stifle a giggle because he always looked as if he was about to burst into song like the gondoliers we'd seen at The Venetian in Vegas. The food was good, though – authentic and generously portioned – and I liked that it wasn't a chain. There were only about ten tables in the place so it was intimate, too. Romantic, for the High Street.

We took our places by the window, which afforded a great view of the bus shelter, where groups of youths – age indeterminate – seemed to gather after dark to vape and kick about discarded burger boxes. I wondered what they made of us, sitting together with the candle between us; the silhouette of a couple out for a romantic meal – if they noticed us at all – then I shut that thought down before it looped back to Grace, and her scathing thoughts about date night.

'By the way, Moira called while you were upstairs,' Rohan said mildly. I forced my hand to carry on with what it was doing: dipping the breadstick in the balsamic vinegar and oil I'd poured, swirling it about and guiding it to my mouth.

'Oh?' I said.

'She wanted to ask "how you were".' He said it in quote marks.

'Okay…' I held Rohan's gaze.

'Abi, is there something you want to tell me?'

I closed my eyes while I tried to frame what I had to say. 'Everything's fine. I'm just taking a break from the hospice at the moment.' Rohan waited for me to say more. 'The painting was consuming me. I wasn't as reliable as I needed to be. It's an important job. I have responsibilities.'

'Is that all it was?' Rohan scratched his ear.

'Yeah. Sometimes I probably looked a bit rough. If I'd pulled an all-nighter. Which I often did.' I didn't mention the times I'd woken up on the attic floor, having passed out through alcohol.

'Presumably drinking?' Rohan said.

I moved my head this way and that. 'A bit.'

Rohan nodded slowly. 'So everything's fine? You're just "on a break"? That's all it is?'

'Uh-huh. Moira's a nurse. It's her job to worry about people.'

'But she doesn't need to worry about you?'

'No.'

'And neither do I?'

'No.'

'Okay,' he said way too mildly. 'If you say so.'

Thankfully the waiter appeared then with our selection of small-plate starters balanced up his arms in a way that defied gravity. He indicated with a flick of his eyebrows and a grunt that we should make space on the table, then flung the dishes down with little care for presentation.

'Anything else?' He looked from me to Rohan and back – he'd

made it clear a long time ago that he was not inclined to chat. I didn't even know his name.

'Just some hot sauce?' Rohan said. 'Tabasco if you have it. And crushed chillies?'

The waiter was across the restaurant in two strides and back with both and then we were alone with our food. I helped myself to some olives and a few pieces of deep-fried mini ravioli with a dollop of its accompanying *arrabiata* sauce.

Rohan broke the silence. 'So does Grace have a boyfriend? A partner? Whatever you call it these days when it's not a husband?' he said, and my heart sank. Could we really not get away from her?

I shook my head. 'Not at the moment.' I paused but he waited, as if he expected me to say more. I swallowed down the lump in my throat. 'She was with someone when she went to Australia, but it didn't work out.' I had to stop myself and take a couple of breaths as my heart banged, too large, in my chest. 'Now she's focusing on settling herself here, and her work. No doubt she'll find someone, though. She always does.' I pinged my fork up and down with my finger, hoping Rohan hadn't noticed how the words fell flat onto the table, like dead flies.

Rohan chuckled. 'And what have you told her about me?' he sucked in his cheeks and struck a model pose. 'That I'm clever, suave, handsome, sophisticated? That you're lucky to have me?'

I laughed. 'All of that.' I took a deep breath. 'I'm going to be stronger with her, by the way. I've drawn up a housework rota.'

'Okay...' Rohan said carefully.

'I admit, she can be a user. But I'm onto it, and I need her for now. I have a plan, and you have to trust me.'

'If you're sure.' He didn't sound convinced.

We lapsed into silence as we ate. Rohan must still have been thinking about Grace, though, because after some time he looked at me with his head tilted sideways.

'Do you remember in the summer when we were having dinner with Mum and Mili, and Mili asked if you had a muse?'

'Mmm-hmm,' I said.

'Can I ask you something? Is Grace your muse?'

I sighed. 'I guess.'

Rohan nodded. 'Okay. Interesting. So, it's hashtag complicated?'

I nodded. Rohan waited for me to elaborate but I didn't even know where or how to start.

'In what way would you say she's your muse?' he said finally.

'I seem to do my best work when she's around.'

'Okay.'

I played with the food on my plate, suddenly not hungry now Grace was back in my head. 'It's hard to explain,' I said. 'It's something to do with how she looks at me – I don't mean "looks" at me – I mean, how she views me; what she expects of me, I suppose. It's like she looks inside me and pulls out something from within, even when I don't know it's there myself.'

'And I don't do that?'

'We're not talking about you,' I said. 'You asked about Grace, so I'm telling you how it is with her.' I pushed a piece of ravioli back and forth in the sauce. 'It's as if she makes me look inside myself. That's where I go when I'm painting. And she's done it for me since we were at university. I think one of the reasons I couldn't paint anything the past few years was because she was away.'

'So it's down to Grace that you've managed to paint these portraits, is that what you're saying?' Rohan asked.

'Yes. I think so. And I think they're all right. They're dark, though, a bit grim.'

'I can't wait to see them. And meet Grace. In fact, can you give me her number? Just in case I can't ever get hold of you. It really worries me when you go AWOL.'

My insides froze, but how could I explain?

'Sure,' I said, and I carried on eating, but Rohan got out his phone right there and then. 'WhatsApp it to me,' he said, so I sent him the number and watched as he saved it.

'Well, despite everything, if she's inspiring your painting, I suppose we'd better toast her,' he said and raised his glass to clink against mine. 'To Grace.'

'To Grace,' I echoed flatly, and the waiter came to clear the plates.

Forty-seven

By the time we'd eaten, Rohan and I were back on familiar territory, the strains of the last two days lost in the warm buzz of a few drinks. Back home, Rohan let us into the house, then he slid his arms around me.

'How about a kiss?' he said, and so we did, tentatively at first, then in a way that made me think we'd soon be moving to the bedroom. But Rohan pulled away.

'You know what I want, don't you?' Before I had a chance to reply, he carried on. 'I want to see your paintings. Now. You did promise.'

'Oh.' Thrown, I smoothed down my top that had become rumpled in our embrace. 'Yes. I guess.'

I led the way up the stairs, suddenly nervous. I felt as if I were laying myself bare in front of Rohan in a way that was far more intimate than simply stripping off my clothes. I paused on the threshold of the attic before unlocking the door and pushing it open.

'Wait here,' I said. 'Let me arrange them.' I wanted him to see the first picture first, as a stand-alone, because this Grace was a happy image. Captured at around five years old, she was full of light and life and motion, her open-mouthed laugh infectious, her eyes bright and her brown hair flying in the wind. You could see she had no cares in the world; it was a rendering of joyous energy, of possibility, the warm light of the sun full on her face, which she tilted upwards like a sunflower.

I wanted Rohan to see this and to drink it in so he got maximum impact from the other portraits. It made me realize that, in terms of the exhibition, this first picture should be in some sort of ante-room or alcove before people saw the rest of the series. I pulled little Grace to the fore, and then tried to look at the other portraits with the eyes of a stranger; I tried to feel what Rohan's first impression might be but I knew the soul of these pictures – I knew every layer of colour, every touch that brush and fingertip had made to the canvases, and it was difficult to get enough distance.

'Cough, cough,' said Rohan from outside the door. 'Can I come in yet?'

So I stepped back and threw a couple of old, paint-stained sheets over the other five.

'Yes.' My heart cantered against my ribs.

Rohan went straight to the first canvas and his face lit up. 'Oh my God, it's amazing,' he said. 'I love how you've created this feeling just from the way you've used the light. Who is she?' He paused then gave me a boyish smile. 'Our daughter-to-be?'

I lurched as if he'd hit me. 'Oh God. No. No! You'll see why in a minute. But no. She's no one. Just a face. Right. Are you ready for the others?'

Rohan nodded so I pulled back the sheet and watched as his mouth fell open and then his hand went to his mouth as he absorbed the pictures, moving slowly along the sequence as Grace aged, to the last one, number six.

'Jesus fucking Christ.' He turned to me.

'Do you like them?' My voice was a whisper.

'Fucking hell, Abs.' He shivered. 'Is this where you've been the last couple of months? Is this why you've been acting so weird? It's just...' He shook his head. 'Bloody hell. Who *are* you?'

'Are they good enough?'

'Good enough? For who? Tate Modern?'

'Oh, just... I know they're not... pretty. I know they're disturbing. But...'

A sob gathered in my throat and I had to blink back tears. Rohan was the first person to see the portraits and it mattered so much what he thought. It mattered that he understood this was art; that this is why I ignored the phone and ignored the door; why I forgot to eat. That this was what I found at the bottom of the vodka bottle. While I was painting things like this, I was hanging onto the edge of human existence by the tips of my fingernails. I was in another dimension; possessed by something otherworldly.

And, yes, I wanted his opinion, but I was also scared of it. I still had three or four portraits to go and my creativity at this point was as fragile as the head of a dandelion at seed; the slightest breeze or negative comment could too easily disperse the tangled wisps of inspiration that created the artwork, and leave me with nothing. It was crucial that he didn't say anything critical.

Rohan swallowed. 'They're... awful... but incredible-awful. Each one is a masterpiece – and then, together, they tell a story. There's so such an impact when you see them together. It's that juxtaposition of beauty and horror as she ages that makes them so, God, *compelling*. I can't stop looking. It's like watching the freeze frame of a car crash.'

I wiped a tear with the back of my hand. 'So, you like them?'

'Understatement of the year. I can see them in some collector's home.' He arced his hands. 'Arranged along a long corridor – God, the feeling you'd get walking past them. Just *wow*.'

He stared at the third picture. Here, Grace's hair was tied back and her eyes were slightly closed as she looked out of the canvas almost knowingly. Rohan tilted his head.

'What's that look in her eyes? Resignation? Or something else?'

The background colours in this image were darker, ominous; clouds gathering before a storm; that sense of waiting you get as a heatwave ripens, ready to break.

'Yes, maybe resignation,' I said. 'Do the colours remind you of anything?'

Rohan's face cracked open with a smile. He pointed at me with his index finger and thumb in the shape of a gun.

'That night at Mr Ho's in the summer, when the weather broke and the rain finally came. It reminds me of that. Right?' I nodded. 'I could look at this for hours,' Rohan said. 'There's something spellbinding about it, something hypnotic, as if it's trying to say more than the sum of its parts.'

Right answer. I smiled, and he moved on, frowning now at the fourth. Here Grace was clearly in her early twenties. Her hair was tied back from her face, and there was a bright, inquisitive look on her face, or on as much of the face as I'd allowed the viewer to see. This was the 'underwater' image, the one in which her features blurred across the canvas as they surrendered to the current. Rohan stared at it, mesmerized, then turned away, pinching the bridge of his nose.

'Whoa,' he said. 'No words. Beautiful. Haunting.'

'That was two words,' I said biting my lips.

As he drank in the fifth, his hand moved to his throat. This was the one in which an older Grace was suffocating under the canvas, trying to claw her way out. Even I could barely look at it. When painting it, I'd had to concentrate on little areas at a time or I'd find myself struggling to breathe.

'Very disturbing.'

Finally, he bent and examined the sixth picture, the one with the melting face. He studied the texture of the paint. 'Abs?' he said. 'Did you mix blood in with this?'

I closed my eyes. I hadn't thought anyone would notice, though the ferrous oxide did add a distinctive rusty tone. Rohan didn't turn around but I could see his jaw clenching.

'How did you get it?' His tone was neutral but I could tell from the way he held himself so still that it was taking all his self-control. 'Did you cut yourself again?'

'No,' I said quickly. 'Well, not like that.' I pulled up my sleeve and thrust out my forearm, showing him the old, healed scars, white worms splayed across the pale skin, and just one new slice, still pink and raw. 'See? Just one. For the art. I promise. It's mainly paint. Otherwise it wouldn't last.'

He stared at me intently and I could see him weighing up this new information; wondering if he needed to take it further. Then he nodded slowly, accepting my words at face value; questioning no further although I knew he would be bursting with 'why's.'

'Okay.' He stood up slowly and moved towards me. 'Baby, I…'

'So what do you think? Of the paintings?'

He rubbed at his forehead. Wiped his hand across his eyes. Looked back at them. Exhaled loudly.

'Jesus, Abs. Francesca's going to be blown away. They're… exceptional.'

He stepped closer, and this time I let him. He slid his arms around me and my body flopped against him, drained.

'You're a genius,' he said into my hair. 'You're going to be a legend of this century.' He rocked me for a bit, then pulled away. 'So – what happens next? I get the feeling death is stalking her. That she's running away from it.'

I took a deep breath, my hand on my chest. 'I'm not sure. It comes from… I don't know.'

'Something dramatic, though. It has to be, after that build-up. But, please, no more blood. You barely have enough for yourself.' He touched the dark circles under my eyes with his thumb then gently lifted my chin. 'Promise?'

I looked away. 'It's art. There's only a couple more. It wouldn't be much.'

'Abi, please.' But defeat dripped in his tone. He knew I would. He knew I had to. My mind was on the next portrait. Rohan was right. Something dramatic was looming. I could feel it building inside me and dread slid through my veins like poison. Rohan would be back in New York when I painted the remaining canvases and I wasn't sure how I would get through the process. *If* I would get through the process.

'Can I take a couple of photos and call Francesca?' Rohan was tapping his phone. Back on safe ground.

'I…'

'She hasn't seen them, has she? I think she should. It'll help her choose the right space for your exhibition. She's going to go crazy when she sees these. Trust me.'

He started snapping, bending low to get different angles. 'Right. I've sent them.'

I flopped onto the sofa, empty, while Rohan paced the attic.

'She's seen them… she's typing… okay. She wants to phone. That's fine, isn't it?'

Moments later, his phone rang. 'Hi, darling. How are you?' he said. 'So what did you think? Amazing, aren't they? Even better in the flesh.' His eyes flicked to mine. Bad choice of word. 'The things she's done… they blow me away.'

I listened to Rohan's side of the conversation. He was animated, pacing, stopping abruptly, gesticulating at the pictures and talking fast. He didn't mention the blood. After he hung up, he came over to where I was sitting, squatted down and put his hands on my shoulders so he could look directly into my eyes. I could smell the beer on his breath.

'She thinks they're incredible. And she never minces her words. She can't wait to see them herself.'

'Only when they're finished.'

Rohan chewed his lip. 'She was hoping sooner, but maybe you're right. Maybe it's better she sees the entire story. Anyway, Abs, the main thing is you're totally on the right track. This is going to be the show of the year. I'm so proud of you!' He plonked himself down next to me on the sofa and started to massage the back of my neck between his finger and thumb.

'But tell me one thing. Where did this come from? What goes on in that head of yours? And what does Grace do to pull this out of you?'

'If I knew how this worked, I'd bottle the idea, sell it and be a millionaire by now.' I smiled, trying to navigate us to safer ground. 'Look, I know the house gets a bit chaotic when I'm painting, but I really am in another world. It's like I forget everything. There's nothing more to it than that. Once I finish the series, everything will get back to normal. You'll get your wife back. And Grace will be gone I promise.' My smile was weak.

Rohan sighed and rubbed his beard. 'I suppose when you put it like that, the state of the house for a few weeks really isn't so important.'

Transcript of interview with Mr Rohan Allerton, husband of Abigail Allerton: 20 December 2019

'How did you feel when you saw Abigail's paintings for the first time?'

'Wow. Well. Absolutely staggered, to be honest. I knew she had something dark inside her, but... they were really something.'

'Were they not what you'd been expecting? Given her last series?'

'How do you ever expect something like that? I thought they were macabre and beautiful. Haunting.'

'Did she tell you at that point who they were of?'

'No. No, she didn't.'

'Would it have worried you, had you known they were, in fact, of Grace?'

'Of course it would!'

'You mentioned to me earlier that she'd used blood in them? Did that surprise or shock you?'

[Sighs] 'Look. I knew Abi had had some issues with self-harming in the past. She has the scars. But she assured me it was a long time ago and that the issues that caused her to do it were resolved, and I kept an eye on her. She hasn't done it at all since

I've known her – I never saw fresh cuts – so I think she was telling the truth. So, yes, I was... worried... when I saw she'd used blood in the pictures, and that she'd cut herself to get it. But she's an artist and, if she wanted blood in the picture... who was I to tell her what to do?'

Forty-eight

After I'd shown Rohan the paintings, I did my 'rounds' down-stairs, checking all the doors and windows, and turning off the appliances and, when I came up, Rohan was waiting naked in bed. He snuggled up to me and whispered, 'Let's try' – and, well, having felt a disconnect for much of the day, I was relieved things were still okay – but I guess the result was that, as we lay together afterwards, he forgot to put in his earplugs.

My dream that night was different. I don't know if it was the food we'd eaten or the conversation we'd had about Grace, but this time I woke with a twitch, a huge twitch that made the bed bounce. 'No!' I shouted at the shadowy figure that dodged, unidentified, between slices of the universe, and then I felt Rohan's hand on my arm, the warmth of his fingers reeling me back in.

'Abs?' he whispered in the dark. 'Can you hear me?'

I turned and took in his face, a dark mass against the white of the pillow; a scent of home.

'Yes.'

'What's not good enough?' he whispered. 'You were saying "never good enough". It's not about your art, is it?'

My mind was blank. 'No idea.' But even as I mouthed the words, the shadowy figure slipping through the blackness between sleep and wakefulness took on the shape of Grace. Something about the flip of a ponytail and the turn of a hip. *Never good enough.*

'Is there anything bothering you?' Rohan whispered. His arm snaked around me, pulling me closer, and I felt his breath on my cheek. 'I mean, your paintings... If there are things that you want to talk about, we can get you counselling or therapy, or something. Something to help you get it straight in your head. It might help with the dreams.'

'I'm fine,' I said, and fell back asleep with Rohan's arm around me but, when I woke to the chattering of the birds in the trees outside, and to the grey of the dawn squeezing around the edge of the curtains as if it were intent on suffocating us, Rohan's eyes were still wide open; his brow furrowed.

Transcript of interview with Mr Rohan Allerton, husband of Abigail Allerton: 20 December 2019

'And so, given what you now know, how did you feel about Grace when you came home from New York that weekend? Did you feel that she could, in any way, be responsible for the changes you noticed in Abigail?'

'Yes. I guess there was something about her that made me uneasy. But I couldn't put my finger on it. Do you know what I mean? I felt that she had some sort of a hold over Abi. But it seemed to be positive, at least in terms of her art. Abi told me that Grace was her muse. To be honest, I was a bit jealous. Why couldn't I inspire her to paint like that? What was it that Grace had that I didn't?'

'But you didn't broach the topic with Abigail?'

'No. No, I didn't. No more than I've already said. Abs was difficult to talk to. Prickly. I guess I just hoped it would all work out in the end. These things usually do.'

Forty-nine

I painted all morning. When I stopped, the light was still flat and grey, the morning sliding towards the tipping point of the day. Outside, the front garden was a picture of sogginess, the weekend's rain having dampened the fallen leaves into a wet mulch. Even next-door's lawn, usually so well kept, looked sorry for itself. I remembered, again, Rohan's instruction to get the tree removed and eyeballed it, willing it not to fall.

I'd been working on the seventh painting. The base was there: a mouth encompassing the whole face, its lips yawning open in a scream. No eyes, no nose. Behind it, the background would be swirling clouds of dark, rusty red. It would take a lot more blood than last time. I'd do it after Rohan had left.

I took one last look at my work, then backed out of the attic, closing the door quietly behind me. The light fell differently on the landing, illuminating dust motes. I paused for a moment but the hairs on the back of my neck prickled with the sense of the paintings gathered behind the attic door. I flew down the stairs, my bare feet silent, and then I heard it: Mili's laugh. In the kitchen. A joyous cackle from Sofia; the deep baritone of Rohan's voice. I dropped down to the bottom step and sat, hugging my knees.

'You're so good with her,' Mili was saying. 'Such a natural.'

'Aww, she's my good girl, aren't you, Sofia?' Rohan replied, then there was a giggle from Sofia. I heard the tinkle of bells and a clickety-clack: toys to keep her occupied.

Mili's voice again. 'Yours and Abi's kids will be gorgeous. You'll make beautiful babies.' A pause, then a lowered tone. 'Are you even trying, or is Mum barking up the wrong tree?'

I held my breath. Rohan coughed and a chair scraped on the floor. 'We're practising,' he said.

'But nothing's happening?'

'Watch this space.' The hope in his voice made me squeeze my arms tighter around my knees.

Hope in the upward inflection of Mili's voice, too. 'She's pregnant?'

'No – well, not that we know of. But you never know. This might be our lucky month.'

'Fingers crossed. You'll make such a great dad.'

There was a clatter and some chattering from Sofia. I stood up, ready to go in, but then Mili's voice again: 'How is Abi, anyway? It's hard when it's not happening. Is she all right?'

'Well…' Rohan cleared his throat. 'I'm not sure.'

I sat back down.

'Okay,' Mili said slowly. A teaspoon chinked on china. 'So tell me. What's up?'

Rohan sighed. 'Have you met her friend Grace? The one who's staying here?'

There was a pause, then, 'Nope. Don't think so. Why?'

'I just… I don't know. I can't put my finger on it. Something's not right.'

'In what way "not right"?'

'I don't know. She's staying with Abi for a while until she finds her feet, but – God, I just don't know.'

'Houseguests aren't always easy.'

'It's more than that. I get the feeling she's using Abs.'

'Okaay,' Mili said.

'And Abi's such a soft touch. She can be a bit "absent" when she's painting. I worry about her without me here to keep an eye on things.'

There was a silence, then Mili said, 'You need to trust her. She's an adult. She can take care of herself.'

Rohan sighed again, and I could picture him running his hand through his hair. A chair scraped back and I tensed, ready to leap to my feet, but Rohan spoke, his voice slightly less audible. Staring out of the window, maybe.

'You've seen how thin she's got. And she's so pale.'

'She's working, Ro. She's not going outside much. Maybe you should book a holiday for when you're back. After the exhibition.'

'Yeah, maybe. Some sun would be nice.' Silence. 'She's changed since Grace's been here.'

'Changed? In what way?'

'Drinking more; not taking care of herself, or the house.'

Mili laughed. 'You mean she's not being a Stepford wife? Keeping house and putting her lipstick on for you? Come on! You said yourself she's painting. I'm sure she doesn't worry about a bit of mess when she's working.'

'It's more than that.'

'Okay, let's gauge this,' Mili said. 'What do you mean "not taking care of the house"?'

Rohan started telling her about the bins, the dishwasher, the dirty dishes and, even to my ear, he sounded a bit whiney;

the henpecked husband with his nose out of joint. 'And why isn't Grace pitching in? That *really* annoys me. It's basic manners when you're a houseguest, for God's sake! And she's living here for free!'

I jumped as a fist slammed on the table. Sofia yelped.

'It's all right, Sofe,' Mili said, making shushing noises. 'But if you're in New York, why does it even matter? Surely the main thing is that Abi's painting. She has that exhibition, right? You can always clean up the house later. Or, God forbid, get a cleaner! Have you seen what she's been painting?'

'Yes. They're… oh my God. Amazing. Incredible. But so dark.'

'Dark in a good way, right? Honestly, Ro, you're so like Mum: always looking for a problem where none exists. You worry too much. How much longer are you in New York for? Two more weeks? That's nothing – what can go wrong? The way I see it, having Abs's friend here while you're away actually works in your favour. At least she's not alone.'

'Yeah, I guess,' said Rohan, but I could tell, even without seeing the clench of his jaw, that he was not convinced.

'Look at it this way,' Mili said. 'It'll all be over in two weeks.'

The thought was terrifying. She had no idea.

When I finally entered the kitchen, a few minutes after Mili had left, I found Rohan rummaging around for something to eat before he left for the airport. I'd taken a shower, done my hair and make-up, and put on a dress. Dutiful wife. If that's what Rohan wanted, I could give it to him.

'No. I'll cook us some lunch,' I said, batting him away. 'Sit down. Relax.'

I pulled two salmon fillets out of the fridge. 'Baked salmon with veg? And I think I have a Sancerre somewhere in here. Fancy a glass?'

I pretended not to notice that Rohan's mouth fell open as I bustled about getting the glasses and opening the wine.

'Sounds lovely,' he said. 'But salmon? Are you actually going
to eat that? You hate fish.'

'Yeah. Grace got me into it. She likes it and it's much easier
than cooking two different meals.'

'Okay,' Rohan said, nodding. I wondered if he, too, was remembering the way I used to say fish were prettier swimming in the
sea than dead on a plate. I turned on the oven, took out a baking
tray and placed the fish on it, spooning a little pesto onto the top
of each fillet. Then I poured the Sancerre and chinked my glass
against his.

'Cheers.'

'Cheers.'

I popped the fish in the oven when it pinged, then rummaged
in the fridge for the veg and started trimming it ready to cook.
All the while, Rohan's eyes followed me.

'So – your pictures,' he said. 'I wonder what Grace will make of
them.' My heart thundered: had I somehow let on that they were
of her? But no. 'Does she know she's your muse?' he continued,
and I managed a shrug that I hoped looked nonchalant. Rohan
swilled the Sancerre around his glass.

'It's a shame you won't see her today. She'll be back later this
evening,' I said and I hoped I sounded sincere.

'How long do you think she'll stay with you? There was a message for her from the estate agent yesterday, by the way – Katie
something? – she's apparently got a place that she thinks is the
perfect fit.'

'Oh, okay. I'll tell her to call.'

'Great.' Rohan paused, swilled his wine again. 'Of course, she mightn't be in a hurry to move out…' There was an edge to his tone. I put down the knife and looked at him.

'Can you please give it a rest?'

He rubbed his brow. 'Just be careful, Abs, that's all.'

'Yep. Being careful.'

'I'm just worried about you. You're my wife.' Rohan dropped his voice. 'And one day you'll be the mother of my children, too – I hope.'

He held the words out to me, a jeweller displaying diamonds on a velvet tray, and I forced a flicker of a smile. Then I turned to the oven and looked through the glass at the food. Rohan got up and slipped his arms around me.

'If you're happy with Grace here, then I'm happy,' he said. 'I'm glad she's here for you.'

'Really?'

'Yes, really.'

But what if I'm not?

Fifty

'Hello! I've got news!' Grace called as her bag thumped down in the hall. I slunk down the stairs, as if I hadn't been watching from the attic window; as if I hadn't been waiting for the sound of the taxi while I cut my wrist carefully, let the pressure out, and swirled the reds for the background of the painting – all the while thinking about how to broach the topic of Alfie. Should I just come straight out and ask her if she did it? And now something else, too: that familiar dread I used to feel when Grace came back to the flat in the old days, sliding through me like tentacles.

'Me too!' I said, stopping three stairs short of the bottom. Grace regarded me and widened her eyes. I was still in the dress I'd put on for Rohan, the fresh cut on my arm wrapped tight with bandage. She was a doctor. She wasn't stupid. I slipped the arm behind my back.

'Had a good time?' I asked.

'Yes! So much to tell you. How was your romantic weekend?'

'Good, thanks. But I have some bad news.'

Grace stiffened. 'What?'

'It's Alfie.' I pressed my lips together. 'My cat? I found him dead.'

Grace snorted a laugh, but recovered quickly. Her features

rearranged into concern. 'Oh, but that's awful.' She reached out a touched my arm. 'You must be so sad.' She gave a little laugh. 'But on the bright side, at least I'll be able to sleep now. Silver linings!'

She sashayed down the hall to the kitchen, where she opened the fridge and took out the open Sancerre. There was just one glass left.

'You don't mind if I have it, do you?' she asked, pouring it. 'I'm parched and I really fancy a glass of something wicked after all that meditation.' She took a sip, rolled it around her mouth and swallowed. I watched so closely I could almost taste it myself. 'Nice,' she said. 'You really should do that retreat. It was amazing. I learned so much about why we should eat more raw food.'

'Aren't you going to ask what happened?'

'What happened to who?'

'To the cat.' I raised my eyebrows. 'His throat was slit.'

Grace pulled a face. 'Eek. Brutal. And who found him?' She drew lines down the condensation on the side of her wine glass.

'I did.'

Grace sighed. 'Honestly. It must have been awful. I'm really sorry.' She took another sip of wine. 'So, anything else happen while I was finding my spiritual self?' She gazed at me over the rim of the wine class and I held her gaze. Energy fizzed between us. She killed him. I knew it. And she knew that I knew. She also knew that I wouldn't say anything. My hands gripped the edge of the counter.

'Nothing major. I realized the house got into quite a state the past few weeks so I decided we should share the chores. I've drawn up a rota. It's there.' My voice sounded fake to me; the words that were spilling out of my mouth utterly meaningless when all I could think about was Grace's non-verbal admission of guilt.

Grace picked up the piece of paper and examined it, then tossed it back down. 'Bins? Loading the dishwasher? Seriously, Abs. We don't need a rota. We're both adults. We can see what needs doing.'

'I know, but...'

'What if I'm out and it's my turn to do something? Will you wait for me to get back to run the dishwasher? Please! If you want me to help, you just have to say. I didn't want to encroach on your territory. You were always so territorial. I was waiting for you to ask.'

I looked down at the table, scenes from our flatshare playing through my mind: me always cooking. Me always cleaning up. Was she lazy and entitled, or was I territorial? Which was it?

'Don't you want to hear my news?' Grace's eyes were bright, her energy like popping candy.

'Sure.'

She took another sip of her wine and I thought about getting myself a glass from the wine box. I could actually do with another vodka but that was upstairs.

'I got back early this morning,' Grace said, 'and I knew I wasn't welcome here till later, so I decided to do some flat-hunting.'

'Oh, okay,' I nodded, ignoring the barb.

'Expensive area, isn't it?'

'Yes. It's got good schools. That always drives up the price. And golf courses – two, actually. Plus, it's rural, but still on the Tube.'

'So I saw. It's got it all, hasn't it? Quite the perfect location.' Grace's tone was acidic. 'You and your perfect husband certainly picked the perfect place. He must be doing very well to afford it. From what I saw, places like these don't go for under a million. Some up to two.'

'Oh, we didn't pay that!' I looked fondly around the kitchen.

'This was a doer-upper! Needed a *lot* of love and attention. Trust me. That's the only way we could afford it.'

Grace sucked her cheeks in. 'So I hear.' She paused and suddenly I knew what was coming. I swallowed.

'The woman in the estate agent told me the story,' Grace continued. 'I had no idea. It's so sad!'

'I know. It is.' I pushed the chair back and stood. 'Right. I should get on.'

'Where are you going?' Grace said. 'I've only just got back. Sit down. Have a drink with me.'

She jumped up and dispensed me a glass from the wine box. 'Here. Cheers.'

I drank deeply. Half the glass in one go. After the Sancerre it tasted dreadful.

'So, about that girl.' Grace shivered. 'I don't know if I could have bought this place – knowing that.' She paused. 'She's buried in the graveyard here. St Michael's, is it? Behind the High Street?'

I nodded. 'I believe so.'

'Have you been?' Grace asked. 'To see it?'

'What?'

'The grave.'

'No.'

Grace sighed. 'Maybe we should go. I kind of feel like…' She breathed in deeply and let it go slowly. 'Those toys. They were probably hers, weren't they? And the little clothes? It puts a whole new spin on it. The parents must have left in such a rush. They moved abroad, apparently. Couldn't bear to live here anymore. Too many memories, I suppose. They probably forgot those boxes up in the attic. It's not as if they would have needed them, really, is it?' She ran her finger around the rim of her glass. 'Where I'm sleeping, it would have been her room, wouldn't it? It's odd to think of them being back in there.'

I turned away, my throat thick with sadness. Of course I'd known the story about the girl of the house. It was one of the reasons I hadn't the heart to throw away her old furniture. She'd been killed in a tragic accident. I knew the story, but I chose not to focus on it. When I pictured the girl, I imagined her growing up here: happy and full of life and hope and plans. She'd been eighteen when she died; her whole life ahead of her.

I didn't want to think about her parents' grief; about the moment they found out she was dead. About the sobbing eulogies in the church from her friends and the sad procession through the churchyard to the grave. I didn't want to think about them returning to this very house after burying their only child; fortifying themselves with sherry as they went through the motions of hospitality. I didn't want to picture them sitting, locked numbly in their grief in this kitchen, untouched cups of tea on the table, listening to the depth of the silence marked only by the relentless tick of the grandfather clock I'd inherited. They'd tolerated it only for a few weeks before packing their bags and moving somewhere warm, as if a bit of sunshine could erase the hole she'd left in their lives. They'd never come back.

Rohan didn't know the story. If he did, he'd never have agreed to buy the house.

'It was all very sad,' I said. 'But you know. Life moves on.' I glugged another mouthful of wine. 'So. How was Kent?'

'Ah, the old stomping ground.' Grace nodded. 'Yeah. Good. It got me reminiscing about the past,' she said.

I focused on the ticking of the clock, but even that seemed to slow down. *Tick... tick... tick.* 'You remember I was born down there?' She paused, her head tilted as she smiled sideways at me. 'You remember the picture we found? With us both in it? Groombridge, wasn't it?'

I nodded. She'd told me about her idyllic summers in the country. Strawberry-picking, her mouth stained with the juices of stolen fruits. Flying her kite in the meadow. Running errands in the village. Horse-riding. Camps built in the woods. Bonfires. Wellies up to her knees and a fishing net to catch minnows in the stream. An idyllic childhood. My hand went to my neck.

'I was always so happy there,' she said, her voice like swathes of golden silk. 'Golden summers they were. Maybe my memory's just playing tricks, but I don't remember a single bad thing. Granny used to get me to do the gardening.' She laughed to herself. 'Mum never knew, but she paid me to do the weeding and trim the edges of the lawn. I spent all of it on sweets in the village shop. Then there'd always be cake or afternoon tea...' Another soft chuckle. 'There was a bunch of kids I used to meet up with. We'd play hide-and-seek in the cornfields before they were harvested.' Grace smiled to herself. 'And, once the bales were in the fields, we'd climb up them and jump off. Mr Denby, the farmer, always positioned a few so they were like a climbing frame for us. Looking back, it was really kind of him, but at the time I just assumed that's what hay bales were for. It's such a beautiful part of the world. Fields for years.' Grace came back to the present, her eyes refocusing.

'Anyway, I was remembering all of that and I thought: this is nuts. Why am I working in London when I was so happy in Kent? Maybe I notice it more for having been in Australia, but London's so choked. So dirty. Overcrowded. Crime-ridden. I don't want to be a part of that. So I decided I'm going to look for a job either in Kent or on the south side of London, and move down there. The commuter lines are great. Even from as far as Ashford you can be in London in forty minutes. What do you think?'

My mouth was dry, my heart drumming. 'Nice,' I said, as levelly as I could. 'Good idea.' I stood up and inhaled deeply through my nose as I stood, using my hands to steady myself on the table.

'Don't go!' Grace said, and was it me or was there an edge to her voice? 'You've still got to tell me all about your weekend. Come on, sit down.' She patted the table next to her. And what could I tell her? About the ruined date night; about the way she'd muscled in between Rohan and me, even when she wasn't there? About the argument? Rohan's doubts about her?

'It was fine,' I said.

She snorted. 'Fine? Is that all? I'd have hoped you'd be swinging from the lampshades with me gone. I'd expect you to be pregnant with twins, at least.' Her tone was dead.

I trilled a small laugh. 'Right, if you don't mind, I was just in the middle of something.' I turned to go.

'But you haven't said anything about my plan? To move to Kent? What do you think?'

'I think it's a good idea.'

'You're not upset?'

'Why would I be?'

'Because it's your neck of the woods. I don't want you thinking I'm stamping on your turf. And I was hoping you'd come house-hunting with me one weekend. Both of us go down there, have a look around. Maybe stop in at the retreat I was at for a bit of R&R. Have you ever done yoga?'

My heart thumped in my throat; blood rushed in my ears. 'I'm busy with my work,' I said. 'The exhibition's less than a month away and I still have three pictures to do. And Rohan'll be back permanently soon.'

'He can come too. I'm sure he'd like to see Kent…' She left the sentence hanging. No reply needed. A smile crept across her face as she nodded. 'Just the two of us, then.'

The roaring in my ears was a tsunami. I ran to the door, scrambled to wrench it open, frantic to get away from her voice, which wrapped itself around me like coils of pond weed intent on dragging me down. Grace's voice followed me, childlike, taunting, as I sank into the depths of the hall.

'What's wrong, Abs? Are you afraid of something?'

Upstairs, I slammed the attic door closed behind me and locked it from the inside. Then I cut my arm again, drawing the blade of my scalpel repeatedly across virgin flesh and leaking my blood into a jar before mixing it with the paint. I had to work quickly, before the blood coagulated, but it was a large area. It would take far more blood than I'd first thought.

Fifty-one

Grace was at work when Francesca came to view the paintings. Nearly two weeks had passed, and Grace had said nothing more about me going down to Kent and I'd focused only on completing the series. The seventh painting was finished, as was the eighth. Here, Grace was no more than a shadow, a smudge of a person, her features indistinct; just scattered eyelashes and the print of her lips; little more than a blur of pinks, lilacs and the greys of her fifty-something hair blended and imploding backwards through the canvas as if she were being sucked out of the universe by an unseen force.

The ninth showed only the edges of what could have been: the sense of a hole; the will-o'-the-wisp that might be a person in the blank canvas of the cosmos. Viewers, I knew, would stand in front of it, tilting their heads this way and that as they struggled to catch the gist of the colours that were maybe there, maybe not. It was an image that made my throat sore and my chest tight. It was an image of extinction.

And then there was picture ten. This was the one that had consumed me day and night for the past ten days. Drained by the way Grace's canvas life had played out to her universal destruction, I'd rewound back to the moments after her birth, when she'd emerged from the womb, crinkled and pink; her eyes, on their first opening, dark pools that knew the truth of life itself; her forehead creased with questions to which we'd never know the answers; wisps of dark hair smeared damp on her scalp; her fingers long and crumpled, her cheeks ready to plump up with milk from her mother's breast. I couldn't look at it without weeping.

Francesca was due at ten. I buzzed about nervously, fiddling with the canvases, tweaking here and there until I could bear it no longer. Downstairs, I slid boxed Chardonnay into a tumbler, and drank deeply, not getting the bouquet; not caring that the liquid was warm.

'What if she doesn't like the paintings?' I'd said on the phone Rohan the night before.

'She likes them. She's seen the photos,' he'd said. 'She just wants to look more closely. Get an idea of size and proportion. You've nothing to worry about.'

The doorbell rang bang on time.

'Hi, Francesca,' I greeted her. A tall and elegant woman, she looked as striking as ever in her signature black. Our house was a long way from her usual stomping ground of Chelsea. She'd never married nor had children herself: the gallery was her main love; the artists whose talents she nurtured, her children.

'Hello, Abigail,' she said, clasping me in her arms putting her cheek to mine so her huge turquoise earrings jostled against my skin. She smelled expensive. 'Isn't this a lovely area? I see why you like it here.' She unwound her scarf and undid her coat. 'And this gorgeous old house.' She looked around the hall and I saw it through her eyes – it was impressive, the high ceiling with its intricate roses; the stained-glass flowers in the front door; the

278

black-and-white geometric floor tiles; the carved woodwork of the bannister showing a little wear and tear from a century of use, but beautiful even under the dust. I watched her face. Did she feel the energy, too?

'Thanks. I managed to persuade Rohan to buy it.'

'He needed persuading?' Francesca laughed.

'He doesn't like old houses.' An awkward silence fell. Was I supposed just to lead her straight upstairs?

'Can I get you anything?' I asked. 'Coffee? Water?'

'I'm fine, thank you.'

'Wine? There's one open.'

'Not before lunchtime!' she laughed, as if I were joking, so I turned and she followed me up the stairs. On the landing, I stopped. I'd arranged the paintings as I wanted them to be seen in the gallery: the young girl first, followed by the others. 'You go ahead,' I said, and I watched as she made her way up the steep attic stairs, then paused on the threshold with an audible gasp.

'Oh my!' Her hand covered her mouth. She moved deeper into the attic, her figure silhouetted in the light from the window, and I followed.

'Oh my,' she said again.

She backed across the attic to take in all the paintings at once, tilting her head and nodding as she looked. Then she scrutinized each one in detail, taking in the way the light rose and fell on each canvas.

'A lifetime on canvas. Incredible,' she murmured, lost in her own world while my nails made marks on my palms. 'What happened? What happened to her?' she murmured as she examined the later paintings. Eventually she stood up and turned to me.

'Abigail, I wasn't sure how you would translate from those... terrifying, almost post-apocalyptic landscapes to portraits, but these are… phenomenal. Really phenomenal.' She chose her words carefully. I bowed my head.

'But what's happening? I see both love and hate. Love in the beauty of her features, and the care you've taken with the brushwork, but then – goodness me… I wouldn't want to be her,' Francesca said. 'There's a *lot* of negative emotion, too. As if you want to wipe this face from existence. And then this one.' She looked at the baby. 'Again, so completely different. So *warm*.'

'This is my favourite,' I said, not knowing that the words were going to come. I touched the baby's face; stroked her cheeks, her rosebud lips. The face was bathed in such golden light I expected the canvas to be warm from the sun. 'So much hope,' I said. 'So much promise. The world unfolding at her feet. Everything there for her to take. Who knows when we're born how it's going to end?' I took another swig from my glass. 'Who knows in life? If only we had the choice to be born, or not…' I broke off because suddenly I was crying. I grabbed a tissue and blew my nose. 'Sorry.'

Francesca touched my arm, her face creased with concern.

I steadied myself, sniffed and swallowed. 'I'm fine.'

Francesca nodded and smoothed her trousers from where she'd been squatting down. 'It must be emotional. I get that.' Another squeeze of my arm. Thankfully not the bandaged one. 'With work of this calibre,' she continued, 'I think we can do a launch specifically for your exhibition – invite the big guns. The media, buyers, some celebrities. I'm seeing champagne, canapés.'

'Really?' My voice was a squeak.

'Yes.' Francesca smiled. 'This is really something. It's really special. Way better than your last one, and you know how well that sold.' She nodded. 'I'd go as far as to say ground-breaking. I think the media will go crazy.'

'Really?' Again, the squeaky voice.

'I have a potential buyer in mind, too,' Francesca continued. 'Someone I know who would be *very* interested. He likes this kind of "anarchy". The destruction will appeal to him.'

Somehow, we ended up back downstairs. I wrote down the date Francesca wanted to have the paintings collected, then called Rohan to tell him the good news, my fingers skidding on the keys, my mood buoyed by Francesca and the wine.

'Now you have professional validation,' he said when I'd finished gabbling everything that Francesca had said. 'Do you finally believe in yourself?'

'Yes,' I said. 'I think I finally do.'

Fifty-two

With the paintings finished, I had time on my hands again. Grace was out at work every day and I rattled about the house trying to remember how I used to fill my days. I'd almost forgotten about the pet portraits – about how het up I used to get about doing them; how stressed. It all seemed a bit ridiculous now. I was a marathon runner who'd crossed the finish line with my new series. The pet portraits felt like the 25-metre race at junior school. Still, I hadn't checked my website for ages. I called it up and clicked listlessly through the gallery that advertised the different styles I could produce, the prices and the submission procedure, but it was like looking at someone else's work, someone else's life, galaxies away. I closed my laptop and stared into space. All I could think about was Grace's words: 'Have you been to the grave?'

It had sounded ridiculous when she'd said it but, now I thought about it, why shouldn't I go? The girl was buried right here in the churchyard that lay directly between the station and our house. And her parents were no longer around so who tended her grave? Her friends? What family? It had crossed my mind before, but to visit when I hadn't known the girl had seemed ghoulish; macabre. So many people who lived in this house – in any old house – would have died – some in accidents – and most people didn't seek out their final resting places, did they? Or was this different because she was young? Because it was a tragedy? I was sure I could feel her energy in the house. I pictured her here. Maybe I should go. I closed my eyes, breathed deeply and felt her smile, that dead girl. No one would know.

With an energy I hadn't felt since I'd been painting, I grabbed my keys and coat and dashed out of the house. My steps hit the pavement briskly as I set off down the road like any purposeful commuter but slowed as I neared the churchyard. I never went to church. Did I have to ask permission, or did I just walk in? What would I say if anyone saw me? Feeling like a burglar, I unlatched the churchyard gate and stepped away from the noise of the street. I'd spent the past four years avoiding this place – refusing to take the shortcut – and now I was here through choice.

A narrow tarmac path led through well-tended gardens toward the church, each side of the path punctuated with gravestones, tombs and memorials that hunkered under towering yews and cedar trees. I knew she wouldn't be here – just a glance told me that these graves dated farther back than ten years – but around the side of the church lay the more recent graves.

I tightened my scarf and, with my hands deep in my pockets, I made my way down the path, around the church and through another gate into another space, where the headstones here were cleaner, newer, better tended. A footpath had been carved through the grass by commuters taking the shortcut to the station and, at the far end, I could see the gap in the hedge they used to bypass the long walk down Albert Road. I stood for a moment to get my bearings, then stepped among the headstones, scouring the names and dates one by one until I found the cool grey curve and neat lettering of the one I was sure must be hers.

Face to face with the tombstone, I read the words. *Dearly Beloved Daughter.* Simple. Factual. Just the dates to jolt the heart; the short lifespan apparent only to those who stopped to notice. The grave looked untended, the weeds of the churchyard taking it over. I stood with my head bowed and thought about the remains of the girl who'd worn the dresses we'd found, the girl who'd played with the toys – surely decomposed now, under my feet, and I felt tears pool. Why was life so cruel? So unfair? I bent and pulled a big weed from the edge of the grave. Then suddenly I knew what to do: there may be nothing I could do for her in life, but I could make her final resting place tidy.

With growing urgency, I pulled at the weeds that grew around the stone. Soil balled under my fingernails as I tugged the roots out of the ground, suddenly desperate to do something – anything – for the girl. On my knees, with the damp seeping through my jeans, I pulled and raked and tidied with fingers that reddened with cold until the area around the grave looked neat.

Loved.

Fifty-three

Rohan had told me not to touch the paintings again; to leave them as Francesca had seen them.

'Do something, do anything, do the gardening, take a sleeping tablet and go to bed, just don't go up there,' he'd said on what we both accepted would likely be our last phone call before he left New York for good. But the pictures were like a scab that had to be scratched – the fingers of my mind itching and rubbing at the thought of the portraits – and I couldn't stop myself from going up to view them again.

I pushed open the attic door and breathed in the familiar smell of my hideaway: linseed oil and paints, turpentine, Liquin and, below that, the pine of the frames, the old wood of my easels, the scent of canvases, and the distinctive smell of the house itself; of hundred-year-old bricks that have baked in the sun and soaked up the rain; bricks that have heated and thawed and heated and thawed while sheltering those who lived within their walls; and finally the smell of the felt and rafters of the roof itself. And then, splayed across the attic, a nightmare on canvas, were the paintings.

The day had largely been sunny, but clouds were coming in now, shifting the light like a movie in fast-forward. As I stood at the door, a sunbeam fell on the fifth painting; on the suffocating, underwater image, illuminating it while leaving the others in shade. I swallowed, my hand on my throat, my chest tight, a diver run out of oxygen too deep to make it back up – always that struggle to breathe. Then the clouds moved and the painting faded, the gloss of its surface bouncing back the ambient light in a way that prevented me from seeing it properly and my breath returned to normal.

I slid down the wall till I was sitting on the floor, the rough rattan scratching my hands as I faced my paintings. As I drank them in, I felt again the emotion that had gone into each of them; yet, together, they were more than the sum of their parts – their impact as an entire collection unfamiliar to me. It was as if someone else had inflicted this orgy of horror onto Grace's life. My body was empty; my soul used up and wrung-out like a holey old chamois.

Rain splattered against the window, a sudden round of gunfire, and downstairs the front door slammed, breaking my trance. Footsteps ran up the stairs. I scrambled to my feet, almost too slow: Grace's head popped around the attic door, her cheeks flushed from the wind outside and her lips parted as she panted after the exertion of dashing up the stairs. She was still in her work clothes and she shoved a strand of hair out of her face.

'Knock, knock!' she called, but already she was peering past me, moving her neck like a meerkat and I was in front of her, my arms wide, sidestepping, trying to block her view. I was fast, but maybe not fast enough. Even as her mouth fell open and her skin drained of colour, I grabbed her shoulders and spun her around, pushing her so hard out of the door that she stumbled down the first few steps and landed hard on her backside.

I locked the attic door, my hands shaky, while she gathered herself and got to her feet, rubbing at her hip. I towered above her on the dark stairs, my heart thumping. Her face was a moon of white below me. How much had she seen?

'I'll just get changed.' Grace turned abruptly, crossed the landing and shut the door with a click. I stumbled after her and lifted my hand to knock, wanting to follow her, wanting to ask her what she saw, wanting to explain, but my hand fell back down. What could I say to her?

I slumped onto the top step, my body scrunched like a child as I hugged my knees to my chest. How could I ever let her see the way I'd tortured and destroyed her in the portraits, suffocating her, strangling her, drowning her, pulling her flesh apart before extinguishing her? Aside from the first two and the last, these images were the antithesis to what she'd imagine. Worse, she'd see, right there in glorious colour, exactly how I felt about her. It was one thing for me to paint those images in private, but I don't know what I'd imagined would happen when Grace finally saw the portraits – as she inevitably would – at the gallery, if not at home.

What had that website said about toxic friends? *Prepare for retaliation.*

I'd buried my head in the sand, losing myself in the creative process and ignoring the inevitable fallout that would follow. But of course, it was an issue. I stiffened, my hand reaching for my phone. I could phone Francesca and call off the exhibition; tell her I couldn't go through with it. But even as the thought crystallized, I knew it wouldn't work. She would argue with me; rope in Rohan. The pair of them would think I was having an 'artistic wobble' or a 'moment'; they'd hustle around me, reassuring me how good I was.

But this wasn't about my faith in myself. I knew those paintings were sensational.

Behind me, Grace's door creaked as it swung slowly open. I closed my eyes and tensed, fully expecting her to strike me somehow; to smash me over the head, to kick me down the stairs, take out her anger on me. Behind me, I sensed her move across the landing towards me and I squeezed my knees tighter to my body, bracing for the impact. She stopped directly behind me and waited. Around us, the house watched.

The grandfather clock ticked, as it always had done, and the deep silence of the hall amplified the sound up the stairs, the seconds passing like gunshots. Then I heard the whisper of Grace's clothes as she took a step, and my nostrils filled with the sickening scent of her perfume. Slowly, she sat down next to me on the top step. Her elbow brushed mine, raising goosebumps on my arm.

'Your husband's back tomorrow,' she said, and I couldn't breathe. 'I don't want to outstay my welcome.'

My heart thudded with each tick of the clock.

'I've arranged some house viewings in Kent,' she said slowly, as if savouring my discomfort. 'And you've finished your paintings now. I'd like you to come down to help me look.' Her words were bullets. 'You'll know all the best places.'

I swallowed. 'It's been years. It'll all have changed.'

'Those villages don't change much.' Grace gave a little laugh. 'They've been the same for hundreds of years. Maybe we can do some sightseeing while we're down there. Make a day of it. We could stop by the house where you grew up, if you like.'

'My dad moved years ago.'

I felt Grace shrug. 'But still. It'd be interesting to see. As we'll be so close. So – you'll come? Tomorrow?'

I closed my eyes against my knees, and squeezed them shut as if the force of my eyelids could squeeze her away, out of my life for good, but she carried on speaking, her voice sliding over me like those thick cobwebs that trail across your face, making you swat at yourself until every touch is gone. Around us, the house held its breath. Through the layers of time, the girl reached out, swirling around me, whispering truths through the ether that I never thought would be told.

'Can you book a cab to take us down?' Grace said, and the clock struck seven sombre notes that reverberated through the house.

Fifty-four

We waited in silence for the taxi the following morning. I hadn't eaten, my insides too fragile.

'By the way,' Grace said as she peered out of the window for the cab, 'I did a bit of research and found out that the accident – you know…' she nodded upstairs, as if the dead girl was up in her room, 'happened quite close to the first property we're seeing.' She named a small village. 'Do you know it? I think I remember it from my own holidays in Kent. I thought we could take down one of her toys and lay it there. What do you think?' She rummaged in her bag and pulled out the pink-and-white dog. 'I just thought it might… *mean* something. I don't know. Reunite her with it – not that she's there. But put something right in the universe.' She shrugged. 'It's better than chucking them in the bin, don't you think?'

Before I had a chance to formulate a reply, she shoved the dog back in her bag and tapped her phone. 'Anyway, the traffic's clear apart from the Dartford Crossing. We should be there in a couple of hours, which is great as our first appointment's at eleven thirty.'

'There's a weather warning for the South East. Did you see that?' I said.

'We're not going all the way down to the coast. And, anyway, it's been downgraded to yellow.' Grace craned her head once more. 'Right. Cab's here.'

I climbed in and the driver headed toward the M25. It was true what Grace had said about the accident. I remembered the estate agent telling me that the girl had been on holiday when it happened. I remembered her mentioning Kent and wondering if I'd ever met her. As we turned onto Albert Road and made our way toward the M25, I put myself in the girl's shoes: how would she have felt pulling away from the house in a car with her family at the start of the long summer holidays? Making this exact drive? I remembered from my own childhood that feeling of freedom and excitement that used to buzz in my stomach at the start of the holidays. Had it been the same for her?

Grace was right: the traffic was clear and, as we joined the motorway, she got a folder out of her bag.

'I've made five appointments for today,' she said, patting the folder. 'Do you think that's too many? I tried to space them out so we've got time to grab something to eat or get a coffee. I'm specifically looking for a two-bedroom place. Ideally a cottage. You know,' she laughed, 'so predictable, right? The chocolate-box house with the low ceilings, the fireplace and the roses in the summer, though I get that that might not happen. So today's a bit of a mixed bag. Some old, some new. More new, to be honest. But this is my favourite.' She held out a picture of a pale, stone-fronted cottage with smart white paintwork and vines twisting around the front door. 'Have a look.'

I didn't take the brochure so she flicked through the pages in front of me and I saw a country-style kitchen-diner with a terracotta flagged floor and a cosy living room with a big open fireplace, but my mind wasn't on her house-hunt and my eyes soon slid back to the car window. The motorway arced around North London, past rolling fields, industrial areas, and the ugly outskirts of satellite towns. And, with every town that we passed — South Mimms, Waltham Abbey, Epping, Brentwood — a ball of sickness grew inside me.

'You're sweating,' Grace said, breaking off her monologue about her dream home as I adjusted the air vent to reach my face. 'Are you okay?'

'No. Can we pull over?' The words rushed out of me like a torrent, my teeth on edge as saliva flooded into my mouth with the rising bile. 'Stop now!'

'Sure,' said the driver, checking his mirrors and pulling onto the hard shoulder. 'Lucky this isn't a smart motorway. You okay?'

I ripped open the door and threw up immediately, my vomit splattering the tarmac.

'Maybe it's something you ate,' Grace murmured, when I climbed back in. There was an interminable queue for the QE2 bridge.

'It's always bad.' The driver gave me side-eye as he peered back to see if I looked likely to vomit again, but there was nothing inside me, and we were finally up and over, past Dartford, Swanley, Orpington and off down the A21 into the heart of Kent. I could feel Grace thrumming next to me, brimful of anticipation for the day ahead. I couldn't understand her ghoulish fascination with the girl who had the accident, but who was I to stop her if she wanted to place a toy there?

My head craned towards the opposite window, taking in quaint pubs, oast houses, big manor houses on impossibly green hills, cows, sheep and ponies standing, bored, in fields of homespun jumps. Against my will, I found myself scouring the landscape for familiar landmarks: that pub, the house on the corner, the scary grey house on the hill that I always thought looked haunted. Finally, the car entered the outskirts of a small country town, and I sat up straighter, peering at the familiar roads.

'Could you just take a left here?' I asked the driver, and he swung down the road I used to live in. It looked smaller, somehow, narrower than I remembered. The grass verge had gone, too, making the street look more built up than I pictured it in my head. My eyes fixed onto the house I was brought up in, its red and brown façade as familiar to me as the back of my hand. The front garden was paved over now, and there was a gate at the end of the driveway, an iron fence drawing a line around the perimeter of the garden. *Keep Out*, it said, and I was more than happy to. The house was something from another life; another me. Dad had moved out five years ago – gone up north to live near my aunt. There was nothing for me there; the whole thing tainted by what had happened.

'Is that it?' Grace asked, following my eyes. 'Do you want to stop?'

'Not here. You can turn around now,' I said to the driver. 'Sorry.'

He rejoined the main road and, within a few minutes, we entered a small picturesque village. Grace looked at the signpost and then pulled the stuffed dog out of her bag and waggled it at me, asking the question with a tilt of her head and a shrug. I leaned forwards, my heart a lump of stone.

'You can stop here, thanks,' I said.

The driver looked doubtfully at the postage stamp of muddy grass that counted as the village green. 'Are you sure? Seems like the middle of nowhere.'

I double-checked the name: yes, I was sure. I paid the driver, and Grace and I got out by a row of village shops. I filled my lungs with the cold, fresh air of the countryside, my breath visible as a puff, and took in the green with its weather-worn benches, the red post box, the row of quaint shops – a quintessential village that seemed untouched by time. I couldn't imagine people here doing anything that wasn't wholesome and pure. My breath was sour with the taste of vomit.

To the right of the green was a small lane: if you hadn't been looking for it, you'd have missed it. I looked down it seeing, at the end, the flash of traffic passing on a busier road. Grace looked between me and the lane, her eyes dark holes in her face, and my heart thumped.

'It's down here,' I said. I could barely hear my voice over the sound of the blood rushing in my head. Grace nodded.

'Lead the way,' she said, so I stood at the top of the lane, picturing for a few moments a girl on a bike, her whole life before her. A girl taking a shortcut on the day she got her A-level results. A girl who didn't stop at the end of the lane; a girl whose bike smashed into a passing car, leaving her broken and dying on the tarmac.

My heart was thumping now, really jumping in my chest, and I had to pause before I could carry on, putting one foot carefully in front of the other, trying not to feel the speed of the girl's bike freewheeling beneath her; not to see her ponytail flying in the wind as she lived the last minute of her life on this very lane.

With every step I was able to see a little more of the main road that lay ahead: a snatch of tarmac, the flash of cars sweeping by, the verge on the other side soggy and brown. It was a busy road, even more so these days, a bypass that fringed the village, connecting bigger towns to each other like the strands of a spider's web. Beyond it, the fields of Kent stretched out, the pale greens and browns of winter and, above them, a straight line of black clouds approaching: the storm about which we'd been warned.

At the point where the lane met the road, I stopped abruptly, centimetres away from the passing traffic: the cars, vans and lorries that streaked by in a hurry, their tyres swishing close to the verge. The strip of green was splattered with mud, summer's flowers nothing more than a memory. On the other side of the road, the hedge was taller, more unkempt, giving just a glimpse of the winter fields beyond. Dark specks of birds beat their wings high above, their raucous screams renting the sky. The trees above me rustled as the wind picked up and, in the distance, above the sound of traffic, there was a low rumble of thunder.

'Is this where it happened?' Grace whispered.

I nodded and steadied myself, checking that I really was here, right now, not just having another nightmare. I bowed my head.

'Apparently, she lost control on her bike,' Grace said. Her face twisted. 'Shot out into the main road. I don't know if it's true, but the estate agent said she'd found out that day that she'd got into UCL.'

'Such a bright future,' I whispered.

For a moment, inside my head, the air ripped with the sound of screaming. I could picture the rotating flash of blue light; the girl lying on the ground, a trickle of blood oozing from her head; the white faces of people waiting bleakly for the emergency services; the hopelessness of knowing there was nothing to be done. Under the tyres of passing cars, the tarmac hissed. It bore no mark, no scar to show what had happened.

'Why don't you do it?' Grace held out the stuffed dog, so

I placed it on the grass at the roadside and, when I stood up, my face was wet with tears. Thunder boomed again, closer this time, and the wind picked up another notch.

'Come on. Let's go,' I said, wiping at my eyes and stuffing the tissue back in my pocket. 'She wouldn't have known what hit her. It would have happened very fast.'

'She might not have known,' Grace said, and my lungs released the air they'd been subconsciously holding. For a moment, I thought we were done. But then Grace spoke again, her voice low. 'But what if she did? What if she realized what had happened and died alone and in pain? Died with no one holding her hand; no one to tell her she was loved?'

As Grace looked at the road, the rain finally started to fall: big, fat drops that pebble-dashed the grey of the tarmac. I looked up at the sky, darker now, and pulled my hood over my hair. Within seconds the road was dark and slick with rain.

'She wouldn't have known,' I said.

'You don't know that. It's what you tell yourself.'

'Grace... please.'

Grace tilted her head as she looked at me. 'I wonder about the driver. How they could ever move on knowing they'd done something like that. How could you live with yourself knowing you'd killed someone?'

Her eyes met mine and I stared back at her, eyeball to eyeball. 'That's enough now. We've paid our respects. Let's go.'

The rain got harder, drumming down and flattening Grace's hair, pasting it to her forehead, which only made her eyes look bigger; more like holes in the pale of her face. She kept my gaze as she gave a sick laugh.

'Don't you ever wish you'd turned yourself in?' Her words were daggers. I twisted away but she grabbed my wrist and pulled me back to face her. 'Don't deny it, Abi. I know it was you who killed her. You were the driver who didn't stop.' I tussled with her but she wouldn't let me go. 'That's why you tried you kill yourself in our first year. Isn't it?'

'I don't know what you're talking about.' I wrestled my arm free from Grace's grip and sidestepped her on the narrow path. Thunder crashed overhead and the rain intensified, running down our faces like a shower.

'You're lying!' Grace shouted. 'You know exactly what I'm talking about! It took a while for me to put it together, but it makes complete sense. Your nightmares. The way you paint! Your first paintings. They were of this road, weren't they?' She looked me up and down as if she were repulsed. 'It explains how you are. What you're like. Why you bought her house!' She stabbed me with the last sentence, each word a staccato jab of pain.

'I'm going now, Grace. Back home.' I pulled away.

'If you were wondering, that's why I didn't let you die,' Grace said, quieter now. Sneering. 'I could have let you take those pills. Could have watched you froth at the mouth and die. But that would have been the easy way out for you. Wouldn't it? That would have been the selfish, cowardly thing to do.'

I stopped walking and stood motionless. I had to concentrate on breathing: in, out, in, out.

'You thought I was saving you, didn't you?' Grace scoffed. 'But why should you get off so lightly? Don't you think you deserve to suffer? You deserve to suffer a lifetime!' She laughed bitterly, and I hated her more in that moment than I ever had before.

'It wasn't my fault!' The words burst out of me like dynamite. 'She shot out of nowhere! I didn't even see her! She hit the car and… I didn't know. I didn't know what to do!' I sobbed. 'I panicked! I was only eighteen myself! I was a child!'

Grace's breath was coming hard. I could see her chest rising and falling; her nostrils quivering as she tried to control her voice. 'You could have done something,' she said levelly. 'You could have taken responsibility. You could have held her hand. You could have made her comfortable. You could have told her she was loved. You could have called an ambulance and waited with her.'

'There was no need for an ambulance.' The words fell like a guillotine.

'You drove off. You left her dead on the road.'

'I was scared!'

'Poor you!'

The rain, already hard, increased its intensity, a frenzy of water pummelling Grace, me and the ground, as if it were trying to wash the memory of that terrible evening from the fabric of the universe.

Ten years of shame ignited inside me. 'How dare you?' I hissed. 'How dare you stand here and throw accusations at me. You have no idea! No idea what it was like! There's not a day goes by I don't think about it! Not a moment I don't think about her. I atone for what I did, *every single day*! Everything I do, I do it for her!' I flung my arms out. 'I've never driven a car since that day! I won't have children because she can't have them! I work at the hospice in honour of her! Is that not enough? Aren't I doing enough because I don't know what else I can do! It's been ten years! Ten years!' I sobbed.

'Yet you've never been back!' Grace shouted, her voice snagging in the wind. 'You've never been to her grave! And don't tell me you apologized to her parents because I know it's not true. You never admitted what you did!'

298

'Please,' I begged. 'I need to move on. She's dead. I can't change that! Let me live my life!'

'You took her life! You don't deserve a life!' Grace stared at me, dripping from the rain, her face ugly with pain, and I realized I would never win. No matter what I did, I would never make this right. My life unfurled ahead of me, and I would never, ever be able to put this behind me.

'I'm going!' I shouted. I ran back up the path to the village green, my finger stabbing at my phone to find an Uber, listening for the sound of Grace's footsteps chasing after me, anticipating the feel of her fists pounding on my back, her hands clawing at my arms. But when the Uber pulled up and I finally dared to look back, I saw the shape of her standing with her head bowed, back at the accident site.

'Let's go!' I snapped as I slammed the door behind me. 'Now!'

Maybe the driver looked astonished. Maybe he said something, but I didn't hear. The rain drummed on the roof of the car and I was far away: I was in Dad's car, ten years ago, on the day I got my own A-level results.

Fifty-five

It's a sunny evening, just before six – I know that because the news starts on the radio just as I slam the front door. It's one of those evenings when you know the last light won't finish its slow fade from the sky till almost ten, and I've had the most amazing day – my A-level results were all that I'd hoped for and I got into my first-choice university. Everything is right with the world and I'm practically tripping with happiness as I yell 'bye to Dad and skip out of the house to the car. It's a saloon, a medium-sized family car, more powerful than many, but I'm a sensible driver, not interested in pushing the boundaries, just in getting from A to B, and tonight I'm nipping into town to pick up a celebratory dinner from the chippy. The table's laid and I'll be back before Dad knows it.

It's been the most glorious summer and the fields along the bypass are incandescent with the yellow of rape flowers; the grass verges are popping with the optimism colours of wildflowers; their scents mingling in the air with the other smells of the country – cow manure, cut grass, the tantalizing whiff of meat being grilled outdoors. The birds are singing, their cheerful voices floating from the trees. I'm not speeding; I'm driving carefully, mindfully, aware of all the details, constantly monitoring the road around me. The windows are open, this is true. Katy Perry's on the radio and my hair's blowing around me. I'm singing along, my heart bursting with the joy of my A-level results when, from nowhere, there's a bang and an impact that makes me clutch the steering wheel to stop the car swerving into the oncoming lane.

The trees form a canopy over the roads and, in that split second, when everything's still all right, I think it's just a low branch.

I think it's just a branch.

I wonder, even, if I have to stop, but then my instincts kick in, knowing somehow that it's more than a tree, more than me having to worry about Dad being cross that I've scratched the paintwork. There was a metallic tang in the sound, and a thud; something that didn't sound like a branch. This registers even as I slam on the brakes, pull to the side, and sit, shaking, for a moment before I open the door.

I get out and look back down the road, and first I see just the bike – it's bent and broken – and, after I've thought how hitting that will definitely have damaged the paintwork, I think: *that's odd.* Why would a bike hit my car? And I take a few more steps and then I see a trainer – an Adidas trainer, and another one, with a foot in it, lilac shorts, brown legs and then there she is, lying splayed in the road; her, and the bits and pieces from her basket scattered across the tarmac. I remember a stick of French bread, and fat, juicy tomatoes, their skins split, spilling seeds, nestled on the verge as if they'd grown there.

And at that moment I still think she's going to get up and brush herself off. I've never witnessed anything like this, and I can't comprehend that she isn't okay. The enormity of the scene doesn't catch up with me. I run over to her and drop down on my knees next to her. Her face is fine, unbruised, her skin a little tanned from the sun, a smattering of freckles across her cheeks, but one earring is missing, knocked out by the impact. I see it on the ground next to her, and I pick it up and hold it out, thinking: 'You'll want that back.'

But the girl can't speak; she just looks at me, her eyes pleading silently with me to do something, anything, to save her. There's a gurgle in her throat and a creeping pool of blood seeping out from under her head but I can't move because I realize then that she's dying. I do nothing but stare at her, paralyzed with shock, my hand clutching her earring, and our eyes are locked at the very moment her life leaves her.

Not only do I kill her, but I fail her, too. Grace is right: the girl dies on the road, without love or comfort, in front of a stranger. Those brightly coloured flowers on the verge are the last thing she sees. Those birds cheeping overhead – the birds that have haunted me ever since – are the last thing she hears, and I know nothing of who the girl is, of what her hopes and dreams are. I don't know that she's my age; that she's just got her A-level results, too. I don't even know her name. What I do know is that she's dead and that there's nothing I can do for her now. Numb with shock, I look around. I see that there's not a single witness, and I edge back towards the car on legs of jelly. I climb into the car, and for another terrified, confused moment, I think. Then I start the engine and make an even bigger mistake: I drive away.

I saw nothing.

I did nothing.

Fifty-six

Of course I find out her name later. The story doesn't make the national news, but it's in the local paper, and her friends write tributes on Facebook. Hundreds of tributes. She wore glasses and she had dark brown hair, the sort that's fine and a little curly, and goes flyaway in certain weather conditions or when you use too much conditioner. She liked to wear it in a high ponytail. She had that type of pale, translucent skin that burned before it tanned. She liked horse-riding, netball, reading, pizza, Beyoncé, and Maroon 5. She was a whizz at maths. She was seeing a boy; it looks like it was serious. Earlier that summer, she'd been to Thailand with her parents. She'd got the results she needed – she'd got into UCL. Her life was about to begin.

These things I find out as I pore over her Facebook page. I don't go to her funeral, so I don't see for myself how popular she was; how loved. I don't see the church packed out, her shell-shocked parents choking back their tears; her friends scrunching balled-up tissues in their fists; the flowers that decorate her coffin, nor the teddy bears and bouquets that pile up at the crematorium. I dream about them, though – I dream about them over and over until it seems to me as if I was there.

And what do you do when you've accidentally killed someone

and failed to report it? How *do* you live with yourself? Around and around in my head went the thought that a girl was dead because of me. That she didn't deserve to be dead.

I sat silently in my room that summer, unable to get out of my head that shuddering moment of impact and the look in the girl's eyes as she died. I had nightmares from which I'd wake screaming, sweating and paralyzed. Heart thudding, I'd lie there and reassure myself that it was just a dream, and, for a split second, everything was okay – and then reality would slam into me, making me cry out loud.

But it wasn't just a dream. My nightmare was true: I had killed someone. I'd lie there, haunted by the thought that that impact I'd felt on the car – that I'd thought was a branch – was one of the last moments of that girl's life. What part of her body had hit the car first?

The imagination can be cruel.

I'd go through the evening – the whole day – from the girl's perspective: the excitement of getting her exam results and confirming her place at university. Her parents proud of her; she overjoyed. Maybe she was picking up provisions for a celebratory barbecue, the French bread and the tomatoes to go with burgers and sausages. I imagined her cycling down that lane. Was she happy? What did she see? What did she feel?

What were her last thoughts?

Did she realize too late what had happened? Did she have that awful moment of wishing she could rewind time? Was she even aware of she'd been hit by a car, or did she just find herself lying on the tarmac looking into the eyes of a stranger while she struggled to gasp her last breath? Did she know, when she was looking at me, that I was the one who'd killed her? Was she in pain?

Did she hate me?

I'd lie awake at two o'clock and three o'clock and four o'clock and go over the events of that evening in my head. Had I been tired? Was I too hungry? Did I need glasses? Had I had a head-ache? Was I distracted? *Why didn't I see her?* Because, despite everything, the facts spoke for themselves: a girl died that day, and she died because of me.

Why me? I pleaded in those godforsaken early hours. Why my car? And then I'd squirm in my bed, feeling selfish for even thinking that because she died, her life cut short before it really even started, while I got to live. I'd go down that horrible, beautiful country road again and again in my head, playing a version of events where there was no impact; where I carried on and made it to the chippy without two lives changing so irrevocably on a country road by a small Kentish village. A version in which I had nothing bigger to worry about than niggling Dad that I wanted to do Fine Art instead of Management Science.

I'd imagine a version where the impact was just an overhang-ing branch. I'd stop and get out, the other cars whooshing past, hooting even, and I'd be dismayed that the car's paintwork was scratched – maybe the roof was even a little dented – and Dad's wrath would be the worst thing I'd have to face. I'd be grounded for a week or two, or have to pay for the damage myself, and that would be fine.

Oh, it crossed my mind to go to the police; to turn myself in. But, in my twisted mind, that would be the easy way out; that would assuage my guilt, maybe, but it wouldn't bring back the girl. Instead, I buried the accident in a compartment deep inside my head and vowed to get on with my life; to live my best life, both for me and for her. But guilt doesn't like to be bottled up.

It's like a genie. It might lie dormant in its bottle but it moulders and festers inside you, and it grows and it turns into a nugget of shame that eats away at you; and the shame and the horror merge together and become something bigger, something black and toxic that eats you from the inside out, like an army of termites.

You're too scared to go out, you jump at sirens, you stop driving, you see every accident waiting to happen, you resolve never to have a child of your own because you don't deserve to be a parent.

You go off to university, and you're relieved, at first, to get away from home, from the daily reminders of what happened, and you hope you might be able to move on with your life. Oh, how much you have to learn.

In your first term, you learn that this is not something you can outrun. That no matter where you go nor what you do, there's a huge ball of grief and shame burning inside you. You're not worthy of being anyone's friend, you're not worthy of going to university, of having an education, a life, a boyfriend. You're not worthy of having any happiness at all.

You lock yourself in your room and obsess about the girl you killed. You spend every waking hour imagining what she'd have been doing if your carelessness hadn't extinguished her life on a sunny summer evening. You stalk the social media accounts of her friends, and you picture what her life would have been like; you look at the places she would have lived, walked and played. You tear yourself to shreds imagining how her life would have been. And still it's not enough. A couple of months after you kill a girl, you realize that you face a choice: either you forget her and move forward, or you die yourself.

It wasn't a cry for help.

Fifty-seven

'Albert Road?' asked the cab driver as we passed the station. It was the first thing either of us had said since I'd told him to drive, and his voice took me by surprise. I looked up to see the familiar shop fronts of the High Street; Mr Ho moving about inside the cosy, pink warmth of his restaurant. Dinners there with Rohan seemed another lifetime.

'Actually, here's fine!' I said suddenly and the driver braked, unsure.

He stabbed at his Satnav. 'We're not there yet. It's just… right here, I think.'

'No, it's good here, thanks. If you can pull over.'

I got out by the bus stop. As the cab pulled away, I crossed the road and hesitated at the gate to the graveyard. The storm lashing Kent hadn't made it here yet, but the light was dampened – flat and expectant – and the air was deathly still. I followed the path round to the grave and stopped in front of it. What could I say to the girl I'd accidentally killed?

I stared at the stone and the graves around me faded from my peripheral vision as my eyes bored through the stone to what lay beneath – through the earth and the coffin – through its wood and satin lining until she was lying below me once more, looking up at me, her limbs splayed, her lips parted, and that tell-tale trickle of blood creeping, ever larger, onto the tarmac beneath her head. From beneath the gravestone she looked up at me and my eyes locked onto the empty sockets of hers. I fell to my knees, my hands touching the cold of the stone as if I could transmit some warmth, some energy, into the depths of her final resting place. If I could bring her back to life, I would.

'It was me. I'm so sorry,' I whispered. 'I didn't see you. There was nothing I could do.'

Around me, the trees sighed and rustled, restless with the approaching storm. An oily black crow flapped and settled on a branch above me, and my hands clutched the edge of the grave-stone more tightly. I waited but felt nothing: no reciprocal energy rising from the depths of the earth.

'I'm sorry. I'm sorry every day of my life.' Nothing. 'Did you see I took your toy dog?' I asked. 'Did you feel me there today?' I waited again for a sign – for something – but there was nothing but the rustling and chittering of the graveyard. 'You know that I care, don't you? Do you see what I do for you every day?' My voice was a hoarse whisper as a decade of guilt clawed its way up from my belly, snagging at my throat.

'I'm sorry I couldn't comfort you when you...' I squeezed my eyes shut and let the familiar sob rip through my insides. 'But I do it for others now. You know that, don't you?' I was talking faster now; begging. 'Every time someone passes, I see your face... I wish I'd held your hand... I could have told you you were loved.' Another sob. 'You were going to be a doctor. You were going to save lives...' My voice trailed off. The tally of lives lost because of the one life I'd taken was a scoreboard rattling inside my head; the grand total multiplying exponentially every day. An ever-increasing number of people she would have saved in the last ten years, who were now also dead because of me.

I keeled forward onto the grave and touched my forehead to the cold, wet stone, then I pressed my lips to it. The wind whipped the trees and rain splattered down: big drops that matched my tears and, within seconds, my hair was flat against my skin, cold rain sliding its way down my neck. I stood up stiffly, brushing dirt from my knees and wiping my hands down my jeans.

'Please. You've got to forgive me,' I said, 'because I don't know what else I can do.'

I walked down Albert Road in a trance as the rain got steadily harder. Above me, the house looked down at the street, the unshuttered eye of the attic reflecting the wet smear of the branches back at me as I walked up the path. At the window, a movement caught my eye: a fleeting shape; the shift of a shadow that quickly withdrew back whence it had come. My hand pressed against the solid wood of the door as I leaned against it for support.

'I'm back,' I murmured as I turned the key. Inside the hallway I got the sense of something hiding, of someone pulling away just out of my sight, of clothes rustling, of breath being held. The layers of the house whispered across the centuries yet, before me, the hall stood empty aside from the grandfather clock, its tick echoing in the stillness of the hall. I felt again the heart of the house; that thrum of energy that came from another time; a different dimension.

The wind caught, tugging at the roof and the rafters, rattling at the letterbox and catching in the branches of the oak tree. I touched the wallpaper, my fingers trailing along it as I went to the kitchen, where I opened a bottle of vodka, sloshed it carelessly into a glass, and drank deeply, wincing as it burned its way down my oesophagus. In my head, there was a jungle of sounds and images: Moira implying I had a drink problem. Me promising to cut back. Rohan's concerned face. The horror of my paintings. The tatty pink dog a symbol of my shame on the tarmac down in Kent. The gravestone. Losing my position at the hospice. The weight of the guilt. The clawing shame of everything.

'Oh, don't look at me like that,' I said out loud to the kitchen, as I put down the glass harder than I thought. 'Don't you think I deserve a drink?'

The house answered only with a creak and a sigh. Outside the wind picked up and a dog howled.

'Come on!' I said. 'I could have lived anywhere, but I chose you! I sought you out and bought you! I did it to keep her memory alive!' I took another slug of vodka. 'I'm taking care of you for her! I kept her room as it was… I know she's not coming back, but…' I drank deeply again as I looked out at the garden, the trees now starting to bend and sway in the wind.

'She played in your garden. She ate right here! She did her homework here. Studied for her A-levels here. Cried over boys here…' I raised my glass too fast and vodka sloshed out of it onto the table. I shoved my chair back and ran to the wall, touching it with my fingertips as if my stroke might bring it to life. 'Her breath touched your walls, your ceiling!' I sobbed. 'You're the same house underneath. I keep you for her!'

I picked up the vodka bottle and went up to the bedroom. There, I dragged the chair across the room, positioned it below the wardrobe and climbed up, clutching at the wardrobe door as I swayed precariously for a moment. Heart thumping, my hand snaked around in the top section that no one could reach, scouting behind the pile of forgotten sweaters for something I hadn't looked at the whole time I'd been married. For a moment I wondered if it had gone; if Rohan had somehow found it and thrown it out, thinking it belonged the house's previous owners, but no: my fingertips pushed the tangle of a skipping rope out of the way and finally lit upon the solid spine of the folder. I slid it out and climbed back down.

I took it up to the attic and gently wiped the dust off the cover. On the first page was a yellowing newspaper article. I unfolded it and drank in the black-and-white face that looked out at me.

GIRL KILLED IN HIT-AND-RUN

'You were pretty,' I said. 'But you knew that, didn't you?' My finger stroked the rough paper, as if I by doing so I could magic the girl back to life, but she stayed stubbornly pixelated, looking out at me with her chin lifted and a laugh frozen on her face, a tendril of hair blowing in a summer breeze. It was a face I knew as well as my own. A face that haunted every moment of my adult life. I turned the page and started to read the thoughts and memories that had been written on her Facebook page. I'd printed them all out. Every single one.

Can't believe you're gone.

To the best friend I could ever have wanted.

You're with the angels now.

Fly high, babe.

Uni won't be the same.

I flicked the pages: there were hundreds of messages, all of which added together to paint a picture of a girl who was loved, popular, clever, going places. There were pictures of her, too: blowing out candles, clutching a drink, with her arms round her friends, wearing bowling shoes, with her boyfriend, riding a horse, with her mouth wide open in a full-bellied laugh.

Downstairs the letterbox clattered, and the doorbell rang simultaneously, jolting me from my reverie. The folder fell out of my hand as I froze.

'Yoo-hoo, Abigail!' came Meena's voice through the letterbox. 'It's me!'

Fifty-eight

The doorbell rang again and again.

'Abigail! Open the door! I know you're there!'

I sloshed another shot of vodka into my mouth, then stumbled down the stairs with the bottle still in my hand, and pulled open the door a little too hard, which caused me to lurch backwards and grasp it for balance. The rain was heavy now, and Meena, huddled into a black coat, cowered as close to the wall as she could, sheltering under the eaves.

I tried to speak but words wouldn't come. My eyes were scratchy from crying.

'Abigail!' Meena exclaimed, and her eyebrows shot up as her mouth opened in shock. She gazed at me with such horror that I looked down to see what she was seeing: my top was stained, my jeans were wet and soiled from the graveyard, and my feet were dirty and bare. My hair, now I thought about it, must be matted against my wet scalp, and my hands were filthy, the nails ragged.

Meena pushed into the house, dropped the bags, shook out her hair and unzipped her coat then turned to face me once more.

'What happened? Your hair's wet. And it's freezing in here.' She shuddered dramatically and peered into my face. 'Is everything okay?'

I put my free hand to my hair and felt its wetness, too. 'I should get changed,' I said, trying out the words carefully. 'Grace'll be home soon.'

Meena scoffed. 'Grace? Ronu's on his way.' She looked at me for a reaction. 'Your husband?' she said, raising her eyebrows and pointing at me with a red-lacquered nail. 'He'll be back in a couple of hours. I'd have come over later, but Daddy and I are going to a bridge night. It's been in the diary forever – everyone's so busy – trying to get a night we can all make is almost impossible.' She tossed her hair. 'Anyway, we thought you'd probably want time alone together…' her voice trailed off as she peered at me. 'Abigail, is everything okay? You really don't look well.'

I closed my eyes and shook my head, feeling my brain ricochet back and forth in my skull. 'I'm fine,' I said. 'Just have a shower and… some make-up.'

Meena shivered again. 'Is the boiler working?'

She hustled to the utility cupboard under the stairs, then came back shaking her head. 'The heating's on. Why is it so cold?' Then she gasped and slapped a hand to her forehead. *'Arey!* It's the energy. *Of course* it's the energy!'

She extended her arms, palms, turned up and closed her eyes, her face a blank canvas. I watched as her eyelids and the muscles around her eyes flickered, then she opened her eyes again and sighed loudly. 'This is bad, Abigail. Very bad.' She paused for effect then carried on. 'I know you think this is all nonsense – silly old Meena and all that – don't think I don't know how you laugh at me behind my back. But you must believe me. I feel something. And it's stronger…' She nodded. 'Yes, we need to do something more. Smudging will be a start.'

She sighed again, as if she had the entire world to organize, then she picked up the bags. 'First let me get these in the fridge for Ronu before everything spoils. I've got all his favourites. The chicken, and even the lamb! It should last you a couple of days.' She bustled into the kitchen and opened the fridge. From inside, I caught a glimpse of the black-and-yellow wine boxes lined up on the two middle shelves.

'Goodness, Abigail,' she said, turning to look back at me just as I dropped the vodka bottle from my mouth and hid it awkwardly behind my back. 'What do you eat? There's nothing in here. No wonder you're so thin.'

'Takeaways,' I said, waving my hand vaguely at the front door. 'Deliveries.' The 'el' didn't sound. I took another swig of vodka.

Meena turned back to the fridge and rummaged about. 'Well, I'm glad I brought these for Rohan. I thought he'd like to have a home-cooked dinner tonight after all that aeroplane food. And, if not, it'll keep a day or two.' She straightened up then put her hands on her hips and looked at me through narrowed eyes.

'Now, Abigail. What are we going to do with you? I'm not happy with you here.'

'I'm good,' I said running my hand through my hair. 'I was just about to get ready. Really.' We stared at each other.

'I'm not sure you should be here alone,' Meena said, 'but… hmm… Ronu will be back very soon.' She pursed her lips as she wrestled between wanting to interfere and wanting to go to her bridge night. 'I'd say come home with me but, as I said, we're going out.'

'I'm fine,' I said.

'Hmm. Well, you've got food in the fridge now. Are you going to be all right heating it up?' I nodded. 'Lay the table,' she said. 'Make it look nice. Put on something nice yourself. Ronu will appreciate that. And we'll sort out the energy tomorrow. I need to look up a few things and get some sage for the smudging.'

I nodded and looked towards the hall and the front door, showing her out with my eyes. Finally, she took my cue and made her way back to the hallway.

'He lands in fifteen minutes,' she said at the door. 'Then probably another two hours till he reaches home. Call me if there's any...' she widened her eyes, 'problem. Okay, bye. Mwah.'

I closed the door behind her, shutting out the wind, the darkness and the rain, and turned to face the house once more.

Now it was just the two of us.

With the vodka bottle still in my hand, I blundered up the stairs towards the dead girl's bedroom and paused at the door. Her things were still there, of course: her bed, her dresser, her wardrobe, the dry, cracked flip-flops she wore around Thailand that last, fatal summer. The old hangers, the child-sized clothes, the wardrobe, the dolls, the flowery curtains: all of it was hers. Grace had put them there to torture me. She'd known what she was doing.

Outside, the wind snarled around the house and a branch of the oak whipped the window, scratching at the glass as if it wanted to come in. I looked at the room, breathing in the smell of the wallpaper and the wardrobe; the smell the girl would have thought of as home. I threw myself onto the comfort of her bed and drew my knees up the foetal position as I rocked side to side, the pointlessness of my existence hurting more than any blow.

'I wish it was me who died!' I cried. 'You were the useful one, the clever one. You were the one who had something to give to the world. What do I do?' I scoffed at the uselessness of my career. 'It should have been me who died.'

Thunder cracked overhead, an explosion that reverberated, and then there was creaking like a hundred wooden doors, slow at first, but gathering in speed and intensity until it was all I could hear, the entire house filled with the deafening roar of tearing and splintering. I flung my arms over my head and ran into the hall, as if getting away from the window might save me as the oak finally crashed down. Seconds later, as stillness prevailed once more, I looked around: the house was still standing. I was alive. I ran to the window of the girl's room and saw the garden entirely full of tree, the smashed remains of the Wendy House at the bottom of the garden barely visible beneath it.

'Cheers to that,' I said and raised the vodka bottle to the garden. I sloshed some into my mouth and felt its fire burn inside me. For a moment the wind dropped and the silence echoed. Then, overhead, there was a sound. Something in the attic. A footstep above. I shivered. Meena was right: it was deathly cold.

I stumbled a little as I made my way clumsily across the landing and clawed at the little door that hid the attic staircase until I prized it open. I bumped against the walls, ricocheting from left to right as I climbed up the narrow stairs, aware all the time that maybe I should be advancing more slowly but, with over half the bottle of vodka inside me, slow and delicate were a stretch too far.

I reached the top step, crashed through the attic door and there she was: Grace.

Fifty-nine

Tall, beautiful Grace was standing with one hand clasped to her chest among the paintings I'd done of her – among the gruesome portraits that ripped her apart, melted her, drowned her, smothered her and wiped her out. I closed my eyes and the room swayed. Nausea rolled in my gut; the vodka too harsh on my empty stomach.

'Why did you do this to me?' Grace said sadly. 'It's as if you hate me. What did I do to make you hate me?' Her jaw clenched. 'I thought we were friends. Together forever. Hey, Abs? Isn't that what we used to say?' She gave a hollow laugh and went over to the picture of her face smashed and distorted, the rustiness of the blood I'd used rich on the canvas. Her hand moved up to her mouth, as if she were physically holding in vomit.

'I think you should leave,' I said.

She spun around. 'Leave?'

'I need you to leave me alone. Stop reminding me all the time. Stop holding it over me.'

Grace shook her head. 'No, no, no. It doesn't work like that. Why should you forget? You killed someone.' She pointed her index finger at me, jabbing at the air.

'It wasn't my fault,' I said. 'I wasn't drunk. I wasn't tired.

I wasn't speeding… it was an accident. It was ten years ago. I need to move on.'

'How can you move on? You took a life! She didn't deserve to die!'

'And I didn't deserve to kill her!'

'Living is your punishment,' Grace hissed. 'And I'll make sure you feel it every. Single. Day.'

'Get out! Now.' I marched to the door and held it open, but Grace put her hands on her hips and shook her head.

'As if you'd throw me out. You need me! You're nothing on your own. You're pathetic.'

'No. You're wrong. I don't need you. I have Rohan.'

Grace rolled her eyes and looked exaggeratedly around the attic. 'Oh yes. Well, where is he now? Where's he been the last few weeks while you slit your wrists and drink yourself into a coma? Let me see… Oh yes: he's been in New York.' The words oozed with spite.

'And did precious Rohan see these paintings?' Grace flung her arm at the collection. 'Did he tell you they were good?' She laughed; a loud, haughty laugh. 'Well, let me tell you something: they're rubbish! Worthless! They're self-indulgent crap! You're kidding yourself if you think you have any talent!

'It's like the emperor's new clothes,' Grace sneered. 'No one will tell you how crap they are because you're so "fragile". No one wants to "upset" you. Everyone's walking around you on fucking eggshells. You do know that your darling Francesca only gives you exhibitions because of your wretched husband, and all he does is enable you to churn out this garbage. You're pathetic!'

'Get out!' I cried. 'Get out of my house! Get out of my life! I mean it!'

Grace rolled her eyes insolently. 'Like last time? Oh yes, this all seems familiar. Haven't we been here before? And then all it takes is a little email: *Dear Abs, I need somewhere to stay…* and you invite me back like nothing happened. You can't get rid of me. You'll never get rid of me! Never!'

'I mean it! Get out!' I screamed.

Grace shook her head slowly as she started to walk towards the door. 'I'll go. But you know I'll be back. I'll never leave you. Together forever, remember?' She laughed again.

'Not this time! This is different!' I grabbed her shoulders and shoved her out of the door and down the stairs.

'I can come, and I can go, but you'll always be a murderer,' she said, disappearing into her room.

I spun around, went back into the attic and slammed the door behind me. Before me were the paintings. She was right. Of course they were rubbish. Who did I think I was kidding? As if I could be a famous artist. I remembered how Rohan had commissioned me to paint his portrait, not because he thought I was a brilliant artist, but because he fancied me. So, was it true? Was he patronizing me? 'Enabling' me to paint as a hobby? As something to keep me busy while he waited for me to get pregnant? And what of Francesca? The exhibition? The buyers, the press? Were they all in on it, too?

I touched my finger to the canvas closest to me, the fourth one, and, as I took in the details of Grace's smashed face, saliva streamed into my mouth and I retched, bringing up the vodka. I spewed the vomit onto the canvas, my bile literally raining down on her.

'Useless!' I shouted, kicking at the canvas, trying to break the frame, but it wasn't enough. 'I'm useless!' I picked up the canvas and hurled it across the room. It hit the wall and bounced, the pine of the frame splintering but, again, it wasn't enough.

'Why me?' I screamed, and I grabbed my craft knife and lunged towards the next canvas, stabbing into Grace's eyes and slicing up her face, then I rampaged on, stamping on the canvases, snapping the frames, slashing the pictures and smearing vomit over what was left. I tipped vodka on them and, had I found matches, would have set fire to them. I rested only when there was just one of my series left to see: the teenage Grace, serene as the *Mona Lisa*, rising above the trampled remains of the others, as if a hurricane had blown through the attic and obliterated everything that she was. Then I collapsed to my knees and crumpled forward onto the floor, spent.

Sixty

'Abs! *Abs!*'

I opened my eyes to see Rohan's face sideways, close to mine, his body crouched low and his face puckered with worry. I realized he'd been shaking my arm urgently and his hand remained there, vice-like. I could feel its warmth through whatever it was I had on. Inside my head, someone beat my brain with a hammer. I could picture him, a tiny man with the steel hammer: *tink, tink, tink.* Somewhere ahead of me, grey and shadowy, there was a memory – Grace? My art? – but it scuttled out of my grasp before I could identify it. The room was dark; through the rain-spattered window I could see clouds moving fast; the oak tree's absence in the sky a glaring blank.

'Thank God! Jesus, Abi! Thank God you're all right! The tree!'

I opened my mouth and closed it again, the insides sticky and dry. My face was squashed against the floor; from this angle I could see all the empty bottles, crisp packets, cigarette packets and food packaging that hadn't made the bin. I closed my eyes. Rohan shook me, harder this time.

'Abi! Stay with me! What happened? Are you hurt?'

I groaned.

'And, Jesus, your paintings? Come on, let's get you up.' He

rolled me over, then slid his hands under my shoulders and lifted me to a sitting position. I slumped forward, bile rising, and propped myself up on my hands.

'Are you okay? Where does it hurt?'

'I'm fine.'

'Jesus, Abi. Just, Jesus. What is this?' He looked around at the devastation of the attic. 'Who did this?'

I stayed still because it was the only way not to be hit by a new wave of nausea. Rohan got his phone out.

'I'm calling the police,' he said. 'Whoever did this… I mean, how did they get in?'

'No,' I croaked. 'No.'

Rohan stopped what he was doing on his phone. 'What do you mean, "no"? Someone did this! We need to get the police involved. Catch them. It's criminal damage. Jesus. Your exhibition…' He shook his head, unable to process that there could be no exhibition. 'Shit. Francesca. We've got to tell Francesca.'

'It was me.'

'What?'

'You heard.' My voice was louder now. 'They were rubbish. You're just humouring me. Both of you. How could you let me embarrass myself in public? I'm not a real artist. I'm not talented. I'm useless. These…' I waved my hand at the destroyed canvases, 'they were crap.'

'You did this?' Rohan's mouth fell open, then his face crumpled. 'No. Why would you? Why would you think they were bad?' He squatted down next to me. 'Who told you that? Who saw them?' He paused and then his face changed. 'Grace?'

I let my head sink into my hands. Rohan shook my shoulder.

'Abi! Who did you show them to? Because these were incredible.

I wasn't lying. I would never "humour" you. These…' He walked over to the desk and I saw too late that the folder was there, open. 'These paintings were the best I'd ever seen. Francesca too. She was blown away by them. I can't believe they're…' He closed his eyes and pulled a hand through his hair.

I struggled to get up but slumped back down as nausea hit me again. In slow motion I watched as Rohan peered at the folder. He was still dressed in the jeans and blazer he'd have worn on the flight. He looked handsome, the man I love, and my heart ached for what we could have been, the two of us and a child. He turned a couple of pages. I couldn't let him. Next to me on the floor was my palette knife. I reached for it and curled my fingers around the handle.

'What is this?' Rohan asked. 'Tributes?' He looked up. 'To who?'

'Don't!' I cried as I struggled to get up. 'Stop!'

But he tilted his head as he looked from the folder to the canvas that still remained, and back again, realization slowly dawning.

'Oh, so you do know who you were painting. It's her, isn't it?' His face softened. 'This girl. What happened to her? Was it someone you knew?'

'Stop it!' I cried again. 'Put it down!'

But Rohan looked back at the folder and flicked the pages backwards until he reached the newspaper article at the front. His face creased with concern.

'"Girl dies in hit-and-run"? Oh no… Abs. How awful.'

'Don't do this! Rohan!' I tried to rise but fell back down.

'Was she a friend?' His face was open with curiosity. He wanted to know; he genuinely wanted to help.

'Stop!' I leaned heavily on the wall as I pulled myself to my feet. The room spun and I lurched toward the desk.

'Put it down!' I shouted but Rohan continued reading. I watched his eyes widen.

'Her name was Grace, too?' he exclaimed. 'Grace Shaw? But isn't that your friend who's staying...?' His brow furrowed and his head tilted sideways again. 'What's going on? How...'

'No!' I screamed. 'Noooo!'

I raised my arm and brought it down against Rohan's shoulder with all my strength. We stayed frozen in that tableau for a moment, our eyes locked, then I felt the warm wetness of his blood under my hand and Rohan's head turned slowly to take in the red stain that was seeping through his shirt.

I pulled the knife out and stabbed it into his shoulder again and again, weaker each time, until the folder finally fell out of his hand and he crumpled onto the floor. I looked at my husband lying next to the folder.

'Sorry,' I whispered. 'I can't do this anymore.' Then I took a deep breath and plunged the knife against my own chest.

Priory Hospital North London: 20 December 2019

Sunlight beams through the high sash window and onto the coffee table, highlighting dust motes that float in the air. I'm sitting in the armchair again today, the one by the window. Every minute, I glance out towards the driveway, then I turn back to the room and start rocking again. There's a solace in the movement; it comforts me, like the feel of a cat purring on my lap. Like the feeling of my Alfie on me. But something happened to Alfie – he's not coming back. The memory's a shadow I can't quite grasp.

It's quiet here today so I hear footsteps in the corridor before Rohan appears at the door. He's with Dr Singh, my consultant. They stop on the other side of the threshold and continue to talk quietly. Rohan's been here all morning, talking to the doctor. They're giving me sideways looks, their eyes flicking to me and back, so I know it's about me and I imagine Rohan's asking when I can come home. I put a hand to my chest – it's still sore, but it's good, apparently, that I only used a palette knife. The blunt blade couldn't go deep. Rohan's arm's in a sling.

'Very high success rate…' I hear Dr Singh say. 'Residential… therapy… psychodynamic…'

'She'd have to stay here?' Rohan asks.

I tune out and my eyes flick once more to the driveway. I rock as I watch the cars, each one a fresh cargo of dread that butterflies and prickles in my belly.

'Abi?' Rohan says and I swivel to see both him and the doctor facing me, concern on their faces. 'What are you doing?'

'I'm waiting for Grace,' I say. 'I know she's coming back. She said she'd never leave me.'

Rohan and Dr Singh look at each other, and Rohan nods. 'Okay,' he says.

Acknowledgements

This book did not come easily. It was only thanks to the foresight, talent and unending patience of my incredible editor, Kate Mills, that it was able to grow into the story you hold in your hands today. Thank you, Kate, for pushing me, for challenging me and for believing in me.

Thank you to Lisa Milton, Executive Publisher at HQ Stories, for making me feel like such a welcome part of the HQ family and for your ongoing support. Endless thanks to Luigi and Alison Bonomi, whose encouragement, brainstorming sessions and constructive critiques keep me on track, and thanks, too, to the entire team at the Emirates Airline Festival of Literature, in particular Ahlam Bolooki and Isobel Abulhoul, and to Charles Nahhas of Montegrappa Middle East.

And, of course, it takes a village to create a book. I'm grateful to every single member of the team at HQ and beyond who plays a part in bringing a published book or audiobook to you, the reader: the teams who work so skilfully in jacket design, editing, publicity, sales, marketing and foreign rights.

Thank you to the bookshops who stock my books, to librarians everywhere, to the book bloggers and reviewers who help make any book a success, and to you, my readers. Thank you for buying, reading and reviewing my books on Amazon and Goodreads. Thank you for engaging with me on social media, for coming to my talks and sharing the love of books.

And, finally, thanks to my friends and family who care enough to ask 'How's it going?' knowing that the answer could expose them to an hour or more of tortured plot discussion – you know who you are. Last but not least, thank you to Sam, Maia and Aiman, who witness me going through the highs and lows that are part and parcel of writing novels, and still put up with me.

ONE PLACE. MANY STORIES

Bold, innovative and
empowering publishing.

FOLLOW US ON:

@HQStories